The Diary at the Last House Before the Sea

BOOKS BY LIZ EELES

LIZ EELES

The Diary at the Last House Before the Sea

bookouture

Published by Bookouture in 2024

An imprint of Storyfire Ltd.
Carmelite House
50 Victoria Embankment
London EC4Y 0DZ

www.bookouture.com

ISBN: 978-1-83525-568-1
eBook ISBN: 978-1-83525-567-4

For our lovely Freddie and Elsie

PROLOGUE
SEPTEMBER 1957

Audrey gasped as water swirled around her knees. It was cold. So much colder than she'd imagined. But she kept on walking, through cresting waves, into deeper water that glistened navy under the darkening sky.

Behind her, lights were starting to shine from the manor house that sat protected in a fold of the land. Soon, Edwin would be looking for her – going from room to room, calling her name and wondering why she wasn't answering him. Her silence would be deafening.

She glanced over her shoulder, her body buffeted by the full tide. What if he saw her from a window, wading through the water that was now swelling around her waist? She was sure he would try to stop her. He would run from his grand house and drag her back onto dry land. But that couldn't happen.

Audrey pushed on more quickly, her body going numb as her shoulders sank beneath the waves and currents beneath the surface snagged at her clothing.

Suddenly, an image of the leather-bound diary sitting on her bedside table swam into her mind. She had forgotten to destroy it. 'Stupid! Stupid!' she muttered, as tears began to stream down her cheeks, mixing with the salt water that was trying to pull her under.

She had always been careful about what she wrote down. But Edwin would find the diary and he might put two and two together. Her oversight had put someone she cared for at risk but there was nothing to be done about it now. There was no way of putting it right.

On the horizon, black clouds were massing – huge, menacing shapes lit from within by forks of lightning. A storm was coming but, when Audrey glanced behind her once more, the manor house remained eerily calm and quiet, as if it was watching her and ready to pass judgement.

The current was tugging at her feet now, lifting them from the sand, but she tried to stand still for a moment. Her mind was whirling with the enormity of what she was doing. The finality of it all.

No more life at Brellasham Manor. No more life as Edwin's wife or Geoffrey's stepmother.

'I can change my mind,' she murmured between frozen lips. She could go back and pretend that this moment of madness had never happened. She could continue with the gilded life she had chosen – a life of luxury, privilege, and secrets. But she knew in her heart that it was too late.

Audrey touched the diamonds at her throat and began moving forward again, into the deep water, and felt her body relax as she surrendered to the push and pull of the heaving sea.

Edwin wasn't coming for her, and this was how it had to end.

1

CLARA

PRESENT DAY

'Clarissa, are you up yet?'

Clara groaned, rolled over and blinked as her alarm clock swam into focus. It wasn't quite seven o'clock and yet her mother was yelling up the stairs for her. *And* she was using her full name, even though she knew how much it wound Clara up.

Perhaps *precisely* because she knew, and it was a ploy to make sure her daughter was fully awake. It was an effective tactic, Clara had to admit, because sleep was impossible when irritation was shooting darts of adrenaline into your bloodstream.

'I'm up!' Clara yelled back, wishing she belonged to the sort of family who woke loved ones with a cup of tea and a whispered 'Time to get up, darling.'

No such luck. Clarissa Netherway had been born into a family who rarely spoke if they could yell instead. They weren't necessarily annoyed with each other. But some Netherway gene, passed through the generations, appeared to dictate that family voices should be raised regularly when communicating. Or maybe it was nurture, rather than nature, and succeeding generations had learned to make their presence felt.

Whatever the reason, the Netherways were loud – her mum, her dad when he was alive, and her brother, Michael, who had the good sense to now live in Canada. He hadn't been saddled with a posh name that got him ridiculed at school.

The bedroom door was suddenly flung open and her mother strode in.

'You're not up,' she declared, yanking back the bedclothes. 'River will be arriving soon and we need to make sure that everything at the manor is shipshape and just so.'

'Why?' muttered Clara, scrabbling the duvet back over her legs. 'It's not a royal visit.'

'It might as well be.' Julie Netherway gazed into the distance. 'The prince returns to his ancestral home after years in the wilderness. It's rather wonderful, don't you think?'

Clara rolled her eyes. 'Nope. Australia is hardly "the wilderness", and River is definitely not a prince. How could he be with a name like that? His Royal Highness Prince River of Heaven's Cove.'

Her mother sniffed. 'I don't know. It has a rugged sound to it, and it's not his fault that his mother saddled him with a name he doesn't like.'

'Mmm.' Clara pondered commenting but thought better of it. 'What are you doing, Mum?' Julie had dropped to her knees and was rifling through her daughter's underwear drawer. 'I can sort my own clothes out.'

'You'd think.' Her mother stopped rifling, a pair of Clara's best pants in her hand. 'However, I'm not sure that's always the case, and today, everything has to be—'

'Shipshape,' interrupted Clara, who, knowing when she was beaten, swung her legs out of bed. 'OK. I'll have a shower and some breakfast and will come up to the manor by eight thirty.' She wilted under her mother's glare. 'Um... eight fifteen?'

'Here's some decent underwear.' Julie got to her feet and

threw the pants and a bra onto the duvet. 'And make sure you wear a dress. No jeans and definitely no scruffy trainers. That pair you wear all the time are a disgrace.' She walked to the door. 'Oh, and I need you to nip into the village to get some Gorgonzola before you come up to the house.'

'Gorgonzola?' murmured Clara with a sigh. 'Why?'

'Because it was always River's favourite and I want him to feel welcome. I've already got French sticks and Devon butter in case he needs a snack after the long drive from the airport.'

She frowned at the hot chocolate stain on Clara's pyjama trousers. 'So that's why you need to get out of bed now, tidy yourself up and get moving. Come on! Chop, chop!'

'OK, you win,' grumbled Clara, miffed that her mother was so excited about the return of her employer's son to Heaven's Cove. Was it such a big deal? She pulled on her dressing gown, her long auburn hair tumbling around her shoulders, and remarked: 'For the record, I didn't get such an effusive welcome when *I* returned to the family home.'

'That's because you'd only been living fifty miles away,' her mother retorted, 'whereas River has been living on the other side of the world from his father. He always was an adventurous boy.'

She smiled approvingly while Clara shook her head at such a jarring display of maternal double standards.

Michael hadn't come under fire for his transatlantic flit, and her mother seemed positively proud of River for having 'adventures' far from his father. Yet, she'd thrown a hissy fit when Clara had moved to the neighbouring county for work. She'd also deemed it simply 'what good daughters do', when Clara had given up everything to move back home after her dad became unwell. The inherent unfairness and sexism of it all had passed her mother by.

Give him his due, Michael had offered – rather nervously –

to come back for good from Canada instead, as their father was fading. But, predictably, their mother hadn't taken up his offer.

'You shouldn't have to uproot yourself, darling, and there's no need anyway because Clara doesn't mind.'

And she didn't mind. Not really. She wouldn't have missed time spent with her father at the end of his life for anything. But being the 'good daughter' sometimes took its toll, especially now Dad was gone and Clara was no nearer to moving out of the family home. Her mother, for all her bluster, was still emotionally fragile and needed support.

The two of them tended to clash but living at home wasn't so bad, Clara had to admit – especially when that home was in the beautiful grounds of a magnificent manor house and only a stone's throw from the ocean.

'Earth to Clara!' said Julie, waving a hand in front of her face. 'Right. I can't stand here chatting. Remember! Manor house. Eight fifteen on the dot. Dress. No trainers.'

Clara gave a mock salute. 'Heard and understood, sir.'

Julie raised an eyebrow. 'Sarcasm doesn't suit you, Clarissa. Oh, I almost forgot. I've got the last of your gran's things down from the loft and you'll need to go through them sharpish or everything will end up in the bin or at the charity shop.'

'Please don't chuck anything out until I've had a look.'

'All right, but you're wasting your time. All that's left are the contents of the drawers in her bedside table. It looks like a collection of old tat but Mum, God rest her soul, always was untidy.' She glared at Clara's jeans which were in a heap on the floor. 'That's presumably where you get it from.'

Then she was gone.

Clara breathed a sigh of relief as the bedroom door banged shut. She loved her mother dearly, but these whirlwind 'chats' left her feeling as if she'd been spin-dried.

She sat quietly for a moment, to recover, and looked around her bedroom. Her teenage posters of the Kaiser Chiefs and Foo

Fighters had long since disappeared – faint adhesive smudges on the walls the only evidence they were ever there at all. But the heavy grey curtains were the same, and the pale blue carpet which was now threadbare in places.

Julie didn't believe in making changes for the sake of it. Her family had lived in this cottage for generations and she found the continuity comforting, particularly since the death of her beloved husband.

Clara pushed herself to her feet and, crossing to the window, peered through the salt-streaked glass. She couldn't see the manor house from here – it was hidden behind a sweep of the gravel drive – but the manor's private cove was visible through the trees.

The sea was a deep shade of turquoise this morning and its waves were topped with white horses, the remnants of a summer squall that had swept through Heaven's Cove in the early hours.

A headland pushed out into the water on the left, its lower slopes thickly wooded and bathed in early morning sunshine. The pretty village of Heaven's Cove lay beyond it: a huddle of whitewashed cottages, a ruined castle, a stone quay-side, and a mini-supermarket which, fingers crossed, stocked Gorgonzola.

A beep from Clara's phone interrupted her thoughts, and she frowned as she pulled the phone from her dressing gown pocket. The message was from her mother: *I can't hear the shower. You need to get a move on!*

Honestly, Michael was so lucky living three thousand miles away!

Clara grabbed her towel and headed for the shower that spat freezing or boiling water at her every morning, depending on what mood it was in. She washed her hair and took extra care drying it, so it fell in waves rather than going frizzy. Then, she put on the pretty cotton sundress that brought out the grey of her eyes, and rummaged in the back of her wardrobe for a pair of flat sandals.

It wasn't that she was frightened of her mother. But she knew that deviating from her mum's sartorial instructions would cause more grief than Clara was prepared to handle.

If River's homecoming was being treated like a royal visit, Clara would play along. But she didn't have to like it.

2

CLARA

Gathergill's Mini Mart *did* stock Gorgonzola! Which meant River would be welcomed home with smelly cheese, and she would escape the displeasure of her mother. Clara pushed the pungent package into her bag, stepped out into the June morning and pulled the supermarket door closed behind her. A salty breeze was blowing through the trees, and seagulls were screeching on the village green as they fought over an empty crisp packet.

Clara walked through the village which was preparing for the daily influx of tourists. Cobbled streets were being washed clean, shop fronts made ready and freshly caught fish laid out on ice in the fishmonger's window.

Dotted here and there were posters for the Brellasham Manor Charity Fete and Open Day. The annual event raised a lot of money for local good causes and was keenly anticipated by the locals of Heaven's Cove – partly because it was the only day of the year when they were allowed to wander around the grand house.

Clara had once suggested that River's father, Geoffrey, open the manor to paying visitors throughout the year. It seemed a shame that its impressive rooms and perfectly proportioned architecture went unseen. But he'd baulked at the idea of 'strangers invading the place and gawping' so she'd let it drop.

It was about time the Brellasham family shared their good fortune, she decided as she reached the ruined castle that sat overlooking the sea.

The castle keep, a square tower of red-tinged stone, rose into the sky and, around it, stone walls, eight centuries old and now fallen into disrepair, marked the boundary of the castle that had once been home to hundreds of people.

What were they like? Clara wondered. These shadowy people who once lived and loved here. Did they have day-to-day worries that sometimes seemed overwhelming? Were their mothers a nightmare too? Talking of which... Clara glanced at her watch and frowned. It was already eight o'clock so she'd better get a move on.

Hurrying down the dip in the land, that had once housed a moat, she set off at a brisk pace.

The weather had been glorious recently, with unseasonably high temperatures, and only puffs of white cloud were scudding across the sky this morning. It was going to be another beautiful early summer's day. The perfect day for a long-awaited homecoming.

Clara sniffed, suddenly weary of her bad mood. River's return was nothing to do with her, and he'd probably disappear again soon. But her mother was happy about it, and that was enough. Anything that lifted her mum's spirits had to be a good thing.

Clara walked on through the village, thinking about her father, who had died twelve months earlier. Then, she tried very hard to focus, instead, on the cobbled street in front of her and the fresh smell of the sea.

It still hurt when the gaping hole left in her life by her father's absence suddenly yawned wide. Some days it threatened to swallow her, but today she needed to be focused on other things – on people returning, rather than people who were gone for ever.

Clara walked on, along the lane that left Heaven's Cove behind. Few tourists ventured past the edge of the village and along this narrow track that led towards the moors.

They didn't know what they were missing, thought Clara, listening to sheep bleating in the fields beyond the high hedge, and a stream tinkling over stones. There was a sense of peace about this place that she loved. A permanence that made her feel grounded.

Clara undid her jacket, feeling warm in the sunshine as a butterfly flitted past. Spring was done and summer had arrived with a bang. Another summer of... who knew what? She could guess. The next few months would bring more hours spent helping Mum at the manor house, intermittent freelance work as a virtual PA – and awkward first dates in The Smugglers Haunt, that led absolutely nowhere.

Finding Mr Right seemed increasingly unlikely and Clara was becoming jaded. It was hard not to be when she met so many Mr Wrongs. She was starting to think the problem was her and she'd never find a man with whom she could imagine settling down. Not that she needed a man to make her life complete, even if her mother didn't agree with her.

Her mood was dipping again, and she deliberately pulled her shoulders back as she reached the tall metal gates of Brellasham Manor.

Beyond them lay the gravel drive that River's car would crunch along in a short while. What would he be like after all this time? she wondered. Would he even remember her, the girl with whom he'd been friends so long ago?

She walked along the drive that was edged with tall poplar trees and past the small cottage where she and her mother lived. Then, she turned a corner and caught sight of the manor house.

She'd seen it hundreds of times before, but this first daily sighting always made her heart leap because the house was just... perfect.

Made of pale red stone, Brellasham Manor sat in the shelter of moorland that rose up behind it.

To look at, the house seemed perfectly balanced with large windows on either side of a stone porch that was held aloft by four stone pillars. A walled kitchen garden sat to the right-hand side of the building, and to its left the lawn fell away, down to the sea. The small, private cove was almost hidden from the house by a line of trees.

On days like today, the sea was a beautiful blue. But Clara had walked on that beach when the water was dark and rough. And it always made a shiver run down her spine.

This bay, far smaller than the public beach that gave Heaven's Cove its name, was where Audrey Brellasham, the lady of the manor, had drowned almost seventy years ago, when she was younger than Clara. Her body had never been found – it was swept out to sea and lost for ever. But in winter, when the wind roared and waves crashed onto the sand, Clara couldn't help imagining that, one day, her bones might wash up on the shore.

Her thoughts were interrupted by the arrival of a lolloping golden retriever that wound its way around her legs, almost knocking her over.

'Hey, Grayson.' Clara bent down and tickled behind the dog's ear. 'What are you doing out here on your own, boy?'

Grayson trotted ahead as she made her way around the back of the house to what Geoffrey Brellasham, the current 'lord of the manor', referred to as 'the tradesmen's entrance'.

Clara found that rather patronising and snobby. But Geoffrey had exhibited a streak of snobbery for as long as she'd known him, which was all her life.

Julie, heavily pregnant with her, had been here, doing the

washing up, when her waters broke – or so the family story went. And the labour progressed so quickly that Clara was almost born on the kitchen tiles.

The ambulance summoned by Geoffrey's father – Edwin Brellasham – arrived in the nick of time, so Clara actually took her first breath in the local hospital. But she still felt an attachment to this old house that went beyond the ties her family had had to it for generations.

She had grown up here, in the cottage in the grounds, skinning her knees as she climbed trees, and playing hide and seek with River, and sometimes his older cousin, Bartie.

Her stomach flipped at the thought of Bartie – handsome Bartholomew – the first boy she'd ever fallen for.

'There you are,' said her mother, poking her head out of the kitchen door. Julie glanced at her watch and frowned. 'You're almost five minutes late.' But after looking Clara up and down, she nodded approvingly. 'That dress suits you. It brings out your colouring. Those shoes could do with a polish but I suppose they're better than your trainers. Anyway, come on in. He'll be here in an hour or so.'

Clara stepped into the large kitchen and carefully wiped her feet on the mat.

'I can't wait to see River again,' said her mother, brushing a strand of greying hair from her face. 'Aren't you excited?'

Clara wrinkled her nose. She couldn't deny that she was curious to see her childhood playmate again. But excited? No. So much had changed since they'd walked together in the manor grounds and hunted for shells at the cove: her grandmother and then her father had died; she'd moved away from the house she'd always called home and come back again; she'd grown up.

Yet, in some ways, nothing had changed at all. Not here at the manor where time seemed to stand still. Her mother was still housekeeping for Geoffrey, the grandfather clock in the hall continued to mark the passing of every minute, and the house stood as it had done for almost two hundred and fifty years. Its rooms elegant and quiet. Its secrets well hidden.

Clara walked softly through the rooms, on a mission from her mother to make sure that nothing was 'amiss'.

Quite what might be amiss, Clara wasn't sure. But, first, she inspected the formal drawing room and the smaller, more cosy parlour – their walls papered with chinoiserie depictions of oriental birds and flowers. Both rooms were immaculate, with marble fireplaces, squashy sofas, and polished walnut tables.

Then, she paused in the grand library to admire its impressive array of leather-bound books, all neatly stored on shelving that stretched from floor to ceiling.

A comfortable armchair had been placed next to the window that looked out over the gardens, towards the cove, and Clara rearranged the cushion – more for something to do, rather than because it needed adjusting.

Geoffrey would often sit here in the mornings, staring through the window and drinking tea. Clara often wondered if he was remembering his son playing out there, before he left for Australia.

No one knew because Geoffrey rarely mentioned River, and there were few photos of him in the house. If he missed his son, he kept it to himself – Geoffrey's thoughts and emotions were a closed book.

'He must be lonely in that big old house on his own,' her mother would say over the dinner table. 'But he's an aristocrat and they don't have feelings like we do.'

Which was bonkers, Clara had realised, even from a young age. Of course the rich and privileged had feelings. The difference was they kept them well hidden behind stiff upper lips.

Time was ticking on so Clara walked up the thickly carpeted stairs to the first and second floors, to inspect the bedrooms.

Each room looked immaculate and, happy that all was as it should be, Clara paused on the second-floor landing. She often stopped here to study the portrait that hung next to the door to the third floor of the manor.

The large portrait, done in oils, showed a striking woman in a beautiful yellow dress: Audrey Brellasham. Her blonde hair was pulled into an elegant bun, and at her throat lay the intricate diamond necklace that had disappeared with her so long ago. The necklace that, rumour had it, was gifted to a long-ago Brellasham by Queen Victoria herself.

Audrey was only twenty-four years old when she died, but the painting made her look older. Clara tilted her head, taking in the faint blush on Audrey's cheeks and the creamy glow of her skin. She was pictured sitting in the library, with a book on the table next to her – *Rebecca* by Daphne du Maurier – and another one on her lap, *Palmer's Grand Dictionary of the English Language*.

Clara pictured the many hundreds of books in the manor's library and frowned. *Rebecca* was amongst Clara's favourite novels and she could imagine it being one of Audrey's, too. However, a dictionary was a curious choice to be for ever immortalised in oil, especially as Audrey's hand was almost cradling the leather-bound volume.

The dictionary had always seemed out of place to Clara, along with the sadness on the face of the woman staring out at her from the gilt frame.

She took a step closer to study the woman's blue eyes that the artist had flecked with gold. Audrey was a beautiful woman, yet she looked troubled.

Why was that? Clara wondered – as she always did whenever she stopped to stare at the portrait. Audrey seemingly had everything: a devoted husband, Edwin; a stepson, Geoffrey; and such a wonderful house. Her life had appeared perfect, and yet she'd walked into a stormy sea on a September evening, fully clothed.

Audrey must have known that she would not survive. That she would never again walk upstairs to the suite of rooms she and her husband shared on the third floor of this house. The suite of rooms that had been closed off ever since the tragedy.

Clara glanced at the door that led upstairs and looked over her shoulder before trying the handle. As always, it was locked. No one ever went up there, except for Glenda, the cleaner, who would not be drawn on what lay above Clara's head.

Even Julie, the manor's housekeeper for decades, had never been up to the third floor, and she seemed reluctant to say anything about it.

Once, following incessant questioning from Clara, she'd told her: 'Your gran was housekeeper at the time of the tragedy and told me that Edwin, Audrey's husband, couldn't bear to go up there after losing his wife. So he blocked off the whole floor and Geoffrey has respected his wishes. It's never been used since.'

Echoes of the tragedy were still reverberating down the years, thought Clara, trying the locked door again, in case it had mysteriously unlocked itself in the last few seconds.

It remained resolutely closed, so she turned again to the portrait.

'What happened?' she murmured. 'Why did you walk into the waves that night?'

Her eyes met Audrey's direct gaze which, immortalised on canvas, kept her secrets safe from beyond the grave. What secrets did she have?

The only person who might know more was Geoffrey but they had never spoken about his tragic stepmother. In fact, they'd never spoken about much, really, even though Clara had known him her whole life.

The sound of hurried footsteps on the stairs broke into her

thoughts and she jumped back from the portrait as her mother hurried along the landing.

'Come on, Clara. What are you doing mooning over that painting again when River will be here any minute? You spend far too long, these days, staring at that picture. You're brewing an unhealthy obsession with a dead woman.'

'No, I'm not,' said Clara, feeling caught out because her mother had a point. She had spent a lot of time, recently, wondering why a woman with seemingly everything would drown herself. Though perhaps the only 'reason' was poor mental health which could affect anyone, whatever their circumstances.

'Grayson ran into the kitchen table and two plates fell onto the tiles and smashed,' said Julie, leading the way down the stairs. 'That dog is a menace. But I'll have to clear up in a minute because I've heard on the grapevine that River's car has been seen in the village.'

'Do you have people standing on watch?' asked Clara, raising an eyebrow.

Julie glanced over her shoulder. 'What have I told you about sarcasm? Belinda was in the bakery and she spotted River's car going by and gave me a call.'

'How on earth did she recognise him? She didn't move to the village until after he'd gone to Australia.'

'She looked him up on the internet and found a photo of him fire-fighting in the bush or something.' Clara smiled, well able to imagine Belinda, the biggest gossip in Heaven's Cove, stalking the returning prodigal son online. 'Anyway, look sharp because River will be here any second and Geoffrey wants us to line up in the hall to greet him.'

'I'm not sure that's a very good idea.'

'Well, Geoffrey thinks it is,' said Julie, shepherding Clara into the large, square hall where a little group had already gathered.

The front door was wide open and sunlight was streaming in across the Victorian floor tiles.

Geoffrey was standing on the doorstep and lined up behind him were Phillip, the gardener, Jean, Geoffrey's part-time PA, Martin, Geoffrey's solicitor, and, bizarrely, Patricia, the chiropodist who came out to the manor house to tend to Geoffrey's feet. Julie joined the end of the welcome line and gestured for Clara to do the same.

Rolling her eyes at the fuss, Clara stood where she was told and watched as a midnight-blue car came into view. It crunched across the gravel and came to a halt outside the front door.

A man in smart jeans and a green sweatshirt stepped out of the driver's seat and Clara felt suddenly as though time was dislocating.

The man in front of them, brushing long, fair hair from his eyes, was undeniably River. He had the same oval face and wide smile. But he was taller and broader with a short, neat beard. His teeth were bright against his golden tan.

She glanced again at the car because someone else was stepping from it. A man in a charcoal suit who looked familiar. And Clara's heart missed a beat as she realised that it was Bartie.

3

RIVER

The house looked exactly the same. River wasn't sure what he'd been expecting. An impressive new extension? A neon 'welcome home' sign flashing above the porch? But Brellasham Manor was just as he remembered it from sixteen years ago, when he'd looked over his shoulder as his mother drove them away for the last time.

And now, he was back. His stomach began to churn and he felt his shoulders stiffen as he drove closer to the house that he sometimes saw in his dreams.

Beside him, Bartie was leaning towards the windscreen. 'Oh, for goodness' sake! Old Geoff has organised a welcoming committee. I wouldn't be surprised if he's killed a fatted calf for you.'

When he laughed, River wished that he'd made this trip alone. It was going to be awkward enough, without his cousin's asides. But Bartie had insisted on coming too and, initially, River had been pleased to have company on the long drive from London. Returning to a house which held so many memories was never going to be easy.

His father, hard to miss in brick-red trousers and a tweed

jacket, had taken a step forward and was peering at the car. He was flanked by two stone pillars and a large dog River didn't recognise.

A line of people was just visible through the wide-open front door. Bartie was right about the welcoming committee, and now he would have to smile and make small talk, when all he wanted was for this awkward arrival to be over.

River swallowed as the car wheels crunched over gravel. Memories of that sound, as he and his mother drove away, were punching into his brain, disorientating him and dragging him back to the past.

He brought the car to a halt at the foot of the wide stone steps that led up to the front door, and took his hands off the steering wheel.

'Are you getting out then?' asked Bartie, undoing his seat belt. 'Your dad's champing at the bit, and I bet you can't wait to set foot again in this impressive pile. Not a bad inheritance, eh?'

'Mmm,' murmured River, before summoning up his courage, opening the door and unfolding himself from the driving seat. A breeze was blowing through the trees and he inhaled the fresh smell of the sea.

River plastered on a smile and said, 'Hello, Father,' before walking up the steps towards him. The older man stepped forward and River had a sudden urge to throw his arms around this man whom he hadn't seen for almost three years. But his father, as always, stuck out his hand to be shaken.

'River, old chap. It's good to see you. You look... tired... but it's a long drive from London.'

'It is,' said River, noting the slight hitch in his father's sentence. He knew he looked tired because he was still jet-lagged after his flight from Sydney. But he couldn't help feeling that 'tired' wasn't the word that had first popped into his father's head. Perhaps the word he'd left unsaid was 'disappointing'. He ran a hand down his jeans, the smartest pair he owned.

His father suddenly looked past him to the car and a smile broke across his face. 'Bartie! You didn't tell me that Bartholomew would be accompanying you today.'

'It was a last-minute decision,' said River, as Bartie bounded up the steps, two at a time.

'Hello, Sir Geoffrey! How marvellous to see you again. It's been too long.'

'It has, indeed.'

Before Geoffrey could say anything more, Bartie pulled the older man into a bear hug and patted him on the back before releasing him.

Geoffrey's face registered surprise at this unexpected manhandling but he didn't look unduly annoyed.

Maybe I should have ignored his outstretched hand and hugged him, thought River, feeling that he'd somehow fallen at the first hurdle.

'Can you stay for a few days, along with River?' Geoffrey asked Bartie, who nodded his head.

'Absolutely. You and I have lots to catch up on and, of course, I'm happy to help with the issue that's brought River home.'

Geoffrey glanced at the people patiently waiting and frowned. 'That's good to hear, but we should discuss that later, rather than here.'

Bartie touched the side of his nose. 'Of course. Mum's the word.'

'And now you must both come and say hello to a few people,' said Geoffrey, leaning over to pat the dog which was running in circles, chasing its tail. 'Calm down, Grayson! I'm afraid he's always like this when he encounters a stranger.'

River supposed that's what he was now, in this magnificent old house that he'd once called home. A stranger making a fleeting visit before jetting back to his real life. A cuckoo in the nest.

As Geoffrey led the way into the hall, Bartie murmured into River's ear: 'Servants lining up to greet us. It's just like *Downton Abbey*.'

Hoping no one had heard his cousin's remark, River made his way along the line, shaking hands and feeling acutely embarrassed by all the fuss.

'River, you must remember Mrs Netherway, my housekeeper,' said his father when they reached the end of the welcoming committee.

So, Mrs Netherway was still here, keeping the house going. River remembered her, all right. Both for her kindness and for the choc-chip cookies she used to make him. He could almost smell them still, as they came out of the oven, caramelised and golden.

She looked much the same – small and slight with dark hair, now greying – but she still had the air of a coiled spring, ready to leap into action. She'd always been a human dynamo, keeping his father and this house going.

'River, it's so wonderful to have you home at last,' she said with a beaming smile. She stepped forward as if she planned to hug him but then stepped back.

River smiled. 'It's good to see you too, Mrs N.'

'And this,' said his father, 'is Clara, who helped out while Mrs Netherway was absent following the sad death of her husband last year. She's Mrs Netherway's daughter. You knew each other when you were children.'

'Yes, I remember,' said River quietly, saddened that Mr Netherway had died and he hadn't known about it. He had fond memories of the man who had taught him to ride his bike and to whittle arrows from fallen branches in the garden.

'Hello, River,' said Clara, her voice low and soft.

He looked at her properly for the first time. The house didn't appear to have changed over the years he'd been away. But Clara certainly had.

Back then, she was a tomboy with scraped knees, who explored the grounds of the manor house with him while her mother worked. They'd swum in the cove together and climbed trees. And he'd told her things. Things that he should have kept to himself.

And now she was grown up. Her dark auburn hair was longer and falling in waves, and her face was leaner. But the big grey eyes were the same. The same colour as the sea when it crashed into the cove in winter.

'It's good to see you again,' she said, holding out her hand, though her solemn face said the opposite. They'd parted on bad terms and the intervening years of no contact had obviously done nothing to mend their relationship.

'You too,' he said, giving her hand the briefest of shakes.

Why was she still here, at Brellasham Manor? River, who'd been sure that she'd be long gone, experienced a pang of envy. She had been enjoying this amazing place while he had been, effectively, banished. But he blinked and pushed the thought from his mind. He had been with his mother. He had been seeing the world. He was the fortunate one.

Clara's eyes suddenly slid past him to Bartie, who had just approached, and her face broke into a wide grin.

'Little Clara. You're all grown up!' Bartie declared, grabbing her hand in both of his and leaning forward to kiss her on the cheek. 'And you've grown up so *well*,' he added, giving her a huge wink that made Clara's cheeks redden.

River stood stiffly, envying the ease and charm that his cousin was displaying. Back at Brellasham Manor for five minutes and he felt like a teenager again. A gauche teenager without a clue. But Bartie had never been afflicted by the insecurity and lack of confidence that had dogged River his whole life.

'Do you work here too, now?' Bartie asked Clara, finally letting go of her hand.

She shook her head. 'No, not really. I help Mum out some-times if Geoffrey has guests, but I mainly work as a virtual PA.'

'That sounds exciting and intriguing.'

Was Bartie being sarcastic? Apparently not because he was gazing at Clara with what looked like genuine interest.

'Those aren't words I'd use to describe my job. It's all very ordinary, really. I basically provide administrative services to clients.'

'Such as?'

'Everything from helping to organise conferences and setting up travel arrangements to buying birthday presents for CEOs' children. I do whatever's needed.'

Bartie stared at her for a moment and then leaned forward. 'I bet you do. And, for the record, I never thought of you as an ordinary girl. You were always rather extraordinary, if I remember rightly.'

River shifted from foot to foot, feeling acutely uncomfort-able. Bartie was very good at flirting but here, in the hallway at Brellasham Manor, five minutes after arriving, was neither the time nor the place.

Mrs Netherway apparently felt the same way because she stepped between her daughter and his cousin. 'Shall I show you both to your bedrooms?'

'I don't want to put you out, Mrs N,' insisted Bartie, shifting his gaze from Clara. 'You didn't know I was coming.'

'No, but it'll only take a few minutes to make up another bed for you. It's no bother. Follow me,' she said, her hand already on the polished bannister.

River gave Clara an awkward nod – though he didn't know why and wished he hadn't – before he and Bartie followed her mother up the wide staircase to the first floor.

They walked past the rainbow window that dated back to the mid-nineteenth century, and into a carpeted corridor that stretched along the west wing of the house. Portraits lined the walls, along with polished tables holding candlesticks and other antiques that the Brellasham family had gathered over the years.

It was all so alien after his years in Australia, and yet so familiar at the same time. River had the strangest sensation that he was walking backwards through a rip in time.

'Hell's teeth!' Bartie muttered beside him. 'I'd forgotten how opulent this house is.'

'I'm surprised you haven't visited for such a long time. Did you say it was more than three years since you were last in Heaven's Cove?'

'Something like that. I've been meaning to visit for ages but, you know what it's like. Work, life, other things get in the way and, suddenly, a few years have whizzed by. But I'm here now.'

Mrs Netherway suddenly stopped next to a dark-oak door and pushed it open. 'Would you be happy in this room, Bartie? I can come along and make up the bed in a short while, once I've shown River to where he's sleeping.'

Bartie looked around the large, sunny room which had cream silk curtains framing a window that overlooked the garden. In the centre stood a four-poster bed, its wooden posts decorated with carved figures of animals.

'I'll be very happy in here, Mrs N,' Bartie declared, kicking off his shoes and throwing himself onto the bed. He pushed himself up on one elbow. 'Tell me, does Clara still live round here full time?'

Mrs Netherway nodded. 'She's back living with me at the cottage in the grounds, though she mentions moving out every now and then. I'm not sure why because the cottage is very cosy and so convenient for the manor.'

Probably because she needs independence and space and freedom, thought River, but he kept his mouth shut. He didn't really know these people any more. He certainly didn't know Clara.

Leaving Bartie sprawled on the bed, River followed Mrs Netherway up more stairs to the second floor.

'I thought you might like to be in your old bedroom,' she said over her shoulder, as they neared the end of the corridor. 'Just let me know if there's anything you need. I'd better go and make up Bartie's bed.'

'Of course.' River stared at the closed door of his room. 'And thank you,' he called after Mrs Netherway, who was bustling back towards the stairs.

When he pushed open the door, a sudden rush of memories took him by surprise. His books and toys had gone, long packed away or disposed of, but the bed was the same, along with the ruby-red curtains and the faded blue wallpaper.

He walked across the room, to the window, and looked out. This side of the house overlooked the gardens that ran down to the cove, where waves were breaking on the red-tinged sand that was common in this part of Devon.

The sea was blue today, a pale blue edging towards turquoise, and the small patch of sand was empty. Grass grew right up to the cove, and the branches of the trees edging it were slanted by fierce winds that blew in with winter storms.

River turned again to the room. It felt familiar, but there were damp stains at the top of the wall, and torn patches of wallpaper that needed repair. The room had become shabby since he was last here. Or maybe it had always been that way but he'd been too young to notice.

He sat down on the bed – its mattress so saggy he wondered if it was the original one from his childhood – and took stock.

The arrival he'd been so anxious about was over, thank goodness, and he felt... River closed his eyes, unsure exactly how to describe, even to himself, the mixture of emotions he was experiencing.

He felt... happy to see his father again after all this time. Perhaps they could get to know each other better over the next few days, though there was always a risk that his father might decide River wasn't worth the effort, just as he had done sixteen years ago.

River opened his eyes and looked around his childhood bedroom. Mostly, he was glad to see Brellasham Manor. Perhaps the place wouldn't haunt his dreams now he'd set foot in it again. But he felt sorry about the approaching upheaval that would affect so many people who were, as yet, unaware of what was about to happen.

An image of Clara suddenly swam into his mind. It was good to see her after so many years. She'd changed, just as he and Bartie had. That was inevitable. But some things remained resolutely the same.

'I'm still jealous of Bartie,' he said quietly, into the empty room. 'And Clara still thinks he's wonderful.'

With a sigh, River got to his feet and wrapped his arms around his waist. He'd forgotten how cold this house got. Even when it was sunny outside, there was a chill that seemed to settle in the bones. It appeared that hadn't changed either – but change was definitely coming and soon everything would be different.

4

—————

GEOFFREY

As Geoffrey watched the two men follow Mrs Netherway up the stairs, the years fell away. The last time River had climbed the flight of stairs leading from the grand hallway he had been a boy. A teenager on the cusp of manhood. Tall and awkward, with limbs that seemed too long for his body.

Now he was thirty-one years old, and even taller, but broader and more in proportion. He was a grown man. When had that happened? How had he, his father, missed so much?

Geoffrey, a man not prone to strong emotion, was surprised by an almost physical lurch of pain that made him shudder.

'Are you all right?' asked Clara.

He glanced at the young woman who'd come to stand beside him.

'Of course I am,' he said abruptly, not happy that anyone had noticed a wobble in his demeanour. He could almost hear his father's voice in his ear: *It's up to us, Geoffrey, to set the tone. To behave in an appropriate manner and keep our feelings to ourselves.*

Geoffrey had certainly made a good fist of that over the years, even when the people in his life had disappeared: his stepmother, Audrey, his wife, Lucia, and River. His upper lip had remained stiff and his shoulders set.

And yet, older age appeared to be undermining him. His emotions were closer to the surface these days and less easy to suppress. But suppress them he must, especially now, when he knew what was coming. Otherwise he and everything around him would descend into chaos.

The girl was still standing there, looking at him with her soulful grey eyes. She bore a strong resemblance to her mother without whom this house would falter. Mrs Netherway almost single-handedly kept the house running, and yet she was blissfully unaware of the changes afoot.

He looked away from her daughter, feeling guilty. 'I think I'll retire to the library for a while. Thank you, Clara.'

Avoiding catching anyone else's eye, he slipped away into the library and sat in the leather armchair that faced the window to the garden.

He loved this room with its old books lining the walls, and a pervading smell of ink and dust. He would sit in here and read as a child when life became overwhelming, and it remained his refuge, even now that he was in his mid-seventies. When had he become so old?

Geoffrey gazed out of the window, across the grass and trees, to a flash of blue sea. He used to sit here and wonder why she did it. Why Audrey, the stepmother he'd loved so much, had decided to wade into the sea one cold autumn evening. Why her life here hadn't been enough. Why *he* hadn't been enough.

He remembered how happy she'd been at the grand ball held here in the ballroom all those years ago. How radiant she'd looked in her beautiful lemon-yellow gown during that exciting evening when the house was filled with music and laughter. That was the last time he'd seen her smile. After that, everything had changed.

Geoffrey gave his head a shake to banish the maudlin

thoughts and tried to focus on the present. His son was home, albeit not for the best of reasons, and he should take advantage of his company. Perhaps he could heal the rift between them, though he feared they had little in common. Even their appearance placed them miles apart – he, pale and cultured, in corduroy and tweed, and River looking rather like a hippy with his long hair, golden tan and jeans.

Geoffrey had to admit he had more in common with Bartie, whose company he had missed over the last few years.

A small cough made Geoffrey jump and, when he looked up, Clara was standing beside him. She was carrying a tray with a steaming china cup on it.

'I thought you might like some tea after the excitement of this morning.' She placed the tray on the side table next to him.

Geoffrey smiled at this unexpected kindness, especially after his brusque reply to her earlier question. Clara usually kept her distance from him. He wasn't sure if she liked him or not. But the tea was a kind thought.

'That's good of you, Clara. Thank you.'

He expected her to leave but she stayed standing beside him. And when he glanced up and followed her gaze, she was staring at the framed black and white photo that sat on the windowsill. The picture was a formal portrait of him as a child, with his father, Edwin, and Audrey standing behind him.

'That's a lovely picture,' she said, before sucking her bottom lip between her teeth.

'It's one of very few I have of my father and stepmother together. My father destroyed a lot of family photographs after my stepmother's death but I managed to salvage a small number.'

Geoffrey stopped talking, surprised that he had said so much.

'It's such a shame what happened to Audrey... your stepmother, I mean.' She paused. 'I'm sorry... I probably shouldn't bring up such a difficult subject.'

No, she shouldn't. And he wasn't about to say any more about such a personal issue, even though Clara had been around the manor all her life. He had never talked properly about it with anyone. Not with his wife, and certainly not with his father, who had burned most of the photos on a bonfire in the garden and placed the painting of Audrey in storage. Her name, after that, had rarely been mentioned.

But Geoffrey had put the painting back on the wall soon after his father had died, and he liked to display this photo that seemed to be interesting Clara. There was some comfort in seeing Audrey's beautiful face that would never grow old as his had done.

'It was all a long time ago,' he murmured to Clara. 'Thank you so much for the tea.'

As he'd hoped, this shut down any prospect of more conversation and Clara walked to the door. But she hesitated, her fingers gripping the door handle.

'I expect you're delighted to have River back home, and Bartie too.'

Geoffrey sat back in his chair, noting the curiosity in her gaze. Clara, always a bright spark, knew there was more going on here than a son's return to the family fold. But she'd find out soon enough.

'It is very...' he chose his words carefully, '...pleasing to see River back at Brellasham Manor. Bartie, too. We have much to discuss.'

'I'm sure you do,' said Clara, giving a tight smile before slipping out of the room.

Geoffrey sipped his tea and went back to staring through the window. There would be lots to do tomorrow but for now he would allow himself the indulgence of remembering the past.

5

CLARA

'Don't you think it's odd, River and Bartie both arriving back at the manor after years away?' asked Clara.

'What did you say?' called her mother, who'd just walked from the sitting room into the hallway of their cottage.

Clara repeated her question at top volume and then winced. Good grief, she was turning into a loud Netherway. She'd be bellowing like Michael next. During his infrequent visits from Canada, he could be heard wherever he was in the house.

'It's not odd, at all,' said Julie, poking her head back around the door. 'It's rather lovely.'

'Yes, of course it's lovely for Geoffrey, and all that. But neither River nor Bartie has been to the manor for ages and then they both turn up together on the same day, and Geoffrey was being a bit shifty when I spoke to him in the library.'

'I'm sure he wasn't being shifty. Don't be ridiculous.'

'He was, Mum. There's definitely something going on.'

Julie pursed her lips. 'Honestly, Clara, you seem determined to assign some ulterior motive to what's simply a wonderful family reunion that Geoffrey's keen to share with us all. Speaking of which, I'll need to sort out the tea and biscuits for tomorrow's get-together.'

'What get-together?'

'The get-together for everyone who's working and has worked at the manor.'

Clara puffed out her cheeks. 'Well, he hasn't invited me.'

Julie frowned. 'You should have received an email about it. Check your junk folder.'

Clara pulled her phone from her pocket and there, lying unseen amongst the junk emails was one from Geoffrey requesting – rather forcefully, Clara thought – that she be at the manor at 10 a.m. tomorrow, prompt.

She looked up at her mother. 'Yeah, I've been invited too but it's not very convenient. I've got a lot of work on tomorrow.'

'A lot' was pushing it, and the work was likely to be tedious – sorting travel arrangements for a business team heading to Switzerland for a conference. But Clara was grateful for any income at the moment. Freelancing had been her only option after giving up her permanent job to move back to Heaven's Cove, but it was proving very hand-to-mouth.

Julie's mouth had set into a firm line. 'It's a good job the get-together won't last long then,' she said in a tone that brooked no dissent. 'Anyway, you need to come along or River will think you're snubbing him, and you used to be such good friends.'

Clara felt sure River wouldn't give a monkey's whether or not she was at tomorrow's event, which was probably some celebration hailing his miraculous return. But a part of her *was* curious to know more about River's life since he'd left Heaven's Cove, and Bartie was likely to be there, too, which might liven up the proceedings.

'So, are you coming?' asked Julie, adding 'Good' when Clara nodded. 'Right, now that's sorted' – her mother pointed at a bulging carrier bag near the fireplace – 'can you sort through that stuff quickly because it's almost time to eat.'

Clara knelt down on the carpet, in front of the TV, and tipped the bag out onto the floor. The contents of her grandmother's bedside table cascaded around her.

'Like I said, it's all rubbish,' said Julie, coming back into the room carrying cutlery. She winced at the mess. 'I tipped the drawers into the carrier when we were clearing out her bedroom, and I have no idea why you want to go through it.'

'We can't just throw it all away without checking it first,' said Clara, rocking back on her heels. She did want to go through her gran's belongings but she was surprised by the extent of the pile in front of her. Who knew a couple of bedside drawers could contain so much? The floor was strewn with what looked like old receipts, plastic toys from the insides of Christmas crackers, and random nails and screws.

'The problem,' said Julie, placing the knives and forks on the table at the back of the room, 'is that your grandmother, just like you, couldn't bear to throw anything away. Fortunately, I've not inherited the hoarding gene.'

That was true enough, thought Clara, starting to go through the pile. Her mother had few qualms about throwing things out and had become more ruthless since discovering Marie Kondo, whom she worshipped as a guru.

'This stuff has been cluttering up my attic for far too long,' said Julie, placing salt and pepper pots on the table. 'Mum, God rest her soul, passed away almost three years ago now and yet her things are still taking up too much space in our small home.'

Clara wrinkled her nose. It *had* been quite a while since Gran had died and she supposed it was fair enough to have a good clear-out. However, her mother had applied a different level of ruthlessness when it came to disposing of her father's possessions. His clothes, his watch, the books he loved – they'd all gone to the charity shop within a few weeks of his death.

They're simply 'things' which won't bring him back, her mother had insisted when Clara had baulked at getting rid of his favourite jumper. *We have our lovely memories of your father, and that's all that matters.*

She was right. And Clara understood that her mother was so grief-stricken she couldn't bear to be faced with constant reminders of her lost husband. But Clara had still squirrelled away his glasses and they sat in the drawer of *her* bedside table, their lenses smudged with his fingerprints that she would never wipe away.

'You should sit in the chair while you're doing that,' said Julie, going back out to the kitchen. 'All that kneeling will destroy the cartilage in your knees.'

Clara glanced at the old armchair where her father had always sat. It was daft but she still couldn't bring herself to sit there. It felt wrong, somehow: an acknowledgement that her father was gone for good.

Clara sat back on her heels. 'I'm fine on the floor, thanks, Mum.'

'You what?' her mother yelled, sounding as if she had her head in the fridge.

'I said I'm fine on... oh, never mind.'

'One word from me and you do exactly what you want,' said Julie, returning with two glass tumblers. 'Oh, did I tell you that Michael rang yesterday to tell me he's been promoted? He's such a clever boy and doing so well out there. I always knew he'd be successful.'

Clara nodded, only half listening as her mother outlined Michael's many attributes for the umpteenth time. She needed to sort through this pile before dinner was ready.

Five minutes later she was beginning to agree with her mother that Gran had been a dreadful hoarder. The haul from the drawers included plastic cutlery, yellowed with age, receipts going back more than a decade, a passport that had expired in 2012, two ancient packs of cards, and a tube of sticky cough sweets.

Clara groaned and adjusted her position on the floor. Her knees were starting to ache but she wouldn't give her mother the satisfaction of moving to a chair.

'Food's ready,' her mother announced, coming into the room with a steaming casserole dish even though it was still baking hot outside and more the weather for salad. 'Have you finished sorting through your gran's things?'

'Just about,' said Clara, starting to scoop the remainder of the pile back into the carrier bag. 'Sorry, Gran,' she murmured, but her mother was right. This was nothing but a pile of old tat destined for the bin.

She paused when her hand brushed against something soft and, pulling aside a half-empty pack of tissues, her fingers closed around a drawstring bag made of purple velvet.

'Come on, Clara. You can finish that later,' her mother called from the table.

'Won't be a sec,' said Clara, opening the bag and pulling out a small book. It was bound in white leather, its pages edged in gold, and there was embossed lettering on the front: *Daily Diary 1957*.

Clara didn't realise that her grandmother had kept a diary. She did a quick calculation in her head. Violet Netherway would have been thirty-two years old in 1957 and working at the manor house as the housekeeper, just as her mother had done before her.

Waiting on the Brellashams truly was a Netherway family tradition, thought Clara. She smiled ruefully, aware of her mixed feelings about the ways in which the two families had become intertwined. Netherway women had shown how independent and assertive they were, as well as ahead of their time, by insisting on keeping their own surname after marriage. Her own father had been sparky enough to take on the Netherway name in honour of his wife. Yet they'd all spent decades fetching and carrying for a family who didn't always appear to appreciate their subservience and hard work.

However, as Clara often told herself, her mother was happy with the arrangement, and her father and grandmother had been too, so it was pointless being chippy about it.

Though maybe her gran's diary would paint a different picture of life at the manor. Clara opened the first page, keen to read Violet's thoughts. But *Violet Netherway* wasn't the name inscribed inside. Written, in large looping letters, was *Audrey Brellasham*.

Clara snapped the book shut. Was this really Audrey's diary and, if so, how did it come to be in her grandmother's possession, hidden beneath a pile of old junk in her bedside table?

'Clara, your food's getting cold,' called Julie, irritation in her voice.

Clara got to her feet and went to the table. 'Sorry, I got distracted. Guess what I've just found in Gran's belongings.' Without waiting for her mother's reply – because she'd never guess in a month of Sundays – she told her: 'Audrey Brellasham's diary.'

Julie blinked and stopped ladling beef stew onto Clara's plate. 'What do you mean, Audrey Brellasham's diary?'

'I mean it's a diary from 1957 and it's got Audrey's name written inside it so I presume it's hers. Look.'

'No,' said her mother forcefully, as Clara went to open the book. 'Please put the diary down and leave it, Clara.'

'Why? Don't you want to know more about the kind of woman Audrey was? No one ever mentions her. Well, Geoffrey did briefly today but only after I commented on the photo of her in the library.'

'You spoke to Geoffrey about his stepmother?' Julie frowned. 'You shouldn't have done that.'

'Why not? I understand that it must have been traumatic

for him when she died but that was almost seventy years ago now, and this diary might contain her final words.'

Beef stew splattered across the table as Julie waved the ladle in Clara's face. 'I meant what I said, Clara. Step away from the diary. Now!'

Her mother looked so panicked, Clara placed the book on the table, unopened.

'What on earth's the matter, Mum?'

'You shouldn't be reading someone's diary, that's all.' Julie pushed it across the table, out of Clara's reach. 'Reading someone else's diary is very wrong. It's a gross betrayal of trust.'

'It's wrong if they're alive. But Audrey has been dead for so long, I can't see that it would do any harm.'

Julie placed the ladle carefully into the casserole dish and swallowed hard. 'You have no idea what harm that diary could do. No idea at all.'

'Then tell me, Mum,' said Clara gently, alarmed by her mother's outburst. 'How can I understand if I don't know what's going on?'

'It's not what's going on now, it's what went on in 1957.' Julie breathed out slowly as if she was coming to a decision. Then, she gave a slight nod. 'It's not something your grandmother ever spoke about but the fact is she almost went to prison after Audrey Brellasham went missing.'

'What, Gran? Prison?' Clara's jaw dropped at the thought of gentle Violet Netherway, an upstanding member of the local community, facing jail. 'What did she do?'

'Absolutely nothing but that didn't stop suspicion falling on her when a diamond necklace went missing at the same time as Audrey. She was accused of theft.'

'Why would someone suspect her of stealing the necklace?' asked Clara, sinking onto a seat.

'She was at the manor house, serving up a meal to Edwin, when Audrey went into the sea, so they couldn't pin that on her. But afterwards, when search parties were trying to find Audrey, your gran was seen by a maid going into the woman's bedroom and coming out with something in her pocket.

'Before he joined in the search, Edwin decreed that no one should go into his wife's room, and your gran always denied being in there. But the police were involved for a while and, though she was ultimately exonerated, mud sticks, doesn't it? It happened a few years before I was born but your grandfather told me she'd had a dreadful time with it all. She almost lost her job but Edwin relented when the police dropped the case.'

'Poor Gran,' said Clara quietly.

'Poor Gran, indeed. The whole thing was totally ridiculous. She'd hardly have stuck around here, cooking and cleaning for the Brellashams, if she'd had tens of thousands of pounds' worth of diamonds stashed away. We'd have all been living it up in the Bahamas.'

Clara agreed that they would have, biting down her anger that such an unfair accusation had ever been made. Violet Netherway had given years of her life to making the Brellashams' lives more comfortable. She'd continued working after getting married and having a child, even though that wasn't the done thing back then, and yet that was how they repaid her.

'The maid was mistaken, of course. I doubt Mum was anywhere near Audrey Brellasham's bedroom,' continued Julie as the stew grew colder beside her.

'Unless she went into Audrey's bedroom for the diary.'

Julie stared at Clara, blinking rapidly. 'What do you mean?'

'She must have taken Audrey's diary. How else would it have ended up in her bedside table?'

'But why would she—' Julie stopped mid-sentence and shook her head. 'None of it makes any sense. It didn't then and it doesn't now, and all I know is that Audrey Brellasham's diary will drag everything up again so you need to leave it well alone.'

'OK, Mum,' said Clara gently, reaching across the table to

pick up the diary which she placed back into its velvet bag. 'Perhaps I should give it to Geoffrey.'

'No. Absolutely not. That man has suffered enough. He was only a young boy when his stepmother drowned and I don't want this diary dredging it all up again for him. Or reminding him and other people in the village about the dreadful rumours about my mother and the Netherway family.'

Clara weighed the book in her palm. It felt heavy with secrets.

'So what *do* we do with it?' she asked.

'We throw it away, with the rest of the rubbish in that carrier bag, and pretend that it was never found.' Julie got up from the table and held out her hand. 'Give it to me, please.'

When Clara handed the diary over, Julie went out of the room and, after a few moments, Clara heard the lid of the kitchen bin clang shut.

'That's done,' her mother declared, coming back into the sitting room, a flush staining her cheeks pink. 'Now, let's eat our meal and talk about something else.'

She ladled out lukewarm stew and Clara, noticing a faint tremble in her mother's hands, changed the subject to River and Bartie's return.

Clara couldn't sleep. The clock at Heaven's Cove church had just struck three chimes to mark ten forty-five, its sound carrying faintly on the wind, but Clara was still wide awake.

Her mother had retired to bed early, after a bizarre evening spent making small talk and never mentioning the elephant in the room – or, rather, the diary in the bin.

Clara had stayed up a little later but had now been tossing and turning in bed for almost an hour as sleep eluded her. There were too many thoughts racing through her mind:

thoughts of River and Bartie's return, her grandmother's ordeal regarding the missing necklace, and Audrey Brellasham's final written words.

After another five minutes of not sleeping, Clara got out of bed and padded to the window. Navy clouds were scudding across an inky sky, and a pale moon was peeping from behind them. Dark water glinted through the trees and a bat flitted past, making her jump.

Clara shivered as moonlight cast shadows across the grass. Were there ghosts in this cottage, which was built at the same time as the manor? Spectres of ancestral Netherways, perhaps, who were for ever tied to this place?

Fortunately, she'd never felt spooked in her home. But Brellasham Manor was another matter.

Clara often caught a shadow at the corner of her eye when she walked through the elegant rooms of the stately home. The manor definitely felt haunted – still inhabited by the souls of people long gone. People like Edwin, Geoffrey's father, and Audrey, whose bedroom remained out of bounds behind a perpetually locked door.

River was still breathing but he seemed like a ghost, too, back in the manor house that he'd left behind so long ago.

Clara's mind spooled back through the years. She'd known that River's mother, Lucia, had been thinking of leaving Brellasham Manor for good – just as Audrey had done, though Lucia was planning a less tragic exit. River had taken her into his confidence and sworn her to secrecy, and it was a secret she'd kept. But when their departure came, it had been swift and unexpected.

He'd promised, if he and his mother left, that he would keep in touch but there had been no letters or photographs from his new life in Australia. Nothing but a postcard a few weeks after he'd gone, with no return address, that said: *Dear Clo* (his nickname for her at the time), *Probably best not to keep in touch now I've moved on. I really hope you have a good life. R.*

The brusque finality of it still made her heart hurt. *I really hope you have a good life.* As if he cared. He had disappeared, and Bartie had soon followed suit. Clara, an emotional fifteen-year-old with a crush on eighteen-year-old Bartie, might have thought she would miss River's cousin the most. But, in fact, it was shy, awkward River whose company she most craved.

Clara did her best to banish both men from her thoughts and turned from the window. She should go back to bed and try to sleep, but she couldn't stop picturing Audrey writing in the diary that was now lying in the kitchen bin.

Perhaps her mum was right and it was best forgotten. But Clara wanted to find out more about Audrey, whose perfect life had ended in such tragedy. A woman who had seemingly been almost airbrushed from the Brellasham family history ever since. Didn't her voice deserve to be heard?

Opening her door quietly, Clara walked down the stairs, switched on the hall light and went into the kitchen. A potent smell of old meat and decaying vegetables hit her nose when she opened the bin. The diary was nowhere to be seen so she put on the rubber gloves beside the sink and pushed her hand into the mess.

'There must be better things to be doing late at night,' she murmured, her nose wrinkling as her hand slid deeper through the squelchy rubbish. 'Sleeping, for a start... aha!' Her fingers had found the diary.

The velvet bag was ruined, its nap stained and smelly. But the diary inside was clean when Clara took off her gloves and slid it into her hand. Pushing the book into the pocket of her dressing gown, she reburied the bag deep in the bin and tiptoed upstairs to her room. Then, she got into bed and placed the diary on the duvet next to her.

Clara felt horribly conflicted. She knew she should listen to her mum and put the diary back in the bin, before her actions were discovered. But another voice was calling from across the years. Was that fanciful? she wondered. Perhaps she really was becoming obsessed with a dead woman.

Clara pulled back her shoulders, tucked away her guilt for disobeying her mother, and picked up the book. Then she opened the diary and began to read.

6

RIVER

It was long gone ten o'clock, but there was still a faint glow in the sky that caught the swell of the ocean. A silver moon was rising above the horizon and casting a path across the waves.

It was beautiful, thought River, sitting on the sand. A damn sight colder than Australia but, on the plus side, there was no risk of sharks lurking in the water.

It was funny, he thought, pulling his knees up under his chin. He'd been dreading coming back to Brellasham Manor, which held so many bad memories – his parents arguing, slammed doors, his mother crying and his father retreating to the library. He'd tried to block them out, over the years. But, without realising it, he'd blocked out the good memories too.

Heaven's Cove was a beautiful village in the midst of glorious countryside. Driving through the village this morning, he'd been struck anew by the never-ending charm of its white-washed cottages and winding lanes. It felt like home.

And being here at the house, seeing Clara again, had reminded him of happy days they'd spent together during school holidays, exploring the moors nearby, climbing trees in the manor grounds, swimming in this cove.

He'd known her for as long as he could remember, and they'd been best friends by the time they hit their teens. She was someone he could talk to about his posh boarding school that he hated, and the deteriorating relationship between his parents. She'd been a good listener and a great keeper of secrets.

They'd been thick as thieves, until Bartie had started joining them. River had never taken much notice of the saying 'two's company, three's a crowd' until then. Clara was dazzled by older Bartie's good looks and confidence, and River couldn't blame her. He'd been rather dazzled too... and diminished.

He glanced through the trees behind him. He could just make out the cottage from here where Mrs N lived and there was a light on in Clara's bedroom. What was she doing? he wondered.

'Penny for your thoughts,' said Bartie, suddenly, making River jump. 'I saw you from the library window, sitting out here, all on your own. Not thinking of wading into the water, are you? I can't believe your return to the family fold has been that bad!'

'It's not been bad at all. Not really,' said River, wrong-footed by Bartie's appearance. 'It's good to see my father again, and this place which has hardly changed.'

'Have you had a good chat with Geoffrey yet?' asked Bartie, plonking himself down on the sand. 'About... you know.'

'No. Not yet. He's been busy on the phone.'

River didn't mention that he'd tried to speak to his father but, several excuses later, had given up. He'd got the feeling that his father was trying to avoid him.

Maybe, River told himself, he was simply being overly sensitive after an emotionally heightened day. But ever since he'd left as a teenager with his mother, the relationship with his father had been hard to maintain. They'd met up a few times, when his father was in Australia on business, but he'd never enjoyed those brief visits that were filled with stilted conversation and awkward silences.

River would sit with Geoffrey in some soulless hotel bar or restaurant, wishing he was at home with his mother instead. His mum's colourful, modern house in Sydney – so different from the manor she'd chosen to leave behind – often rang with her warm laughter. He hadn't heard his father laugh for a long time.

'Old Geoff does seem busy but I managed to nab him for ten minutes.' Bartie grinned. 'He doesn't change. Still the same old curmudgeon.'

'Did you discuss his plans?' asked River, experiencing a twinge of jealousy because his father had found time for Bartie.

His cousin adopted a more serious expression. 'We did, and he seems determined to go through with it. It's a shame, of course.'

River nodded. 'It's a real shame. I understand why he sees it as the only way forward but it'll break his heart.'

'It's for the best, though, don't you think? The best for all of us.'

River supposed so. He hugged his arms around his legs because it was chilly out here, even though Bartie had come outside in his shirtsleeves.

Bartie nudged his shoulder against River's. 'Hey, changing the subject... what about Clara Netherway then?'

River glanced at Bartie, who was staring out to sea. 'What about her?'

'I didn't think she'd still be living in Heaven's Cove so it was a pleasant surprise to find her here. What did you think of her?'

'What did I think?' River hesitated. 'I thought it was good to see her again.'

'It certainly was,' snorted Bartie. 'She was an annoying teenager the last time I saw her, with braces and dreadful plaits. But, boy, she's changed for the better. You could drown in those big grey eyes and I loved her slightly arsey attitude. There's something rather... naughty about her, don't you think?'

'Mmm,' said River noncommittally. She'd been slightly

arsey with him, but he hadn't noticed her being the same with his cousin.

'I know you and Clara were close, back in the day, but I was wondering, do you mind if I have a crack at her, while we're here?'

River shifted round in the sand until he could make out Bartie's face in the moonlight. 'A *crack* at her?'

Bartie had the good grace to look a little shame-faced. 'Sorry, that was rather ungentlemanly of me. What I mean is, do you mind if I try to woo her?'

River blinked. 'Your love life is none of my concern.'

'I suppose she might be married...'

Was she married? wondered River. Had Clara found the love of her life while he was ten thousand miles away?

'But she wasn't wearing a wedding ring,' continued Bartie. 'And when I was talking to Mrs N, while she was making up my bed, there was no mention of her daughter having a boyfriend or anything. She's the type of woman to mention it too.'

'What about your girlfriend? Mary, was it? You mentioned her during our drive down from London.'

Actually, Bartie had passed the time from Wincanton to Yeovil – a good thirty minutes – telling lurid tales of his love life. It all sounded far more exciting than River's, which Bartie hadn't enquired about beyond ascertaining that he was currently single.

'You mean Mariella, my beautiful fiery Italian. She's not really my girlfriend. It's just casual between us. We both do our own thing, if you know what I mean.'

River raised an eyebrow, wondering if Mariella realised that their relationship was 'just casual'.

'But what about you, mate?' asked Bartie, giving River's shoulder another nudge. 'You've been very tight-lipped about your love life.'

'There's not much to tell. I've gone out with a few

Australian women but there's been no one serious.' Except Kitty, who had broken his heart two years ago. But he wasn't about to tell Bartie that. He doubted that Bartie had ever had his heart broken. He was the heartbreaker in his relationships.

What if he broke Clara's heart? River pushed down his concerns because Bartie was right. Clara was all grown up now – a very different person from the girl he'd known all those years ago. And her heart was her business and hers alone.

'Well, that's great we've got that sorted,' said Bartie. He got to his feet and slapped River on the back. 'And it's so good to be back at Brellasham Manor with you. If only for a short while.' He looked around the shadowed beach and at the black waves breaking onto the sand. 'It's a bit weird sitting on your own in the dark so don't stay out here too long.'

'I won't. I'll be in, in a minute.'

River watched Bartie make his way through the trees and cross the grass, silhouetted by light coming from the library. Then he turned his attention once more to the sea.

It felt surreal to be sitting here, with an owl hooting in the trees behind him and the sand growing colder. Audrey had left Brellasham Manor, and his mother had, too. Neither of them would ever return but here he was, back in his childhood home that held so many memories. He could only hope that coming back hadn't been a horrible mistake.

7

CLARA

Audrey's first diary entry, on the day that heralded the start of 1957, was brief: *A new year beckons and I'm filled with hope for new beginnings. The gardens will soon be in bloom again and days will be long and carefree. Who knows what the coming twelve months will bring? I'm excited to find out.*

Clara swallowed and brushed her fingers across the neat handwriting, her skin touching paper that Audrey had touched.

It was so sad that Audrey would not live to see all of those twelve months. She would be dead by the autumn of 1957. But on January the first of that year, she sounded so vibrant and alive.

Clara stopped reading, her heart pounding when she heard her mother's bedroom door opening. She balled her fists as Julie walked past on her way to the bathroom, landing floorboards creaking with every step. Would she notice the light under Clara's door?

'Don't come in,' muttered Clara, knowing that one look at her guilty face would give the game away. She pushed the diary under the duvet and held her breath.

A couple of minutes later, the flush sounded and floor-boards creaked as Julie made her way back to her own room.

Clara exhaled slowly when she heard her mum's door close and fished the diary from beneath her bedclothes. She had to do this quickly because her nerves were in shreds. Even the hooting of an owl in the trees outside, usually a comforting sound, was making her jumpy tonight.

Swiftly turning page after page, Clara began to leaf through the diary. Audrey was not a prolific diary writer and had penned only a few lines each day. But she spoke of walks on the moors, spending time with young Geoffrey, and meals with her husband, Edwin, whom, she noted more than once, was an incredibly busy man.

No friends were mentioned and Clara wondered if Audrey had been a lonely woman in her grand house, with only her stepson and busy husband for company. Though there must have been other people in the house, back in the 1950s. Her own grandmother, Violet, for a start, who must have had some sort of relationship with the 'lady of the manor' or she'd never have spirited away her diary after her disappearance.

Clara turned another page – now in March – and frowned. There were the usual few lines, in Audrey's flowing writing, reporting on a walk taken around the manor gardens. But there was something else beneath them. A row of numbers: 159-37 50-21 285-17 76-03.

Clara studied them for a moment but the numbers meant nothing to her.

She turned another few pages and there were the numbers again – different ones this time, but written in the same style: a number followed by a dash and a second number, and then a space.

She flicked through the pages. Numbers were written beneath several diary entries through to July. Were Audrey's words on 'number days' any different from other days when no numbers appeared?

She re-read the diary, from January to the end of June, but nothing leapt out at her. Audrey's daily entries became even shorter as the year went on, with little mention of her family. But there was a shift in tone, Clara realised. The vibrancy of January was gone by June. Something appeared to be affecting Audrey's mood. But still the numbers made no sense.

Clara stopped reading and looked out of the window. The sky had cleared and the silvery moon was shining bright. The same moon that had lit up the night sky over Brellasham Manor more than six decades earlier, as Audrey had written these words and numbers in her diary. Time had slipped through Audrey's fingers, and Clara had the strangest sensation of it slipping through her fingers too. Who knew what lay ahead for any of them?

She gave her shoulders a shake, to anchor herself in the present, and went back to the diary and its tales from the past.

There was a marked change in Audrey's mood from mid-July, thanks to a grand ball that was being arranged for early September 1957. She sounded happy and excited, and the strange series of numbers, Clara noticed, had stopped.

The dance Audrey was so looking forward to was due to take place in the manor ballroom which was now used for little more than taking afternoon tea. Clara leafed on through Audrey's animated entries. They mentioned everything from the guest list, and what food and music was planned, to what she and Edwin would be wearing.

She had chosen to wear a dress she already owned but had hardly worn. And as Clara read her description of it – a gown of pale lemon satin with a strapless bodice and a full skirt with chiffon overlay – she realised it was the same dress that Audrey was wearing in her portrait.

Her outfit would be completed, Audrey noted in the diary, with the Brellasham family diamond necklace that Edwin had gifted her on their wedding day.

Clara lay back on her bed and imagined the woman in the portrait, all dressed up for the ball, with diamonds at her throat, coming to life. She must have been so delighted as the ball began. Did she have a wonderful evening?

Clara needed to know and turned the pages until she came to September the seventh.

It's now two in the morning and the ball is over, but what a marvellous evening we had. It was everything I could have wished for, to see the house so full of life. Such a wonderful change. Geoffrey had fun and Edwin seemed happy, too. I wished that the ball could go on for ever.

Clara smiled, happy to know that the dance had lived up to Audrey's expectations. But there was no diary entry on September the eighth. The page was blank. Perhaps she'd been suffering with a hangover or had slept all day so had nothing to report.

But the following day's entry brought Clara up short: *Everything is black and broken and it's partly my fault. Life cannot go on this way so perhaps it's time.*

Time for what? Clara bit her lip, realising that Audrey had walked into the sea around a week later. Something must have happened after the ball to bring Audrey's mood crashing through the floor. And the numbers were back. More numbers now, scrawled untidily across the following pages, until Clara reached September the seventeenth, the day of Audrey's drowning.

I'm cruel to leave Geoffrey, she'd written. *He won't understand my actions or that his life will continue well without me in it. But Edwin will care for him, I'm sure of it. That's the only reason I feel able to leave this life.*

Clara swallowed, a lump in her throat. There must have

been little to no mental health support for women like Audrey back then. Women who, from the outside, had everything: a family, a magnificent home, amazing balls and fairy tale dresses. Yet, beneath it all, she was no different from Clara, whose mood often dipped although she, too, had a comfortable if rather less grand life.

'It's so sad,' said Clara out loud, still puzzled that the diary had been amongst her grandmother's possessions.

There was no mention of Violet within its pages, and while she and Audrey might have been friends, that seemed unlikely between the lady of the manor and the housekeeper. Even today, there was a clear delineation between 'upstairs' and 'downstairs'. Her mum had worked for Geoffrey for years but there was still a formality between them which put Clara's teeth on edge.

Clara groaned because all of this guesswork was getting her nowhere and time was ticking on. She picked up the diary and closed it with a snap, wondering whether to put it back in the bin and leave it there. What was the point in resurrecting such unhappiness? But a scrap of paper fluttered down from the back of the book.

Clara picked it up and frowned. The paper contained nothing but another string of numbers: *49-6 197-23 74-29 224-1 14-33 279-17 199-8 289-2*

They were written in the same format as the others in the diary. But these were written by someone else, Clara was sure of it. The figures were smaller and neater, but what on earth did they all mean?

Clara pushed the piece of paper back into the diary and shoved the book into the drawer of her bedside table. She felt as if she'd opened a can of worms, and her head was beginning to ache. She should have listened to her mother and left the diary to rot with the vegetable peelings. At least then it couldn't mess with her mind.

After switching off the bedside lamp, Clara lay in the darkness. Sleep took some time to come that night but, when it did, she dreamed of a woman in a lemon-yellow dress, sinking beneath a grey sea, her body entwined in strings of numbers that tightened around her limbs.

8

CLARA

Clara was sitting next to her mother in the room that had once echoed to the sound of Audrey's grand ball. The dance, so keenly anticipated, that seemed to have sparked the chain of events that led to her death.

'What's the matter with you?' Julie leaned closer and stared into her face. 'You look a bit peaky this morning.'

'Thanks, Mum.' Clara ran a hand through her hair, hoping she didn't look too much of a fright. 'I didn't sleep too well last night. I had bad dreams.'

'Sparked by a bad conscience, I dare say.'

Clara swallowed. 'What do you mean?'

'You promised to finish the washing up before you came up to bed but there were still a few dirty pots on the kitchen counter when I got up.'

Clara's jaw unclenched as she realised her late-night forage through the bin was still a secret. 'Sorry, Mum. I forgot. I'll do them before I start work.'

'No need. I did them before you got up.' Julie looked around the room, which was buzzing with the hum of conversation. 'I didn't realise that Geoffrey had invited so many of us. He must be absolutely delighted by River's return and keen to share his excitement.'

'Maybe,' said Clara, who found it hard to imagine Geoffrey – a man not known for being emotional – being excited, let alone wanting to share it.

In all the years she'd known him, Clara had never seen Geoffrey lose his temper and had rarely seen him smile. He always seemed level, distant and somewhat cold – a combination that River had found difficult to cope with as a teenager.

Clara, who'd had a close and loving relationship with her father, had sometimes felt sorry for him back then: the poor little rich boy wanting for nothing, save paternal approval. His Australian mother, Lucia, was the opposite – vibrant, caring and tactile – so it was little wonder that her marriage to much older Geoffrey had come to such a messy end.

Her mum nudged her arm. 'This is a beautiful room, don't you think? It's such a shame that it's hardly used these days.'

'It is,' said Clara, taking in the portraits of long-gone Brellashams, the twinkling chandeliers, huge windows overlooking the gardens, and the opulent flocked wallpaper.

Sometimes, when the house was quiet, Clara would stand in here and imagine dancers in beautiful crinolines, being whirled around the floor by their beaux. Their faces lit by flickering candlelight while an orchestra played. Sometimes she fancied she could hear strains of the music – violins soaring to meet the intricately plastered ceiling. And now she knew that Audrey and Edwin had danced on these floorboards on September the seventh 1957.

Everything is black and broken. Audrey's words written in her diary two days later sprang into Clara's mind. What had happened here in this room to cause such a catastrophic change in her mental health? she wondered, as the past and present began to collide.

A sharp dig in the ribs from her mother's elbow cut into Clara's thoughts.

'I hope there will be enough refreshments for everyone. Geoffrey seems to have invited every tradesman who's ever worked on the house.' She tutted. 'I wish he'd given me a better idea of numbers.'

'Don't worry. I'm sure people won't expect much, and I can give you a hand with making tea and coffee later, if you'd like,' said Clara, whose guilty conscience about fishing Audrey's diary out of the bin currently outweighed any worries about getting her freelance work finished.

'That would be helpful. Thank you. Oh, here they are!' Julie tilted her head towards the door. 'It's so lovely to see the boys together again, isn't it? Don't they both look handsome!'

A hush fell over the ballroom as River and Bartie walked across the floor and sat in two of the three chairs that had been placed in front of the windows. They bent their heads close together in conversation and Clara had a chance to take a good look at the two men she'd once known as boys.

In appearance, they were chalk and cheese – short-haired Bartie with his dark, leading man good looks, and River, with his thick, fair hair reaching to his shoulders. He wasn't as conventionally handsome as Bartie but, Clara had to agree with her mother, he was good looking too. Once all limbs and sharp features, he seemed to have grown into his body. Now he was a strapping man of thirty-one, with a golden tan that accentuated the soulful brown eyes he'd inherited from his mother.

Overall, he looked far more like his mum than his dad, thought Clara, studying him closely. Geoffrey wasn't bad looking, in spite of his tragic comb-over, but he'd become paunchy over the years. Whereas River looked taut and lean, as if he'd been working out in Australia. His shoulders were broad and the muscles in his upper arms were well defined.

He suddenly glanced up and caught Clara's eye. 'Awkward,' she murmured to herself, looking away and feeling embarrassed.

Fortunately, Geoffrey chose that moment to make his entrance and everyone's attention turned to him as he walked to the windows and stood beside his son.

It was good to see the two of them back together, Clara realised, though their close proximity only exacerbated their differences. River was still wearing jeans, with a pale blue T-shirt hanging loose. Whereas Geoffrey had on a checked shirt and mustard-yellow trousers, as if he was trying to live up to the stereotype of an aristocrat.

Beside them both, in smart grey chinos and a crisp white shirt, Bartie leaned back in his chair and gave Clara a wink. Clara swallowed and shifted in her seat.

'Stop fidgeting,' hissed her mother as Geoffrey stepped forward. 'He's about to speak.'

Geoffrey stood for a moment, looking out at the expectant gathering and cleared his throat.

'Thank you all for coming,' he said in his booming voice. 'I have a few things of importance that I'd like to impart.'

When he clasped his hands together, Clara realised that he was nervous, and a shiver went down her spine. Why were they really here, a ragtag group of employees, past and present, in a room that had once rung to the sound of festivities?

'Thank you all for coming this morning,' he said, unclasping his hands. He winced. 'I do believe I've said that already. Anyway, it's wonderful to have my son, River, here, and Bartholomew – Bartie – too, of course.'

He cleared his throat again. 'You all know and love Brellasham Manor, as do I. This house has been home to my family since it was built, more than two hundred years ago. However, unfortunately, that is the problem.'

He glanced at Bartie, who gave him an almost imperceptible nod. 'It has become increasingly expensive to manage the upkeep of this house, especially as it is so close to the sea and is battered by ferocious weather every winter.

'You all do a marvellous job in keeping this house, and me, running. You have done over the years.' Geoffrey looked at Clara's mother and gave her a faint smile. 'But frankly, it's all becoming too much.'

People in the room had started exchanging glances. Clara looked at River, trying to read his expression, to anticipate what was coming next. But he was staring resolutely ahead, his face neutral. Was his father stepping aside so that he could take over as 'lord of the manor'?

Geoffrey turned his palms towards the ceiling. 'Basically, the situation cannot continue as it is. It's taken me some time to come to terms with that fact but' – he swallowed – 'it's now time to move on and pass this house into other hands. It's time to sell Brellasham Manor.'

A collective gasp echoed around the room and Clara's stomach did a flip.

Geoffrey held up his hand to staunch any comments from the floor. 'Obviously, I don't want to sell this house but I have come to understand that it's the only way forward. It's time to pass it on to a developer who can make this house work, as a new type of accommodation. Bartie has some ideas about that. It seems that the manor could be transformed into a number of luxury apartments.'

He raised his hand again to quell a hum of dissent from his audience. 'I realise that this will come as a shock to you, and leaving this house will be' – he paused – 'difficult, but it appears to be the only option.

'I will, of course, keep you informed as I appreciate that your livelihoods will be affected, and for that I am sorry.' He stopped and studied his feet for a moment, before raising his head. 'But we will do our best to ensure that none of you are left in the lurch. I'm afraid that needs must and, while I may not like it, I learned from my father, who never shirked from doing what was necessary, that hard decisions sometimes have to be made.'

He sat down, his audience now stunned into silence. Clara blinked, hardly able to believe what she'd just heard. *Luxury apartments* – meaning swanky homes that locals like her could never hope to afford.

Clara loved this house. It had been a part of her life since she was born, and the thought of not being able to walk its rooms, or dangle her feet in the stone fountain on hot days, or sit on the sand and gaze at the ocean, took her breath away.

Then, she felt guilty because both Geoffrey and her mother faced losing far more – though it was hard to feel as sorry for Geoffrey as it was for her mum. It was devastating, of course, that he would have to leave a home that had been in his family for generations. But the money from the sale would mean he could live out his days in comfort.

Whereas, her mother would lose both her home and her job – a job which had helped to keep her life turning over following the death of her husband. She would have to find rented accommodation somewhere else and, if new work was hard to come by, her finances would take a battering.

When Clara reached across and clasped her mother's hand, Julie squeezed her fingers. She'd gone pale and was blinking, as if she might cry.

Being the housekeeper here was more than a job to her. The Netherway family had been a part of Brellasham Manor for so many years. They'd maintained the grounds, kept its occupants fed and – Clara thought of the diary in her bedside table, and its strange sequences of numbers – they'd kept its secrets safe.

'There will be time for questions later,' said Geoffrey, speaking from his chair. 'But first, let's hear from Bartie, who, along with River, will be managing the sale.'

All eyes turned to Bartie, who slowly got to his feet and smiled at the upturned faces in front of him.

'Hi, everyone. I'm related to the Brellasham family. What's our connection, Geoffrey?' He turned to Geoffrey, who was staring at his hands clasped in his lap. 'First cousin twice removed? Second cousin once removed? Something like that.'

He turned back to his audience, with his easy grin that lit up his handsome face.

'But I'm also a successful entrepreneur who dabbles in property and I have a variety of contacts in the development market. So, when I heard that Geoffrey was enduring stressful financial challenges, I said I'd be happy to help him seek a viable solution.

'We all know that this house is wonderful but it's also, not to put too fine a point on it, a money pit. Damp is an ongoing problem, utility bills are increasingly onerous, and the roof, despite patch-ups here and there over the years, has increasingly fallen into disrepair. It's now reached a state where most if not all of the roof needs to be replaced and that's no easy feat. We have to use expensive slate tiles, which means the bill is likely to be eye-wateringly high.'

He smiled again which seemed jarring in the circumstances. 'In short, I'm afraid there's nothing to be done other than sell the house. And I'm here to help ensure that Geoffrey receives the best possible price, while also preserving the special feel of this amazing house that has been a haven to me ever since I was a child.'

It might have been a haven when he was a teenager, but Clara didn't think he'd been back here for a good few years. Perhaps she was wrong and her mum hadn't mentioned his more recent visits.

Phillip, the manor's part-time gardener-cum-handyman, raised his hand, as if he was at school.

Bartie glanced at him. 'Yes? Did you have a question?'

'Yeah, I do. I can see why Geof... Mr Brellasham is finding the house a handful. Not meaning to be rude but he's getting on a bit.'

'That is quite rude,' muttered Julie, but Phillip continued unabashed.

'To be honest, I have enough trouble making ends meet and I live in a cottage – I'm in the old harbour master's place by the lifeboat station.' People around him nodded. 'But why doesn't the son take the house on?' He glanced over at River. 'Sorry, I can't remember your name, mate. Storm, or something?'

'It's River,' said Bartie, twisting his mouth in amusement. 'I think River feels that... Actually, why don't we hear from the man himself? River, over to you.'

Bartie sat down, clearing the floor for River, who got to his feet.

'Thanks, Bartie, and thanks to, um, Geoffrey.'

He'd used his first name. River and Geoffrey had never been particularly close but, sixteen years ago, at least he'd called him 'father'.

'Thank you to all of you for being here.' His eyes briefly settled on Clara and then moved on. 'I'm sorry that we've had to give you bad news today.'

He shifted from foot to foot and cleared his throat. 'For those of you who don't know me, I spent the first years of my life in this house before my mother and I moved to Australia when I was a teenager.' The Australian twang in his voice was unmistakable.

'Though I've seen my father in Australia since then, I've never been back to England. However, I recently became aware of the difficulties that Geoffrey is facing with this house so I've come over to offer what help I can. Along with my cousin Bartie, who, like me, has links to the manor but, unlike me, has the expertise to push a sale forward. I don't think my work as a software programmer has equipped me for striking a hard-nosed property deal.'

He gave an awkward laugh as Clara remembered River's interest in computers and IT as a teenager. So, he'd made it his career.

'But couldn't *you* stay and take on the house?' urged Phillip.

River shook his head. 'I'm afraid not. The financial difficulties posed by this house would be exactly the same for me, and my work and life are back in Australia. Brellasham Manor isn't my home and it hasn't been for a long time.' He glanced at Geoffrey, who was still staring into his lap. 'Anyway, that's all we know at the moment but we'll keep you informed.'

'Yes,' said Geoffrey, pushing himself up from his chair. 'We wanted to make you aware of the situation and we'll keep you abreast of our plans to sell and how your jobs will be affected. Thank you for coming.'

'Well,' said Julie as a discontented murmur rose around them. 'That's that then.'

'I can't believe it,' muttered Clara, trying to make sense of what they'd just been told. 'Are you all right, Mum?'

'Of course I am.' Julie stood up abruptly and smoothed her hands down her skirt. 'All good things come to an end. Isn't that what they say? Well, there's no point in crying over spilt milk. Worse things happen at sea.'

Clara blinked at the deluge of platitudes. 'If you say so, Mum, but don't you think—'

'It's best not to think, I find,' said Julie tartly. 'Now, we'd better get refreshments organised for everyone. You said you could help me with that.'

'Of course I can, but—'

Julie raised a hand. 'Let's get on with it, then. There's absolutely no point in panicking because I'm sure that someone will pull a rabbit out of a hat and come to Brellasham Manor's rescue. Don't you think?'

'Um... probably. Possibly.'

Julie nodded towards River, Bartie and Geoffrey, who were surrounded by people asking questions. 'Perhaps Bartie will come up with a solution, or River will decide to stay after all.'

'Mmm.' Clara twisted her mouth. 'I doubt it, to be honest, Mum. He said himself that he doesn't feel he belongs here.'

'Then perhaps Katrina will change his mind,' said Julie, raising an eyebrow at the village vamp who had once done some work for Geoffrey and was now standing far too close to River.

'I hardly think so.'

There was a strange fizzing feeling in Clara's chest. River would never fall for Katrina's outrageous flirting, would he? She was totally wrong for him, though Clara didn't know how she could be sure of that after so many years.

Back when they were teenagers, River took little notice of the pretty girls in Heaven's Cove. He said he preferred 'interesting' girls with stories to tell. Though he was probably only being kind to Clara, who felt like an ugly duckling, with her unruly, thick hair and freckles. They'd got on so well back then. Clara had trusted him implicitly, and he'd entrusted her with his secrets. But then he'd let her down.

However, none of that mattered now, thought Clara. The manor was going to be sold and its link with generations of Brellasham and Netherway families severed. River would head back to Australia, after having a fling with Katrina or not – and, however brave Julie was about the situation, nothing would ever be the same again, either for the Brellasham family or for the Netherways.

9

CLARA

Everyone had disappeared an hour later, leaving dozens of dirty tea cups in the ballroom and biscuit crumbs scattered across the polished wooden floorboards.

Clara was supposed to be helping her mum clear up but, right now, all she was doing was gazing out of the window, trying to make sense of the bombshell that had just been dropped.

Her mum was still in denial over the news that she faced losing her job and her home. And then there was Geoffrey.

Clara closed her eyes and tilted her face up towards the sun whose warmth was penetrating the glass. How was it possible to hold two such opposing feelings at the same time? she wondered.

She resented Geoffrey's sense of entitlement and the hold Brellasham Manor appeared to have had on her family for so long. She also felt strongly that her mother had deserved to find out news of the imminent sale ahead of time and in private.

Yet she also felt sorry for Geoffrey, who was, in essence, a lonely old man rattling round this place with no family to love him.

In many ways he'd made a hash of his privileged life. But maybe he'd been damaged by his stepmother's death when he was only a child – younger than River had been when he'd left Brellasham Manor for good. And trauma like that cast a long shadow.

Where would he go if the house was sold? She couldn't imagine him in some posh residential care community, or living alone in a penthouse somewhere. And his shaky relationship with his son meant he'd hardly be heading to Australia for a new start.

I should be more compassionate and understanding, thought Clara, opening her eyes. That was something she didn't like about herself – her propensity to judge other people when she had plenty of faults of her own.

After all, she was, in effect, lying to her mum about Audrey's diary which was now nestling in her bag in the corner of the room.

What would Audrey think about the house being sold? she wondered. Perhaps she wouldn't care because she hadn't been happy here.

The chiming of the grandfather clock on the landing brought Clara's thoughts back to the present and she began to tidy up before her mother caught her slacking.

After piling a teetering mountain of china onto a tray, Clara walked out of the room, down the stairs and towards the kitchen which was at the back of the house.

The freelance work she had to get done today was beginning to make her feel stressed and she needed to get back to the cottage as soon as possible. That was why she'd piled the cups so high – a decision she was now regretting with every tentative step. Especially when Grayson suddenly bounded out of the kitchen towards her.

'What's the matter, boy?'

She raised the tray higher, trying to keep it balanced as he jumped up and down. The daft dog seemed agitated and even more frisky than usual.

Clara placed the tray on top of a low cupboard in the corridor and bent to tickle behind Grayson's ear. And that was when she heard a strange gulping sound.

She walked softly to the kitchen and peeped around the door but there was no one there. The large room, with its glistening black Aga and rows of copper pans hanging from a ceiling beam, was empty and yet the sound – a faint gulping and sniffling now – persisted.

It was coming from the store room which housed non-perishable food and cleaning equipment. Clara pulled the door open and her heart lurched at the sight of her mother sitting on an upturned crate, sobbing quietly.

'Oh, Mum.' Clara rushed forward, knelt down and put her arm around the older woman's shoulders. 'I'm so sorry.'

'I'm... fine,' gulped Julie, trying to catch her breath.

'You're obviously not fine. You don't have to be brave about all of this.'

'But I do.' Julie sniffed and dragged her sleeve across her nose. 'I can't go to pieces. It's too hard to put myself back together again. After your dad... after your dad...'

When she began to sob again, Clara gently rubbed her mother's back and let her cry. At last she was all cried out and she pulled a tissue from her sleeve to blow her nose.

'Sorry about that,' she said, her face puffy and eyes red. 'It's just it's been hard since your dad died. It's taken me a while to adjust, and this has all come as a shock. So many memories of your dad are in our cottage. It'll be so hard to leave.'

'Did this all come completely out of the blue?' asked Clara. 'Surely Geoffrey said something to you about difficult decisions having to be made.' Julie bit her lip and shook her head. 'So there was no hint of it at all?'

'No, or I'd have told you.'

'Then he *should* have told you. I mean, you've worked here for ages.'

Julie rounded her shoulders and leaned forward. 'It must have been a very difficult decision for Geoffrey to make, and why should he tell me ahead of time? I'm nothing special.'

'Don't say that.' A knot of anger had lodged in Clara's chest. 'You've kept the manor and the Brellasham family going for years, and Gran did the same before you. He should have had the courtesy to speak with you privately so you didn't find out the news with everyone else, especially as you live in the grounds. This is your home too.'

'It would have been nice but I suppose he's had a lot on his mind. I don't blame him.'

Her brave smile almost broke Clara, who rocked back on her heels. 'It must cost a lot to keep this house going but I thought Geoffrey was loaded.'

'There have been some rumours about bad business deals recently but—' Julie pressed her lips together as if stopping any further words from tumbling out. Then, she said quietly: 'It's not for me to speculate or to pass on gossip. That's not my job. Talking of which...' She got to her feet and pushed her tissue back up her sleeve. 'It'll be lunchtime soon and I need to poach Geoffrey's salmon. Life goes on, doesn't it.'

'I'm sure it won't matter if his lunch is late for once.'

'Maybe not, but it'll matter to me.'

'Why don't you go home, Mum? I can cook Geoffrey's lunch.'

'No, thank you. He likes his fish cooked just so and you wouldn't get it right. I'll do it.'

Julie walked into the kitchen and Clara followed, the anger in her chest still knotted and tight.

'Are you going to speak to Geoffrey about all of this?'

'What's the point?' Julie was banging pans around, her brisk, no-nonsense demeanour restored. 'There's nothing I can do about it. I'll see you later, Clara. Didn't you say you had work to do?'

Clara left her mother searching for salmon in the fridge and walked to the front door of the manor house. She had lots of work to do, work that would bring in much-needed income if she and her mother were about to become homeless.

But first... She paused at the door and swallowed. First, there was something else she had to do. Something else that needed to be said.

10

GEOFFREY

That had been more difficult than he'd anticipated. Geoffrey pulled in a deep breath as he sat ramrod straight in the drawing room armchair that faced the fire.

Today the temperature was nudging 27°C outside so it was unlit. But sitting in front of the stone fireplace, where huge fires roared in the winter, felt comforting somehow. Would he still be here this winter to warm his toes?

He closed his eyes for a moment, hardly able to bear the thought of his wonderful house being knocked about by the developer who would buy it. But Bartie was right, there was no other option.

Sadly, Geoffrey hadn't inherited his father's business acumen, and the business deals he'd made a few years ago had recently come back to bite him. So, in reality, the fault was his. Brellasham Manor would have to be sold because of him.

You've failed, Geoffrey. That's what his father would say if he were still here, his nostrils flaring with disappointment. *But then I never did hold out high hopes for you.*

The door to the drawing room was open and Geoffrey noticed Clara walk past towards the front door. He waited to hear it open and close but silence stretched and contracted around him.

Suddenly, she appeared in the doorway. 'Can I get you anything? A drink of water, maybe?'

Geoffrey shook his head. 'I'm all right, thank you.'

'Mum is busy cooking your lunch.'

There was an edge to her tone that Geoffrey didn't recognise. But he and Clara rarely spoke these days. When she was younger, he'd avoided her because she reminded him of River and what he'd lost. He'd asked once if she was still in contact with his son and she'd said no, although he hadn't been sure she was telling the truth.

In more recent years, after growing used to River's absence, he'd liked having Clara around. She brought some life to the house. But the damage was done and she often seemed to avoid him, as he'd once avoided her.

Clara was still standing in the doorway, shifting from foot to foot.

'Was there anything else?' Geoffrey asked, pushing himself out of his chair.

Clara stared at him for a moment before stepping into the room and closing the door behind her. Geoffrey blinked, unsure what was going on.

'First of all, I'm very sorry that you have to sell this house,' she said, swallowing as if she was nervous. Did *he* make her nervous? He hoped not.

'Thank you. It's very sad and, of course, I regret that it means your mother will lose her job.'

'And her home, too.'

He nodded. 'Yes, that's another source of huge regret for me.'

He did regret it, deeply. Mostly for Julie, but partly for himself because it would be strange to live in a place that didn't have her in it.

'This has all come as a great shock to her,' said Clara, clasping her hands together.

'I'm sure it has.' He tried to imagine how shocking the news must have been for his housekeeper. 'How is your mother doing? Perhaps I should have talked to her in private about what was happening, rather than have her hear it with everyone else.'

'Yes, you should have.'

'Excuse me?'

'My mum has given you years of loyal service, as her mother did before her, and she's devastated by today's news that you didn't have the decency to tell her about beforehand.'

Clara swallowed loudly and clasped her hands so tightly her knuckles blanched white.

'I mean,' she continued, 'first, your family wrongly accuse my grandmother of stealing, and then you upend my mother's life without giving her any warning of what was coming. It's not an acceptable way to treat people.'

Geoffrey narrowed his eyes. Not many people criticised him, especially not his staff, although Clara wasn't technically in his employ. She helped her mother out sometimes and she was currently back living in the grounds' cottage. Which meant that she would lose her home, too.

Geoffrey sighed, any fight suddenly going out of him. The whole situation was awful and this girl was right, he hadn't handled it as sensitively as he might have.

'I'm sorry,' he said, sinking back into his chair. 'I'll apologise to your mother the next time I see her.'

'Oh.' Clara blinked, seemingly surprised by his apology. 'Right. Well, I'm sure that would be appreciated, though if you wouldn't mind not telling her that I... well, you know...' She tailed off, twisting her mouth.

'That you collared me in my drawing room and tore me off a strip?'

The corner of her mouth lifted. 'Yeah, something like that.'

'I think I can manage that request.' His mind flitted back to Clara's admonishment. 'What did you mean about your grandmother being accused of stealing?'

Clara blushed pink and pushed a hand through her fringe. 'I didn't mean to mention that. Though I don't suppose it matters now we're all leaving.' She paused before continuing. 'My grandmother, Violet, was accused of stealing the diamond necklace that went missing at the same time as your stepmother, Audrey.'

'Was she?'

Geoffrey, only a child at the time, was so sad and confused after Audrey's death, he'd hardly registered what was happening around him.

'She didn't do it, of course,' said Clara, frowning.

'Of course she didn't.' He remembered Violet – a tall, thin woman with kind eyes – baking cakes for him and asking how he was in the aftermath of the tragedy. Had his father really accused her of stealing the necklace? 'Violet was always loyal to my family and very good to me after the death of my stepmother.'

'I'm glad to hear that she helped you.' The anger was gone from Clara's voice and there was a look of her grandmother about her when she said quietly: 'It must have been a terrible thing for a child to go through – someone you cared about simply disappearing.'

'It was...' Geoffrey fought to control the emotions rising inside him. 'It was a difficult time.'

Clara gave him a sympathetic smile. 'I'm sorry to have brought it up again.' She paused. 'Anyway, I've said what I wanted to say and you're going to have a word with Mum so I'll leave you in peace.'

She'd reached the door before Geoffrey said softly, 'I saw her, you know.'

He hadn't intended to tell her. He'd never told his wife or

River or Bartie. But they'd never really asked about Audrey and that tragic day.

Clara stopped and looked back. 'Who did you see?'

Geoffrey stared out at the garden bathed in bright sunlight. The weather had been very different that day. 'Audrey. I was sitting at the library window and I saw her walk into the sea. That was how we knew what had happened to her when she disappeared.'

Clara was looking at him, with her mouth open.

'I shouldn't have been in the library at all,' he added. 'I was meant to be having dinner with my father but was excused to read a book because I felt unwell.'

'Was Audrey on her own at the cove?' Clara asked.

'Yes, quite alone.'

Outside, a chaffinch was calling, and there was the distant hum of a lawnmower. But time was reeling backwards for Geoffrey.

'She was standing at the water's edge with her back to me and I could hardly make her out. I remember it was getting dark and a storm was coming in. I watched her for a while, and then she began to walk into the waves, fully clothed.

'She was walking quickly and, by the time I'd got to my feet, I could only see her head and shoulders above the water. I called out for her to stop and she turned towards the house for a moment. But she couldn't hear me, of course, and she began to move away, further out to sea.'

'What did you do?' asked Clara.

'I ran to find my father, who accused me of seeing shadows, until he couldn't find Audrey in the house. Then he believed me but it was too late. She'd been swallowed by the waves by the time we got to the cove. It was dark and had started to rain so visibility was poor. My father got local people out searching in boats and along the shore but her body was gone, pulled out to sea by the current.'

Geoffrey's shoulders slumped. He had watched something unfold that he couldn't fathom. Something that he still didn't understand.

Clara took a step towards him. 'I'm so sorry.'

He shrugged. 'It was a long time ago.'

But time suddenly held no meaning for Geoffrey. He was a child again, being sent back to boarding school soon after the loss of Audrey. His father had mourned his wife for a while but had soon married again. He wasn't a man prone to displays of emotion.

Just like me, thought Geoffrey, suddenly seeing himself through the eyes of this young woman in front of him, who, somehow, was bringing up memories that he'd buried deep. But he couldn't focus on them or he would be lost.

He couldn't afford to relive the heartbreaking moment when Lucia and River had driven away from him and this house for the last time. He couldn't dwell on the years of togetherness that he and his son had lost since.

'Why are you so interested in my stepmother?' he asked, his tone harsher. 'You mentioned her the other day when you saw her photograph in the library.'

'I'm not quite sure.' She hesitated. 'The truth is I feel a kind of... connection to her.' A connection? With a woman she never knew who had died almost seventy years ago? Geoffrey noticed that Clara was blushing again, as she well might. 'I'm really... I mean, I'm sorry,' she stumbled. 'I know that probably sounds ridiculous.'

'It does, rather.'

Clara's expression hardened. 'I'm interested in her life, that's all. But I am sorry if I've overstepped the mark.'

Geoffrey held her gaze for a moment, then looked away, past the voile curtains that were billowing gently in the breeze coming through the windows.

'Perhaps it's a good thing that Audrey is still remembered

sometimes. However, I've learned that it's best not to focus on negative events of the past. It's far better to let sleeping dogs lie. And now, if you'll excuse me, there's a lot to do, as I'm sure you can imagine.'

He stood up and strode through the room, past Clara, and let the door bang shut behind him.

How did other people cope with emotions? he wondered. How did they deal with tragedy and heartbreak? He'd learned from an early age to push his emotions down. It was either that or end up like his father. Though it was clear that, business acumen aside, he'd turned out just like his father in many ways.

Geoffrey walked through the hall to the grand stone porch and stood on the front steps that led down to the gravel drive.

He tried to still his mind by focusing on the trees bending in the breeze. The gardens brought him solace – they always had, from an early age – but soon those gardens would belong to someone else, along with the cove where Audrey had walked into the sea.

Geoffrey breathed in and out slowly and pushed his emotions down until he felt like himself again. There was such a lot to organise and he couldn't afford to fall apart. He had coped with adversity at the age of nine and, later, when his wife and son had left him, and he would cope again.

Clara knew she should be working. She should be arranging flights to Geneva for the business team who had hired her free-lance services. But she was currently at the cove, sitting on the rocks that jutted out into the ocean. The sea was lapping around her bare feet but she barely registered the chill of the water.

Her mind, instead, was filled with snapshots of what had just happened in the drawing room: speaking her mind, Geoffrey apologising, his surprise that her grandmother had been accused of theft, then his bombshell that he'd seen Audrey walk into the waves that night.

Clara looked around her, at the seagulls wheeling overhead and the sun-warmed sand. Today the cove seemed benign, as if nothing bad could ever happen here. But, once upon a time, Audrey Brellasham had stood right there, at the water's edge, and made the decision to keep on walking.

What a terrible thing for a young child to have witnessed, and it haunted him still. Geoffrey had tried to hide it but she'd glimpsed strong emotions beneath his perpetually cool façade.

Clara pulled the diary from her bag and ran her fingers across its leather binding. She should give this book to Geoffrey, whatever her mother said. It would upset him but he deserved to read his stepmother's words.

She turned to the last entry: *I'm cruel to leave Geoffrey. He won't understand my actions at first or that his life will continue well without me in it. But Edwin will care for him, I'm sure of it. That's the only reason I feel able to leave this life.*

Perhaps knowing that some of Audrey's last thoughts had been about him would bring him comfort.

'Hey, Clara!' Bartie's voice drifted across the cove and Clara turned quickly. He and River were walking towards her across the sand.

Pushing the book into her bag, she returned Bartie's wave and steeled herself for the awkwardness to come.

11

RIVER

'There she is,' said Bartie, as they reached the cove. 'Hey, Clara!' he called across the sand. 'I wondered where you'd been hiding.'

Clara, sitting on the rocks, her auburn hair blowing in the sea breeze, glanced over her shoulder. She seemed startled by their arrival but returned Bartie's wave.

He was already walking towards her, undoing another button on his shirt as he moved across the warm sand, and River followed behind.

Sunbeams were dappling through the trees at the cove's edge and River realised that he was literally walking in his cousin's shadow, just as he always had metaphorically.

'What are you reading?' asked Bartie when they reached Clara.

She finished stuffing a small white book into the handbag lying next to her and looked up. 'It's nothing. Just a notebook.' She cleared her throat. 'What are you two doing out here?'

'Looking for you.' Bartie smiled at Clara. 'We were worried about you. We thought you might be upset after hearing Geoffrey's news. Isn't that right, River?'

River nodded, though he didn't think that worry about Clara was Bartie's sole reason for seeking her out.

Clara sniffed, her face pale. 'I'm shocked about it, to be honest, and my mum is distraught. It's all come out of the blue.'

Poor Mrs N, thought River. He'd assumed his father would have told her before the big announcement but shock had ricocheted across her face as Geoffrey had imparted the news to everyone.

'I can see why your mum would be upset after working here for so long,' Bartie sympathised, his hands on his hips. 'And you must be upset, too, because you're both going to lose your home. It's such a terrible shame, the whole thing.'

Bartie sat down next to Clara. He was so close their arms were touching but she didn't move away.

'Poor Geoffrey has been struggling with the situation for a while,' he told her, pulling sunglasses from his pocket and putting them on. He looked even more like a leading man in shades, thought River ruefully. 'But Geoff didn't want to burden anyone with it at first. Not even River, here, which is understandable seeing as he was ten thousand miles away. But I was honoured when he reached out to me and asked for my help. That's when I suggested that River should be involved.'

River scuffed his feet into the sand. That wasn't exactly what had happened. Bartie had heard on the grapevine from his mother – a second cousin of his father's – that Geoffrey was having financial difficulties, and it had been Bartie who had contacted Geoffrey to offer his services.

In the meantime, River had received a letter from his father, outlining his dilemma with the manor and asking him to visit. So his trip to England was already planned by the time Bartie got in touch with him. But it seemed that his cousin wasn't about to let truth get in the way of a good story.

'It's really kind of you to help him,' said Clara, turning to Bartie, who brushed a strand of hair from her cheek.

'I'd do anything to help Geoffrey, who's always been like a second father to me.'

River rolled his eyes because Bartie was laying it on a bit thick. From what he'd gathered, his cousin had hardly visited over the last few years. But then he, himself, had never visited at all.

River turned his face to the sea and focused on the puffs of white cloud scudding towards the horizon. The sky here was china blue, less vibrant than the bright blue he was used to in Australia. It was prettier, more delicate. A lot like Clara, sixteen years on. She'd grown into an attractive woman. The freckles were still there, scattered across her nose and cheekbones, which he was glad about. He'd always liked her freckles though, back then, she'd complained about them bitterly.

He glanced over his shoulder at Bartie and Clara, who were deep in conversation, Bartie seemingly engrossed in whatever she was telling him.

Did this constitute 'having a crack at her'? River feared that it did and turned his attention back to the sea. He'd always felt protective towards Clara but they were no longer great friends and it wasn't for him to look out for her. Perhaps she welcomed Bartie's attentions anyway. She'd hung on his every word back when they were teenagers.

'What do you think, River?' Clara asked suddenly.

He turned. 'About what?'

'I was asking Bartie if selling Brellasham Manor really is the only option. It seems a bit nuclear.'

'And what's Bartie's opinion?'

'He reckons the house costs too much to run and is a lost cause. But surely there are ways of making money. You could open the house to visitors. Market the place and get tourists in. Do tours. Set up a café and a playground for little kids. Hold weddings, and events like the annual village fete that's happening soon.' She winced. '*If* it's still happening soon.'

'I've been racking my brain for various ways to boost income,' said River, 'but they all involve strangers at the manor and my father would never agree. He's always guarded the house jealously and the annual village fair is about as far as he'll go.'

'He might change his mind if it would save the place and mean he could stay here.'

'It wouldn't,' said Bartie bluntly. 'The amount of money needed to bring Brellasham Manor up to scratch in the first place, so it's fit for tourists and weddings, is substantial. And that's money that Geoffrey doesn't have. So I'm afraid selling is the only option. I wish there was something else that could be done.'

'Me too,' said Clara, her face glum. 'There are so many memories in that house. So many echoes of people long gone.'

'Yeah, right,' said Bartie, frowning slightly. He clearly thought Clara was being over-dramatic but River knew what she meant. As a sensitive teenager, he'd sometimes imagined history seeping from the walls.

He looked behind him, at the gardens and manor library just visible through the trees. He'd arrived yesterday, glad at the thought of being shot of this place for good. Hopeful that bad memories of the house would disappear when it was sold. But already his feelings were more mixed.

Back in Australia, the manor had seemed almost dreamlike. A place he'd once known that was mired in tradition and an outdated class system. In a younger country, enjoying the sunshine and a new start, he'd felt that it had nothing to do with him any more.

But he couldn't deny the increasing pull he was already feeling to this house, to Heaven's Cove and to the people who lived here.

Bartie's phone suddenly rang and he pulled it from his trouser pocket, glanced at the screen and winced. 'Sorry, I need to take this. Honestly, I'm only out of the office for a few days but they can't cope without me.'

He took hold of Clara's hand, held it to his lips and kissed the pale skin on the inside of her wrist. 'It's so lovely to see you again, Clara. Such an unexpected pleasure. I hope we can spend more time together, now we've renewed our friendship.'

Good grief, it was all so cheesy. River waited for Clara to roll her eyes or even raise an eyebrow, but instead she smiled up at Bartie and nodded. His legendary charm appeared to be working.

Bartie got to his feet and hurried away, speaking animatedly into his phone. The words 'high-level mergers' drifted back across the sand towards them.

Once Bartie was out of sight, River cleared his throat. This was awkward. It shouldn't be. He and a former childhood acquaintance were simply enjoying the view – they'd sat here together enough times in the past, chatting and laughing. But that was then and a lot had changed since.

'How do you think your father's announcement went?' asked Clara, gazing at the waves rippling towards the shore.

'As well as could be expected, I guess,' said River, who had found the whole event stressful. Everyone in the audience, including Mrs N, had been visibly shocked by the news and several had looked at him hopefully. As if he might be their knight in shining armour who would save the day.

Phillip, the gardener, had put their thoughts into words. *Why doesn't the son take the house on?* And River had seen the disappointment on their faces when they'd realised the truth: he wasn't here to save Brellasham Manor. He was here to help his father and Bartie sell it.

'Do you *want* Brellasham Manor to be sold?' asked Clara. She'd always been forthright and that obviously hadn't changed.

River pondered his answer because the situation was complicated. He didn't want the house. He never had. And he and his father had a relationship that was challenging. River had little in common with the austere, often cold man who had played only a minor role in his life since adolescence.

Geoffrey had made some efforts to keep in touch, and River, too, had sent birthday and Christmas cards plus the occasional email. However, he'd never been sure that his father liked him that much, whereas his father's love for the manor house was evident. How ironic, thought River, that the old man appeared to love a pile of bricks more than his flesh and blood.

'Or would you rather have the money?' asked Clara when a silence stretched between them.

River stared at the girl to whom he'd once opened his heart. She'd known him so well once upon a time but now she didn't appear to know him at all.

'After we left here, Mum took me to live in what I suppose you'd call a commune, in the Australian outback. Money didn't feature in our lives then and it hasn't much since. I haven't needed it to be happy. So, no, I wouldn't rather have the money from this house.'

Clara held his gaze for a moment before looking away. '*Have* you been happy?' she asked quietly.

River nodded. 'Mostly. What about you?'

'Mostly.' She swallowed. 'You know that my dad died last year.'

'Yes. I was sorry to hear it. Your dad meant a lot to me.'

Clara blinked and pursed her lips. She looked like she was fighting back tears, and River had an urge to put his arms around her. To let her rest her head on his shoulder and weep for the parent she'd lost.

But he'd given up the right to comfort her the day he'd let her go.

A piece of paper, caught by the breeze, suddenly danced across his feet and River bent to pick it up.

'Is this yours?' It was a small scrap bearing a string of numbers.

Clara's eyes opened wide as he handed it over. 'Oh, yes. It must have fallen out of my book. Thanks.'

'What's with the numbers? Are you taking a maths course or something?' He grinned, aware that maths had always been Clara's nemesis at school. The subject that she would rail against at length as they sat here in this cove, back when they were younger and life was full of possibilities.

'Yeah, something like that,' she said tersely, pushing the paper into her open handbag. 'It's nothing important.'

She was lying to him. He could tell by the way she twisted her mouth and began to bite her lip, just as she used to do. But he let it go and gave her a faint smile.

'I suppose I'd better get on.'

'Yeah, you and Bartie have a lot to sort out.'

He should move – go back to the house and try to speak to his father. But his feet seemed planted in the sand.

'So, tell me,' he said after a while, 'what will you do?'

'Me? Oh, I have work to finish. Well, start, really. Flights and accommodation to organise in Geneva.'

'Are you going to Switzerland?'

'Sadly, no. I've been working as a virtual PA since moving back in with Mum, before Dad died, and I have some travel arrangements to organise for a client.'

'Right. But actually I meant what are you going to do when my father sells the house and you and your mum have to move out of the cottage?'

'Oh.' Clara puffed air through her lips. 'I guess we'll find somewhere else to live, in the village, hopefully, and Mum will need to look round for a new job. We'll be all right.'

Would they? River hoped so.

He tried to think of something else to say, but the atmosphere was strained and he couldn't take much more stress today. So, he said goodbye and left her, and he only looked back once.

She was still sitting on the rocks, turned away from him, with her shoulders slumped. But she'd taken the mysterious piece of paper from her bag and was staring at it closely. Brellasham Manor, as always, had its secrets.

12

CLARA

Clara hurried across the grass, sand escaping from the sides of her sandals, and let herself into the cottage. Her laptop was sitting on the hall table, ready for her to do some work, but she walked past it and up the stairs to her bedroom. Booking the flights to Geneva would have to wait.

Dropping to her knees, she began to root through a box in the bottom of the wardrobe: her treasure box of mementos that was crammed with photos, cards and gig programmes. She ran her hand across a picture of her dad and then began to pull everything out onto the carpet.

Memories tumbled around her – her first holiday abroad, her mum's fiftieth birthday party, going with Michael to see the Stereophonics in London. But the blasts from the past weren't what was making her jittery.

She felt at sixes and sevens following the news of Brellasham Manor's fate, and after her encounter at the cove with River and Bartie.

But, most of all, she felt shaken by what she had noticed as she sat by the sea. The numbers written on the scrap of paper that River had handed back to her looked more stark against white paper in bright sunlight. And there was something about the way the numbers were formed – the curve of the six and the nine – that rang a bell. A louder bell this time. The writing had seemed vaguely familiar before, but now she had an idea why that might be.

Rooting through the now almost empty box, Clara at last found what she was looking for.

'Here you are,' she murmured, pulling out a handful of birthday cards from her grandmother, Violet. 'I knew I'd kept some of you.'

Clara caught a slight waft of lavender as she opened the last card that Violet had sent her before she died. The sight of her grandmother's handwriting, especially on what was turning out to be a ridiculously emotional day, left Clara sniffing back tears. Violet had always been a loving gran and she was sorely missed by her family.

Clara squinted at the writing – *Have a lovely birthday, Clarissa* – and smiled through her tears. Violet had turned Clara's dislike of her full name into a running joke, which had served to take the sting out of it when she was a child. But was her writing the same as on the scrap of paper found at the back of Audrey's diary?

Clara opened the other cards from her grandmother and compared their writing with the numbers on the paper that she pulled from her bag. The heaviness of the pen stroke and the neatness looked similar and yet... Clara frowned because the evidence was inconclusive. There was nothing concrete to confirm her suspicion that Violet had been the author of the mysterious note.

She began piling her precious mementos back into the box, her body warmed by a patch of sunlight that was falling through the open window. And then she saw an image she'd thought lost for ever.

It was funny, she thought, picking up the photo that had

attracted her attention. It was funny how at ease she and River had looked in each other's company twenty years ago when nowadays they were, in many ways, strangers.

Clara thought she'd ditched her photos of River after he'd left for good, but this one had survived. Grainy and partially faded, it showed her and River sitting by the stream that flowed through the manor grounds. They must have been about ten, in shorts and T-shirts, and they were laughing as they trailed their toes in the water: her hair dark and pulled into a ponytail; his fair and close-cut, ready for his return to boarding school.

Those were happy days, she mused. Before people left and people died, and the future of the manor house and their cottage was put in jeopardy.

Placing the childhood photo carefully in the box, she piled her grandmother's cards on top, closed the wardrobe door and stood up. It was a shame that Violet's writing proved inconclusive, she thought, flexing her aching knees. If only there were numbers that her grandmother had written down to compare with the ones on Audrey's scrap of paper.

'Of course!' said Clara, swinging her bag onto her shoulder. 'I know just the place.'

Julie was still in the manor kitchen, where she seemed to spend most of her time, and Clara was pleased to see that she was looking brighter.

'Are you OK, Mum?' she asked, surreptitiously shaking out the last of the sand from her shoes before she got any closer.

Julie looked up from the table where she was poring over a large ledger. 'I can't just sit back while Geoffrey has to sell his home, so I'm going through the household expenses to see where I can make cuts.'

'That's great.' Clara sat at the table and put her hand on top of her mother's. 'But I think it's going to take more than cutting back on cleaning products and switching off a few lights to save this place.'

'Perhaps, but I have to try. Geoffrey has been here for generations. Our family, too, keeping this house and its occupants going. I was hoping that you would take over as housekeeper when it's time for me to retire.'

Was she? Clara blinked, not sure that she or Geoffrey would ever want that. But she said soothingly, 'I know, Mum. I'm so sorry.'

'There must be a way to save this beautiful house. I can't bear the thought of its rooms being ripped apart and turned into apartments.' Her eyes lit up. 'Though, if that does happen, perhaps you and I could buy one of them, so the Netherways are still here in a sense. Or Michael could.'

'That's a lovely idea, Mum, but none of us could afford to buy a flat here. The manor is in a beautiful location and has such history that apartments will sell for top prices. Finding a flat we can afford to rent in Heaven's Cove, when we lose the cottage, is going to be challenge enough.

'But,' she added quickly, seeing her mother's face fall, 'I'm sure we'll find something and, who knows, maybe the Brellasham Manor apartments won't cost as much as I'm anticipating.'

They would. Probably more. But there was no point in making her mother even more despondent.

Julie gave a wobbly smile. 'Let's hope not. Oh, you'll never guess what happened when I took Geoffrey his poached salmon. He asked how I was and apologised for not speaking to me before the meeting this morning. He was very sorry that he hadn't had a chance to make me aware of the situation in private. That was nice of him, wasn't it?'

'Mmm.'

'It was very unexpected. I don't think Geoffrey has ever apologised to me for anything before in his life.'

'Gosh,' said Clara, taking a sudden interest in the open ledger on the table. 'That *is* nice.'

'Gosh?' Julie leaned forward. 'I don't think I've ever heard you say "gosh" before.' Her eyes narrowed. 'Did you get to him?'

'Did I *get* to him?' Clara spluttered. 'I don't know what you're talking about.'

Julie leaned closer and stared at her daughter for a moment before slumping back in her chair. 'You did, didn't you? You said something to Geoffrey. Not content with mentioning his poor, dead stepmother to him the other day, you told him I was upset that he hadn't spoken to me first.'

'Not really,' said Clara, cursing her guilty face and deciding not to tell her mother that she'd also mentioned the theft accusation levelled at Violet. 'All I did was tell him *I* was upset that he hadn't spoken to you.'

'You shouldn't have done that.'

'Why? I know he acts all high and mighty sometimes but he's just an ordinary man who needs to think more about other people's feelings.'

'I certainly hope you didn't tell him that.'

Clara wrinkled her nose. 'Not in so many words, no. I was very polite.'

Julie raised an eyebrow. 'Well, I'm still not at all happy about it. You can't go around speaking on behalf of other people. It's not right.' She glanced at the floor and frowned. 'Are you scattering sand everywhere?'

'Nope,' said Clara, pushing her feet under the table. 'Can I ask you something?' she said quickly, trying to avoid another telling off. 'Do the numbers on this piece of paper look familiar to you?'

She pulled the paper from her bag and passed it to Julie, who scanned it quickly and then placed it on the table.

'Where did you get this?'

'I found it and I'm not sure what it is.'

'*Where* did you find it?'

'In that carrier bag of Gran's possessions. Do you think that might be Gran's writing?'

Julie's lips drew into a thin line. 'I wish I'd thrown that bag away without telling you about it. Why does it matter if your grandmother wrote this...' – she peered at the paper again – 'incomprehensible string of numbers? There's enough going on right now without harking back to the past.'

'I know, Mum, and it might not matter at all but it's intriguing, don't you think? And I'd like to find out. I wondered if you still had the ledgers that Gran wrote in when she was the housekeeper here? So I can see how she wrote her numbers.'

'You're not going to let this drop, are you?' Julie's shoulders slumped. 'You always were a stubborn child. Michael never dug his heels in like you did.'

Michael was actually stubbornness personified, but Clara said nothing and Julie finally nodded towards the store cupboard she'd retreated to a couple of hours earlier.

'The old ledgers are in there, in the tall cupboard that's against the back wall. Geoffrey doesn't like us to throw any records away, though quite what he's going to do with them when he moves, I don't know. You're wasting your time, Clara.'

'Probably but I'd like to check it out.'

'You're so like your father,' Julie muttered. 'Stubborn. Determined. He could never let anything go either.' But she sat back in her chair and shrugged.

Taking that as grudging assent, Clara went into the store room and straight to the cupboard that stood in the corner. She'd never looked inside before, and judging by the dust that rose into the air when she pulled the door open, hardly anyone ever did.

Piles of hardback ledgers were stacked onto the shelves.

Dozens and dozens of them. She pulled one down and recognised her mum's neat figures set out in the right-hand column on each page.

> *Electricity bill paid – £1,453*
> *Food shop – £85*
> *Repair to downstairs WC – £140*

The list of expenses went on and on and included an increasingly large number of repairs to the manor. No wonder Geoffrey's financial problems were stacking up.

Clara replaced the ledger and searched through the others until she came to one with 1957 inked onto its spine: a year when her grandmother was working here as housekeeper – the same year that Audrey had died.

She pulled out the ledger, opened it and ran her finger across pages filled in by Violet as she'd balanced the books. It was hard to imagine the elderly white-haired grandmother she'd known writing this back then, when she was hardly older than Clara was now.

Leaning closer until her nose was almost touching the paper, Clara carefully studied the figures that were neatly written in the right-hand columns. Then she closed the ledger, carefully replaced it in the cupboard and went back to her mother.

'Well?' asked Julie, dark shadows beneath her eyes. Today was proving too much for her.

'The figures in one of Gran's ledgers and on the piece of paper I showed you look the same, especially the way the sixes and nines are written. It wouldn't hold up in a court of law but I'd say they were written by the same person. By Gran.'

'Which means what?'

Now was a good time to confess that she'd pulled Audrey's diary out of the bin and read it. Tell her that the book contained more of these mysterious numbers, and the scrap of paper, apparently written on by Violet, had fallen from it. But Clara couldn't add to her mother's stress. Not today of all days.

'It probably means nothing at all,' she said, pushing the paper into her pocket. 'And now, I don't care how much you rail against it, I'm taking you home so you can rest.'

'I have to make dinner for Geoffrey, River and Bartie.'

'They're grown men who are completely capable of making themselves a meal.'

Clara put her arm around her mother's shoulders and, when she pulled her to her feet, Julie didn't resist. 'Well... I do have a bit of a headache. I suppose I could have a little rest before I come back and make dinner but I'll need to let Geoffrey know. After all, he is my employer.'

Not for much longer, thought Clara, keen to get her mother home as quickly as possible. 'I can hear Phillip mowing the lawn. We can ask him to let Geoffrey know once he's put the mower away.'

Fifteen minutes later, while her mother dozed on her bed, Clara sat by the stream and dangled her bare feet in the cold, rushing water.

It had been a shocking, surprising and frustrating day. The manor was going to be sold, her mother would be out of work and both of them homeless, Bartie was being surprisingly flirtatious, River was being awkwardly awkward and, though it now seemed likely that her grandmother had written the strange note, Clara was no nearer to knowing what the numbers meant. Or the numbers in Audrey's diary, for that matter.

Leave it, Clara. She could almost hear her mother's voice whispering in her ear.

Clara closed her eyes and turned her face towards the sun,

knowing that the stubbornness she'd inherited from her father wouldn't let her leave it alone.

The present was hard going enough but she could feel tendrils of the past wrapping around her and pulling her back to a woman's disappearance almost seventy years ago, and to the housekeeper wrongly accused of theft.

13

RIVER

River stepped into the library and ignored an urge to turn tail and step straight back out again.

His father was sitting in the leather armchair, next to the window that overlooked the gardens. A flash of bright blue sea was visible through the trees.

'River,' he said, his face solemn.

'Father,' River replied.

A silence fell across the room now the two of them had ascertained that they knew who each other was.

'Um, I was looking for Bartie,' said River when the silence began to stretch.

'Bartholomew was here. We had a good chat, but he's gone off now to ring his office or do whatever it is he needs to do, to make sure that wheels are in motion regarding the sale.'

We had a good chat. His words cut through River, who had long suspected that Geoffrey would rather have Bartie as his son.

Perhaps Clara suspected the same thing, especially now that Bartie had grown into a successful businessman handling 'high-level mergers'. Whereas he, beneath his Australian tan and broader shoulders, remained the same old unconventional screw-up. His work as a software developer wouldn't set the world on fire and, to be honest, he was only averagely good at it.

'I think the announcement this morning went as well as could be expected,' his father said, adjusting his gold cufflinks.

'I think so, too, though it was a huge shock for everyone, including Mrs N.'

His father glanced up and caught his eye. 'Indeed. I've apologised for not giving her prior warning.'

Had he? His father apologising was a first.

'So,' said Geoffrey. 'Did you sleep well last night?'

'Yes, thank you. Though it's strange being back in my old bedroom.'

'I expect it is. Truth be told, it's rather strange having you back in the house. You and Bartie back together. Just like the good old days.'

The good old days? Had he forgotten arguing with his then wife and berating River about his exam results? Or that Bartie had once shut River in the windowless coal cellar and left him there for hours?

Bartie had claimed it was just a joke, and Geoffrey had told River to grow up and stop being over-sensitive after his shouts were eventually heard and he was rescued. But, even twenty years on, River still shivered at the thought of those hours spent trapped in the dark.

Being back at the manor house was strange and discombobulating, like stepping back to a time when he'd been confused and unhappy. He hadn't set foot in the place for almost two decades and yet... He'd realised last night, as he lay in bed thinking about it all, the prospect of this grand, solid house being sold felt like someone was standing on his chest.

He'd believed that Brellasham Manor had faded into obscurity during his time abroad. But now he understood that the knowledge it was trundling on, unchanged for decades, had given him a feeling of stability. Perhaps he'd always assumed subconsciously that he would return one day.

River swallowed. 'If you've got half an hour to spare, perhaps you and I could have a chat and a catch-up. It's been a while since we properly talked.'

'We talked at dinner last night and it'll be dinner time again soon. There'll be plenty of time to chat then,' said Geoffrey briskly.

'Yes, but Bartie will be there as well. I was thinking that maybe we could have a word now, just the two of us.'

An emotion flickered across Geoffrey's face and was gone. It looked like fear but River knew he must be mistaken. Why would his father be frightened of him? He was more likely annoyed by River's apparent 'neediness' in wanting to talk.

The door suddenly banged open and Bartie bounded into the room.

'Well,' he announced. 'Good news! The developer contact I mentioned to you is *very* interested in buying Brellasham Manor. So interested, in fact, I wouldn't be surprised if she were to match the market rate for the property immediately, or even exceed it if we exerted a little pressure.' He tapped his nose. 'If you know what I mean.'

River didn't know what he meant. Thumbscrews, perhaps?

Geoffrey murmured, 'That is very good news,' though his face told another story.

Leaving this place which his family had called home for generations would kill him, River realised, before inwardly berating himself for being overly dramatic – something else his father could not abide.

'It's early days,' Bartie continued, 'but a very good start that could come to fruition relatively swiftly. It's going to need a lot of work on my part, but that's something I've never been afraid of and, of course, I want to do the best for you and the manor.'

Geoffrey smiled. 'It's very good of you, Bartie. I would ask

Mrs Netherway to make us a pot of tea but she sent me a message some hours ago saying she'd gone home with a headache. She promised to come back to cook dinner but I haven't seen her.'

'If she's still not feeling well, I can cook for us,' said River, wondering how his father was going to manage after the sale without the help he was used to. He doubted that Geoffrey knew how to boil an egg.

'That would be—' Geoffrey stopped mid-sentence when Mrs N rushed into the room, with Clara at her heels. 'Ah, you're back, Julie. I assume that your headache has gone?'

'No, not really,' said Mrs N, tapping her foot over and over on the carpet. She was a ball of nervous energy. 'It's still pounding away because I can't relax.'

Clara stepped forward. 'Mum, I don't think—' But she was silenced by an imperious wave of her mother's hand.

'No, Clara, it needs to be said and I won't relax until it has been.' Mrs N turned to his father, her foot still tapping. 'I understand that my daughter took it upon herself to castigate you for not telling me about selling the manor before this morning's meeting.'

Had Clara given his father a telling off? River bit back a smile at the thought. Bartie's grin was less well hidden.

'Well,' Geoffrey harrumphed. 'She did have a word with me.'

'Then she shouldn't have and I'm sorry.'

'Mum, you don't *need* to say sorry,' said Clara, her cheeks flushed.

She glanced at River as if seeking his support, but Geoffrey was already speaking.

'Your daughter's right. There's no need to apologise, Julie. As I told you earlier, I should have been more sensitive to your situation.' River felt his mouth fall open and he quickly closed it again. 'Actually, Clara and I ended up having an interesting chat.'

When Geoffrey glanced at Clara, River frowned. What was that look the two of them had just exchanged? As though they had some kind of understanding.

'Anyway, I hope your headache will now ease,' Geoffrey continued. 'However, if you feel unable to cook dinner, my son has offered to take over your duties.'

River tried hard not to be offended by the disbelief and horror that registered on Mrs N's face.

'Absolutely not. I wouldn't dream of not cooking your meal,' she spluttered, silencing her daughter's protestations with another wave of the hand. 'I'm heading for the kitchen right now and dinner will be at the same time as usual.'

She bustled out of the room but Clara remained, shifting from foot to foot.

'Actually, while I'm here, I was wondering if you had a minute?'

She was looking at River but Bartie stepped forward. 'I always have time for you, Clara, and your entertaining mother. How did she know we'd be in here?'

'Everyone seems to gravitate towards the library because it's the most comforting room in the house.'

River glanced at the shelves filled with books, the faded Persian rug that covered the floorboards, and the leather armchairs whose seats had become squashy with age. He found this room, that smelled of sandalwood polish, comforting too.

Outside, the sun was glaring, giving the green of the lawns and the blue of the sea a fever-dream vibrancy. River had been back to Brellasham Manor in his dreams. He'd dreamed of the echoing rooms with high ceilings and the cove with waves lapping at the sand. He'd dreamed of Clara.

'Earth to River!' Bartie's voice was loud.

'Sorry, what did you say?' River asked, feeling foolish.

'I was telling Clara that plans are progressing regarding the sale of this place. She needs to know because of how much it will affect her and her mother.'

'Thank you. It would be good to be kept up to date.' Clara pushed her hair behind her ears. 'But actually, I wanted to know if the charity fete and open day is still going ahead, only there are a lot of arrangements still to make if that's the case.'

'I don't imagine it'll still go ahead.' Bartie looked at Geoffrey. 'What do you think? There doesn't seem to be much point, and do you really want to be overrun with people when you're trying to organise a move? People won't be aware of the situation.'

'I don't think that's true,' said Clara. 'I imagine your news has already spread around Heaven's Cove like wildfire. It's hard to keep anything quiet around here.'

'Small villages really are a hotbed of gossip, aren't they?' said Bartie, curling his lip. 'Small towns, small minds, I'm afraid.'

Clara frowned. 'I don't think that's fair. Local people like to be informed about what's going on in their area because they care about where they live.'

'Yes, of course,' said Bartie quickly. 'I wasn't trying to diss the village. Of course people are interested, and I'm sure the fete would be good fun. But I'm just not sure that it would be a good use of our resources at the moment.'

'It doesn't use many of the manor's resources, other than this place being the venue on the day. The event is organised by a village committee which I belong to, and, as I live here on site, I oversee the final arrangements. Everyone gives their time for free because it's for such a good cause. A number of local charities benefit from the money raised.'

'Which is all very admirable,' said Bartie, 'but I still think it's best if the fete is cancelled, now that we're focusing on selling the manor. And I'm sure Geoffrey and River agree.'

Clara turned to River. 'Do you?'

River hesitated because it was clear that the fete meant a lot to Clara and to local people.

'Not necessarily,' he said, ignoring his cousin's groan of exasperation. 'These leads you're following are going to take some time, Bartie, even if everything pans out as you're expecting. So where's the harm in letting the fete go ahead as usual? It can be a swan song, if you like. A final goodbye from the Brellashams to the village that's been their home for so long, and it'll raise money for charity, which has to be a good thing.'

'The harm is that it risks us taking our eye off the ball when there's a lot to be done regarding a potential sale. Plus, it seems somewhat bizarre to be hosting a happy event, with everything that's currently going on.'

'I'm sure Clara will be doing the lion's share of any work involved in the fete, and there's no harm in spreading a little happiness, is there?' River turned to his father. 'But it's up to you, of course.'

Geoffrey waved his hand as if he couldn't be bothered with such an inconsequential issue. 'Yes, let it go ahead.'

Bartie's mouth set into a thin line but then he smiled. 'Of course. You're absolutely right, and I'm focusing too much on the sale. The Brellasham family have been a part of the local community for years, and the fete would be a fitting end to their association with the village. In fact, as penance for taking such a strong line against it initially, I'd like to help with any remaining arrangements, if I can. Maybe you and I could have a chat about what's planned, Clara? Somewhere away from the manor, for a change. Is The Smugglers Haunt still open?'

Clara nodded, seemingly unfazed by Bartie's swift change of heart, as River pictured the pub in Heaven's Cove where he used to down half-pints of lemonade. It was impossible to drink a sneaky beer when the landlord knew full well that he was only in his mid-teens.

'We could meet there tomorrow lunchtime to discuss your plans,' Bartie was saying. 'Or what about a picnic instead? Everyone loves a picnic in this beautiful weather. I'll provide the food. We could meet at the beach in Heaven's Cove.'

'We could, but it'll be heaving with tourists.'

'Ah, that's a shame, 'cos I'd love to meet up. I was hoping to surprise you with my packed lunch.'

Did River imagine it or did Bartie wink at Clara? The man was shameless. Everything was in turmoil but he was still trying to get off with Clara, using pathetic innuendo. She'd definitely see the funny side and tell him where to get off.

But instead, Clara, eyes widening slightly, said: 'I suppose we could try Heaven's Cove green, near the church?'

Bartie smiled. 'Excellent idea. Lunchtime tomorrow? Does one o'clock suit you?'

'It does.'

'Great! Then it's a date.'

Clara turned towards him. 'What about you, River?'

The shadow of a frown crossed Bartie's face. 'Yes, River,' he said very deliberately, 'what about you?'

River knew that Bartie was expecting him to bow out. To leave the coast clear for him to unleash his charms on Clara, who, judging by her lack of reaction to his cousin's innuendo, seemed to have lost her mind over the last sixteen years. But Bartie's seduction technique wasn't why they were here at Brellasham Manor.

'That time sounds fine to me,' said River. 'I'm looking forward to it.'

Geoffrey went into the drawing room after everyone had left and pulled open the bottom drawer of the Victorian dresser that sat in a corner. The dresser was polished to within an inch of its life but no one ever delved into this drawer, which was filled with books deemed too tatty for display in the library.

They should be disposed of and no doubt would be during his move from the manor. As would the dresser that would dwarf any room in a smaller property. It would never fit into sheltered accommodation. *He* would never fit into sheltered accommodation, either, but he supposed that was the ultimate fate for a man with no wife and no children to take care of him. River would soon be heading back to Australia and so much would remain unsaid.

Geoffrey sighed and pushed his hands beneath the books until he reached a small tin box that had once held toffees. Inside were the photos he had squirrelled away as a boy, while his father was burning pictures on a bonfire, along with images from his own marriage that had not lasted.

He rarely looked at them. In fact, he never looked at them. But today he had an urge to open the tin and drown in the past. Clara's interest in Audrey had brought up memories that were refusing to lie quiet and still.

Geoffrey flicked through the photos, his heart fluttering at the images long unseen. He spent several seconds studying a photo of Lucia with their newborn, who, she'd insisted, must be called River. She was a beautiful woman, glowing with maternal pride at the bundle in her arms. He had been so proud the day she brought their son home from the hospital. So determined to look after the both of them for ever. And look how that had turned out.

Pushing that photo back into the tin, Geoffrey turned his attention to a picture of Audrey and his father, Edwin. This one must have been taken during their early courtship, at some kind of dance. Audrey, much younger than her husband-to-be, looked radiant in a dress with a tight bodice and full skirt. She was gazing up at him with adoration in her eyes as he placed a protective arm around her waist. It was sad but Geoffrey never remembered them going out dancing after they were married and Audrey had moved into the manor. Except for the ball held here in 1957, and that was swiftly followed by the tragedy of her death.

His mood dipping, he began to leaf more quickly through the images before deciding to stop dredging up the past and put the photos away. What was the point of all this pain?

'Hello. Where are you?'

River's voice drifted into the room from the hall.

Startled, Geoffrey dropped a handful of photos which scattered across the floor.

'Damn!' he muttered, getting onto his knees and sweeping the photos into a pile which he crammed back into the tin. He pushed it back beneath the books and closed the dresser drawer quietly. River had gone into the library looking for him but it wouldn't be long before he was discovered.

'Come on, Grayson,' he said to the golden retriever which was slumbering on the sofa. 'Time to go.'

Geoffrey slipped out of the open French windows and walked with the dog across the grass, towards the moors which rose up behind the house. He felt guilty for deliberately avoiding his son but the thought of a heart-to-heart chat filled him with dread. When they'd met up over the years, it had always been in a public place at his instigation – a busy restaurant or the bar of an airport hotel, where deep conversation was unlikely. But here, in the peace of memory-laden Brellasham Manor, it would be different.

And while Geoffrey knew what he should say to River, he also knew that he never would. He never could. So it was better, right now, to avoid spending time alone with his son at all.

14

CLARA

Clara turned away from the portrait of Audrey. River had just reached the top of the stairs and was walking along the landing towards her.

'Have you seen my father?' he asked, his feet making no sound on the thick carpet.

'Afraid not. Do you need him urgently?'

'No. I was hoping to have a chat with him but he seems to have disappeared again. I'm beginning to think he's avoiding me.'

That was very possible, thought Clara, who had once been convinced that Geoffrey was going out of his way to avoid her too. But she wouldn't add to River's suspicions.

'I expect he's just gone for a stroll with Grayson to try and clear his mind,' she assured him. 'There's a lot going on and he usually goes to the moors when he wants some peace and quiet. I'm sure he'll be back soon.'

'Yeah, I suppose so.'

'Thanks for backing me about the fete, by the way. It's a tradition that people in Heaven's Cove look forward to every year, and it won't be held next year, of course, so...'

Clara tailed off as the fact that this would be the last ever Brellasham Manor Fete properly hit her. This house had been a part of local life for so long, but soon it would be carved up into expensive apartments. And the cottage she shared with her mother, which was old and in need of repair, would probably be razed to the ground.

'You're welcome,' said River, peering at her closely. 'Are you all right?'

'I'm fine, thanks. It's just been a long day.'

'You can say that again.' River's mouth turned up at the corner. 'Did you really tell my father that he'd behaved like an arse?'

'Not in so many words but' – Clara grinned – 'sort of, yeah. He took it quite well, considering.'

'Which is surprising. My father isn't a man who handles criticism well.'

'I think he's changed a bit over the years,' said Clara, surprised to find herself standing up for Geoffrey, but she couldn't shake the image of him as a child watching a woman he loved walk into the sea. Trauma like that must change a person.

'Maybe. I wouldn't know. We've hardly exchanged more than a few words since I arrived.'

'Hopefully you'll get a chance to talk soon.'

'Yeah, I hope so. I won't be here for too much longer.'

River brushed his fringe from his face, something he used to do all the time as a teenager. Clara swallowed, feeling a pang for the past when life was less complicated and they were still friends.

'Why didn't you tell me before the meeting about the manor being sold?' she asked, trying to keep any hint of accusation out of her voice.

'I assumed my father had already told your mum, and I wasn't sure you wanted to talk to me anyway. You didn't seem overly happy to see me again.'

You know why, thought Clara. But she wasn't about to have that conversation here, where people might overhear them. She might not have that conversation at all before he returned to Australia. What was the point?

'Do you know much about Audrey Brellasham?' she asked instead.

River blinked at the change of subject. 'Who?'

'The woman in this portrait. Your dad's stepmother, who drowned in 1957 after walking into the sea.'

'I've not heard much about her although I know it was a terrible tragedy. Why do you want to know?' When Clara paused, weighing up how much to share, River added: 'We used to tell each other everything, back when we were kids. You can still trust me, you know.'

Clara raised an eyebrow because it was trust that River had shattered after leaving the manor for good. But the secrets she was carrying were beginning to drag her down.

'Have you ever been up to the third floor?' she asked, nodding towards the locked door that led to the rooms above.

'The ghostly rooms upstairs? Nope. I presume they're still out of bounds?'

'That's right.'

'My father's always respected his father's wishes that no one should ever go up there. Edwin must have really loved his wife and been grief-stricken to shut off the entire floor.'

'Maybe.'

This time it was River who raised an eyebrow. 'Maybe? What exactly are you getting at, Clara?'

'Don't you think the whole thing is a bit strange and there's more to it?'

'Not really. I suppose Edwin wanted to avoid seeing anything that would remind him of the tragedy. And, as well as being grief-stricken, there was more stigma around suicide back then so another good reason for Edwin to distance himself from the whole thing. Why are you bringing all of this back up?'

Clara took a deep breath. 'I found something, in my gran's possessions after she died.'

Confusion flitted across River's face. 'What did you find?'

'This. Audrey's diary from 1957, the year she went missing.'

She pulled the book from her pocket and handed it over to River. He stared at the diary for a moment, as if it was likely to explode, and then he began to leaf through the gold-edged pages.

'This is amazing, Clo,' he said, looking up from Audrey's flowing writing. 'But why did your grandmother have it?'

Clara ignored the use of her nickname, even though hearing it from his lips again took her by surprise.

'I reckon Gran went into her bedroom on the third floor, after Audrey disappeared, and took it. She was seen coming out of her room and accused of stealing the diamond necklace that went missing at the same time as Audrey, but she must have been there for the diary. And the scrap of paper I found in the back of the diary – the one you picked up for me at the cove – was written by Gran and contains a coded message, though I haven't worked out what it means yet.'

'Woah!' River held up his hand. 'Hang on a minute. Lost diaries, stolen diamond necklaces, coded messages... what on earth are you going on about? I feel like I've been catapulted into an episode of Sherlock.'

Clara slowed down her breathing and her words. She was starting to gabble.

'The diary contains strings of numbers that make no sense, and the piece of paper also contains similar numbers. I can tell by the writing that the numbers in the diary were written by Audrey whereas the numbers on the piece of paper were written by my gran, who didn't steal any necklace, by the way.

The numbers must mean something, and Gran was using them to send a message to Audrey.'

'Before she took her own life.'

'Yes.' Clara paused, a half-formed idea flitting in to her mind. 'If that is what happened and how she died.'

River snorted in disbelief. 'So, what do you reckon? My grandfather murdered his beautiful young wife and buried her body under the apple tree in the garden?'

'Or upstairs on the third floor.'

'Oh, for goodness' sake!' River pushed the diary back into Clara's hands. 'Edwin Brellasham wasn't the easiest of men by all accounts. As far as I can gather, he wasn't a great father either. But I'm sure he didn't go around killing people.'

'OK.' Clara winced at her overactive imagination and tendency to speak without properly thinking things through. Geoffrey had been clear about what he'd seen. 'Sorry. That was a step too far. But don't you think it's strange that Audrey has been almost airbrushed out of Brellasham family history?'

River jabbed his finger towards the painting. 'There's an enormous portrait of her right there in front of you.'

'Which your grandfather refused to display. It was only put up, after he died, by your father, who was badly affected by Audrey's death. I mean, he saw—'

Clara stopped and bit her lip.

'You mean he saw what?' asked River.

'I don't know,' murmured Clara.

Geoffrey's admission that he'd seen his stepmother that fateful night had been raw and unexpected, and Clara didn't feel right sharing it with anyone. Not even his son.

River frowned and folded his arms. 'You're getting too caught up in all of this, Clara. It's not some conspiracy theory you can solve. Audrey was a woman with mental health issues. What happened back then was terribly sad and, yes, it's a bit odd that the third floor is still kept locked and boarded up, but that will all change when this house is sold and the developers move in.' He paused, looking pained. 'Everything will be opened up.'

'And any evidence will be destroyed.'

'Evidence? Listen to yourself, Clara. You're looking for confirmation of a crime that never happened. You need to get on with organising the fete that you're so invested in and let the past stay where it should, in the past. This is all plain... stupid.'

Clara was winded by his telling off, and River's face softened. 'Look,' he said, reaching out his hand and briefly touching her arm. 'I don't mean to be harsh but there's so much going on in the here and now, why fixate on a woman who's long dead? OK?'

Clara nodded. Perhaps he had a point and she *was* becoming obsessed, as her mother had warned her.

'Does my father know about the diary?' River suddenly asked.

'No. My mum thought it would upset him to see it, and she didn't want rumours about my gran being a thief – *allegedly* a thief – resurfacing.'

'I can see what she means but I think he should have it, don't you? Audrey was his stepmother, after all.'

'Yes, I know you're right. He deserves to have it and I will give it to him, though I might wait for the right moment, seeing as he'll probably kick off about my gran taking the diary in the first place.'

'It's always best to pick your moments, I find, when dealing with my father. He's not the easiest of men, either. Or the most understanding when people, like me, don't measure up to his high standards.'

River tried to smile but it was so filled with pain, Clara felt a rush of protectiveness towards him.

'He can certainly be tricky.'

'You can say that again.'

'He can certainly be tr—'

'Oh, please!' interrupted River. 'I thought we were both grown-ups now.'

But he laughed, which warmed Clara's heart.

'Anyway.' River twisted his mouth. 'I'd better go in search of my missing father, and I'll see you at one o'clock tomorrow at the picnic, if not before. I imagine Bartie's looking forward to it.' He paused, a frown on his face. 'Do you know much about Bartie these days? You know... about what he's been up to? What he's like?'

'Not really. I hadn't seen him for years until he arrived with you. Why?'

River shrugged. 'No reason.' He hesitated but then pulled himself up tall. 'Right. Don't stand here staring at that picture. It makes you seem weird.'

'Understood,' said Clara, turning her back on Audrey.

But she turned towards the painting again as soon as River was out of sight. River had been dismissive about the whole thing, and perhaps she was being obsessive, but she couldn't get this woman out of her head.

'OK, Clo, that *is* obsessive,' she told herself, giving a sardonic smile.

She rattled the door handle to the third floor once more but the door remained locked, as she'd known it would be.

Who knew what lay undiscovered above their heads? The only way to find out, she realised, was to get hold of the key and find out for herself. Before the developers did their worst and stripped the whole place bare.

15

RIVER

River only felt himself properly breathe out when he reached the hall and Clara was two floors above him – no doubt staring at that portrait again.

He hadn't expected to see her on her own at the end of the landing and he'd almost turned quietly and gone back downstairs.

But he'd decided to put on his big boy pants and have a word. It was ridiculous to run away. They'd been friends once. Good friends – and there was a time he'd hoped they might be more. But he'd just been fooling himself.

His mind flitted back to his first and only kiss with Clara when they were both fifteen. It was initiated by him after he'd realised that his feelings of friendship towards Clara had changed somewhere along the line into love. At least it felt like love back then. But Clara hadn't felt the same way.

'Idiot,' he said out loud into the hall before looking around to make sure he hadn't been spotted talking to himself. Bartie would think he was losing his mind.

But he *had* been an idiot to risk ruining his friendship with Clara. Especially as he'd known by then that he and his mother would soon be leaving for Australia. Though perhaps that knowledge had given him the confidence, or the desperation, to lean in and kiss her as they'd sat talking by the stream one September evening. His heart had been full of how much he was going to miss her.

At first, she'd moved back, startled, as his lips touched hers, which was hardly surprising. The idea of leading up to the kiss gradually hadn't crossed his mind. It was more a case of 'now or never'. But then, she'd seemed to lean into it – into him – and kiss him back. Though he couldn't swear to it later because the whole thing had been so brief and awkward.

Mrs N had suddenly called out Clara's name, letting her know it was time to go home. And though the two of them couldn't be seen in the darkness, Clara had leapt to her feet, gabbled a goodbye and hurried off.

He'd never had a chance to talk to her about it because his mum had decided she could cope with Geoffrey no longer and had driven them away for good the very next morning. And though River had sent a text to Clara about their hasty flit, she hadn't turned up to say goodbye. That was when he'd fully realised that his clumsy lunge at her hadn't been welcome.

Did she remember it still? he wondered. Probably not, after all this time. He was no doubt giving it far too much significance and she'd forgotten all about his adolescent faux pas.

'Nothing to do, River?' His father had just stepped into the hall from the garden. He shook soil from his shoes which tumbled across the floor tiles. 'I'm sure Bartie would welcome a hand with making arrangements for his developer contact to visit.' He tilted his head towards Bartie, who had followed him into the hall.

'Of course,' said River, wondering if the two of them had been walking together. 'But maybe you and I could have a cup of tea together first? We can talk about what you're planning to do after the manor's sold. Or not, if you'd rather have a break from it all. I can tell you about what I've been up to recently in Australia.'

Geoffrey regarded him for a moment, an emotion that River couldn't read playing across his face.

'I'd love to, but I'm afraid I have a lot of paperwork to get through before we can advance the sale.'

'Would you like me to help you with it? I'm a whizz with paperwork.'

River smiled but his father, looking solemn, shook his head.

'No, no. Thank you for your offer but I'm sure I can manage, and Bartie has offered to help if I get stuck. So I'll see you at dinner time.'

He turned into the library and shut the door behind him. The sound of the closing door felt like a slap across River's face.

'All right, mate?' asked Bartie in a very bad Australian accent. 'Phew, it's warm out there. Not as hot as you Aussies are used to, but boiling for us Brits.'

River dragged his attention back to his cousin. 'I'm still a Brit too.'

But Bartie wrinkled his nose. 'Nah, not really. Your life's over there now, with your mum and your girlfriend.'

'I told you in the car, I don't have a girlfriend.'

'That's a shame, but there's nothing wrong with choosing to be on your own.'

'I was in a serious relationship for a while, with a woman called Kitty,' said River, keen to wipe the patronising pity from Bartie's face. 'She was lovely but it didn't work out.'

'How long ago did you break up?'

'The summer before last. It was tough at the time but I'm over it now. Anyway,' said River, wishing he'd never brought up the subject of his ex-girlfriend, 'I've been thinking about the development of this house and wondered if there's any chance of Mrs N's cottage being saved? I know my father's keen to preserve the grounds, whatever deal is made, so where's the harm in keeping the cottage?'

Bartie frowned. 'It'll be a bit of an eyesore for the owners of the new top-of-the-range apartments who buy here.'

'It can't be seen from the manor house, and it's a pretty, historic cottage. It'll add charm to the whole development.'

Bartie's mouth twisted, wrinkling his nose. 'I don't think so, mate. I know how these things work.'

The implication being that he didn't have a clue, thought River, wishing that his cousin would stop referring to him as 'mate'. But he did his best to smile. 'Do you need a hand before the developer arrives?'

'Nah, I think good old Geoff and I are getting everything sorted. So you're not needed.'

Wasn't that the truth, thought River as Bartie wandered off. All that was required was his acquiescence to the sale so his father could sell Brellasham Manor, minus any guilt that he'd acted behind his son's back. And he was definitely avoiding River, which was upsetting but also strangely liberating. If his father couldn't be bothered to make an effort, River decided, then neither could he.

After dinner, during which Bartie regaled them with examples of his business prowess, River sat in the drawing room at the computer. He'd planned to investigate flights to Australia, so he could get his return home booked – his father didn't need him, not with Bartie around. But he'd started looking up Audrey Brellasham instead and had quickly fallen down a Google rabbit hole. Twenty minutes later, he was still researching the woman who had been his step-grandmother.

There was very little online about her, and what there was River presumed that Clara had already found: a few newspaper mentions of her marriage to Edwin, and two reports of her disappearance. Both of these reports skirted around the details of what had happened and made oblique references to her drowning in 'tragic circumstances'.

There were several internet pieces about Edwin, most of them regarding his later marriage to a London socialite, which had ended in her death ten years after they'd walked down the aisle. That was three wives who had died at a relatively young age.

River pushed aside the whisper of suspicion that was swirling round his brain, because he wasn't about to start fabricating hideous crimes, like Clara. Instead, he went in search of the filing cabinet that used to be in the rarely used office at the back of the manor.

He pushed open the office door and smiled. Nothing changed. The room was arranged exactly as it had been sixteen years ago, with an old wooden desk at its centre and the filing cabinet in a corner. A huge spider plant in a yellow ceramic pot was the only new addition.

The cabinet was unlocked and crammed to overflowing with certificates, documents and pieces of paper. This wild goose chase was going to take some time. River sighed and, sitting cross-legged on the floor, began to sift through the cabinet's contents.

Fifteen minutes later, he'd found what he was looking for: a marriage certificate for Edwin and Audrey that showed they'd got married in April 1954 at St Augustine's Church in Heaven's Cove. He put the certificate to one side and continued searching but that was the only mention of her that he could find. It wasn't much but it gave Audrey's maiden name, which Clara might find useful.

Why was he helping her with this obsession of hers? he wondered, getting to his feet. To get back in her good books?

Possibly. But the truth was that Clara's story of a lost diary, unfounded rumours and unintelligible numbers had piqued his own interest in the woman who'd once lived in this house. Audrey, who stared out so enigmatically from her portrait, was getting under his skin, too.

River folded the certificate carefully into his pocket and went back into the drawing room to turn off the computer. But as the screen faded to black, he noticed something on the floor that was poking out from beneath the sofa. It was a colour photo taken of his father in middle age, he realised. Geoffrey, no more than fifty, had a full head of dark hair and was smiling broadly at whoever was taking the picture. It was hard to remember him being so full of life and happy.

River bent to pick up the photo and noticed another two. These had slipped farther under the sofa and he had to scrabble in the dust to grab them.

The first black and white photo was smaller than the picture of his father and was of a woman bending over the reading table in the library. River held the photo up to the lamp and squinted at what he'd found. The woman's face was in profile but it was clear that she was the same woman depicted in the painting on the second floor. Audrey was peering at a large, open book that took up much of the table space and seemed unaware of the photographer.

She was in the second photo too but wasn't alone this time. Edwin was standing next to her and Audrey's hand was resting on the shoulder of the child in front of them. River realised with a jolt that the child must be his father. Edwin was staring directly at the camera, a look of pride on his face, but Audrey's gaze had wandered. She was looking out of the picture and her mouth was twisted, as if she was biting the inside of her cheek. She looked distracted and unhappy. Did she have a premonition of her future?

River knew that he was getting too caught up in Clara's ridiculous notions. But he put the photos with the marriage certificate and kept hold of them nonetheless.

16

CLARA

The sun was absent this morning, hidden from view by high grey cloud, but the day was still hot and humid. Clara turned her face to the sky for a moment and breathed in the smell of the sea. It was a perfect day for a picnic, but first she had someone to speak to.

Weaving in and out of the tourists thronging the quayside, Clara made her way to a small whitewashed cottage squeezed between two larger buildings. Lobster Pot Cottage was where former fisherman Claude lived. She'd known him all her life, but there was no guarantee he'd have anything to do with her today.

Claude was curmudgeonly, reclusive and unpredictable. But there was something about him, a vulnerability that surfaced occasionally, that meant she'd always liked him.

Her knock on the front door was greeted by a volley of barking from inside and a loud yell: 'Give it a rest, Buster!' Then the door was opened a crack and Claude peered out. His shock of grey hair, once long and wild, was more tamed these days and his beard less bushy, but he still looked like the local eccentric.

'What is it?' He gently pushed his dog to one side with his foot.

'Hello, Claude. It's Clara, from Brellasham Manor. I wondered if I could have a quick word with you.'

'What about?' he asked, his eyes narrowing.

'I want to talk to you about a body.'

'Killed someone, have you?'

Clara blinked. 'What? No. Of course not.'

Claude stared at her for a moment more and then opened his door wider. A dark, narrow corridor lay behind him.

'We can have a word but I don't want to invite you in.'

'That's fine. Maybe we can have a quick chat in your garden instead?'

'Garden' was pushing it. The tiny space in front of Claude's house was paved with cobblestones and the only greenery was provided by a withered hydrangea in a large pot. Rumour had it that an old lady friend of Claude's had given him the flower to cheer up the front of the cottage, but he'd obviously forgotten to water it.

'I'll only take up a few minutes of your time,' urged Clara, bending to pat Buster's head.

'All right,' grunted Claude, stepping out of the cottage and pulling the door to behind him. 'What's this body, then?'

'I'm trying to find out more about Audrey Brellasham. She's the woman who drowned in the manor house cove in 1957. Do you remember it happening?'

'Might do,' said Claude, sitting down on the low stone wall that surrounded his garden. 'Why?'

'I've been finding out a bit about it and I'm surprised that Audrey's body was never found. I thought you might have some knowledge about that.'

Claude sniffed. 'Dunno what makes you think I'm an expert in body disposal.'

'I thought you might have some knowledge about local tides,

having fished in these waters since you were a boy. Wouldn't Audrey's body have washed back to shore if she'd drowned?'

'It depends on weather conditions and the currents that night. I'd expect her body to wash up somewhere, but maybe it wouldn't. It might still be trapped on the seabed, though it'd be nothing but bones now, stripped clean.'

Claude glared at a tourist who was taking a photo of the fraying lobster pot next to his front door. 'People'll take pictures of anything these days. The world's gone mad.' He tickled Buster behind the ear, still watching the tourist, who'd taken one look at Claude and wandered off. 'So why d'you wanna know about something that happened so long ago?'

'I'm just interested.'

'Is that right?' Claude gave her a searching look. 'It was a strange business. I was young at the time and never saw Audrey around the village. I wasn't sure she really existed. The current squire was only a kid too. Hardly saw him neither 'cos he went to some posh school up country.' He paused. 'Wasn't there some trouble involving Violet Netherway after Audrey vanished?'

'No,' said Clara quickly. 'I mean, there was an issue but it was all a misunderstanding.'

'Makes sense. Life's full of 'em.'

'Was Edwin, Geoffrey's father, around the village much when you were young?'

'Oh yeah, he appeared often enough, lording it about over the rest of us. I didn't much like him. Dead eyes. Mind you, local people pandered to him.'

'In what way?'

'With lots of bowing and scraping. There's not so much of it these days which is just as well. It's only an accident of birth them living in that big house while the rest of us are slumming it.' Clara was minded to agree but she held her tongue. 'He insisted that his wife was going swimming but not everyone believed him. I know posh folk can do stupid things sometimes but who, in their right mind, would go swimming at that time of year at that time of night?'

'Maybe she wasn't in her right mind.'

'Maybe not,' said Claude gruffly. 'Happens to the best of us that life gets too much sometimes.'

Did life ever get too much for Claude? Clara wondered, sneaking a sideways glance at him. But he was getting to his feet.

'Is that everything? I can't spend all morning answering your daft questions.'

'Yes, that's all. Thanks very much for your time.'

Claude grunted in reply and had reached his front door when he said: 'I hear the current squire is selling up and moving on.'

'That's right. He's sad about it but he can't afford to keep the manor going.'

'So you and your mother will lose your cottage, I dare say.'

Clara nodded. 'That's right. It's going to be all change for everyone.'

'Not much about to rent in the village, and you won't want to be moving away from Heaven's Cove.'

'Mum definitely won't want to go far but we might not have a choice.' Clara breathed out slowly. 'Brellasham Manor Fete is still going ahead next Saturday, Claude. You should come along, to say goodbye to the place.'

'I don't suppose I will but I appreciate the invitation.'

And with that, he stepped into his cottage, ushered Buster to follow him inside, and slammed the front door shut.

'OK, then,' Clara murmured to herself.

She glanced at her watch and, leaving Claude's cottage behind, began making her way towards the village green. It was only just midday but Bartie had brought the time of the picnic forward by forty-five minutes and she didn't want to be late.

Weaving her way past groups of tourists, Clara thought

about the information that Claude had shared. Audrey was rarely seen after moving into the manor, and Edwin was full of himself and claimed that his wife had been swimming on that fateful night.

She remembered River's words about the stigma surrounding suicide in the 1950s. Perhaps Edwin had lied to save his wife's reputation, or his own face. Or maybe he was so grief-stricken, he couldn't bear to admit what had really happened. If that *was* what had really happened?

Clara tried, unsuccessfully, to calm the thoughts tumbling through her brain, and quickened her pace. The more she delved into Audrey's fate, the less she seemed to know for sure. It was probably a colossal waste of time when there were more pressing things to occupy her – finding a new home, for one. But her mother was right about her stubborn streak because she couldn't let it drop.

17

CLARA

Bartie licked his ice cream and shifted on the picnic rug. 'I bet tourists go ape over that church. What is it, three hundred years old? Four hundred?'

'Older than that,' said Clara. 'Eight hundred, I think. We can have a look inside if you like. And the graveyard's interesting, if you fancy finding out more about the people who used to live in this village.'

'No, you're all right,' said Bartie, amusement crossing his face. 'I tend not to visit graveyards when I'm on a date.'

Were they on a date? wondered Clara, lifting hair from the nape of her neck so the breeze blowing through Heaven's Cove could cool her skin. If so, it was the hottest date ever, though not in a good way. The clouds had parted in the last half hour, the sun was blazing down and the temperature was rising.

Bartie, looking as cool as ever, finished his ice cream, stretched out on the picnic rug and put his hands behind his head.

'So, Heaven's Cove is just as I remember it – quaint and pretty, like something out of a fairy tale.'

'A fairy tale peopled with hundreds of tourists,' laughed

Clara, watching a group of visitors peering at the Mourning Stone, an old stone on the green which marked an ancient local tragedy. The summer season was burgeoning and Heaven's Cove was bustling. 'Anyway, shall we start discussing the fete? Or would you rather wait for River? You did tell him that the picnic was at quarter past twelve rather than one o'clock, didn't you?'

'Yeah, I mentioned it to him this morning but he was busy at the time.'

'With his dad?'

'No, some long-distance phone call from a girlfriend,' said Bartie airily, wiping drips of ice cream from the neck of his T shirt.

'Really? I didn't know he had a girlfriend. He never mentioned it.'

'He's keeping it quiet while he's here. Not too keen on the old man finding out for some reason. But I get the feeling that it's serious.'

Clara felt bizarrely let down. Of course River had a girlfriend waiting for him in Australia, and there was no reason why he would have mentioned her. Once upon a time, Clara and River had known everything about each other's lives, but it was different now.

'Do you know what? I'm not sure River will turn up at all,' said Bartie. 'He can be quite unreliable these days, now his life's elsewhere, but let's give him another five minutes.'

He sat up and stretched his arms over his head, causing the bottom of his T-shirt to ride up, revealing a toned stomach that had presumably seen plenty of action at the gym. He smiled and shuffled a little closer on the picnic rug.

'In the meantime, what's happened to you over the years, Clara Netherway? As my grandma used to say, are you courting?'

'Me? No. I've had boyfriends, of course.'

'But no one serious?'

'Not really. I seem to have kissed a lot of frogs in my time. Well... not *lots* of frogs.' She stopped. Did that make it sound as if she was going out with every Tom, Dick or Harry who asked her? 'What I mean is—'

'I know what you mean,' said Bartie softly, leaning towards her.

'What about you?' Clara asked, her voice sounding higher than usual.

'Footloose and fancy-free.'

'So no one special then?'

A shadow crossed his face. 'There was a woman a while back who broke my heart.'

'What was her name?' When Bartie hesitated, Clara kicked herself for asking. 'Sorry. It's none of my business.'

'No, you're fine,' said Bartie, stroking her arm. 'She was called Kitty and we broke up last summer. It was tough at the time but I'm over her now. Just about, and finally deciding to risk my heart again.'

Clara swallowed because Bartie really was very close, and he was staring into her eyes.

'Anyway,' he murmured, 'enough about me. What else have you been up to since we were teenagers way back when?'

'Not a lot,' she managed, not breaking eye contact. 'This and that. You know. Stuff. Grown-up stuff.'

She stopped talking, feeling stupid. Sixteen years ago, she'd dreamed of Bartie taking an interest in her life, not realising that it would turn her into an incoherent idiot.

'Grown-up stuff.' Bartie raised an eyebrow, and leaned forward until his mouth was almost brushing hers. 'That sounds exciting. What kind of grown-up stuff?' he whispered.

'Responsibilities, really,' said Clara, feeling distinctly jittery. 'My dad had severe disabilities following a stroke, and he and Mum needed my support until he died last year.'

'Oh, right.' Bartie sat up straight again. 'That sounds very... erm, grown up and challenging.'

'Yeah, it was,' said Clara, berating herself for ruining what had appeared to be 'a moment' between them. Bringing up death was always going to do that. 'Tell me more about you,' she said, trying to rescue the situation.

'Well, what is there to tell?' said Bartie languidly, a smile playing on his lips.

'Have you been to Brellasham Manor much over the last few years? I haven't seen you.'

The smile faded. 'Not as much as I'd have liked. Life gets in the way, doesn't it. Especially when you're working to build your career, as I've been doing. I'm doing rather well now – lots of irons in the business fire, a flat in London and a great social life. But, without someone special to share it with, it all feels a little hollow sometimes. Do you know what I mean? I'm still looking for that one person who gets me for who I truly am. That's why I feel drawn to you, Clara. Not only have you turned into an extremely attractive woman – a swan, if you like – you know me. After we've been friends for so long, you really *know* me.'

Clara wasn't sure that she really did, but she nodded anyway, glowing at being called a swan. Though that did imply she'd once been an ugly duckling.

'Clara Netherway, are you listening to me?' asked Bartie. He gently brushed his finger beneath her chin. 'I don't know what it is but there's something about you, some magnetism, that's attracting me. Don't you feel it too?'

He was so close now, Clara could feel his warm breath on her cheek. Her fifteen-year-old self would have been thrilled, and her thirty-one-year-old self felt pretty excited about it too.

Bartie leaned ever closer. He was going to kiss her. That was obvious. And Clara wanted him to kiss her. Who wouldn't want dashing Bartie to pull them into an embrace? So why was her first thought, as his lips landed, *I hope Mum isn't walking past right now?*

Her mother probably wouldn't approve of Clara fraternising with what she deemed the 'upper classes'.

Concentrate! Clara told herself, closing her eyes as Bartie's arm snaked around her waist and he pulled her hard against him. *This is what your teenage self could only dream about.*

Bartie's hand was pushing through her hair now, and the kiss was lovely, if she actually let herself focus on it. A bit forceful, perhaps. He was pressing her backwards, lowering her down onto the rug, and she felt his heavy body cover her as the kiss went on.

This was all very unexpected and exciting, but not entirely appropriate for a public place at lunchtime in Heaven's Cove.

When Bartie's hand slipped beneath her T-shirt and she felt his fingers on the bare skin at her waist, she opened her eyes and shifted her head slightly.

'You OK, babe?' he asked, still heavy on top of her.

'I just feel a bit awkward. It's very public around here. I thought we were meeting up for a picnic and a chat. I didn't realise that... you know.'

Bartie stared at her for a moment, his expression unreadable. Then he rolled onto his back and put his hands behind his head.

'Sorry, Clara. I didn't mean to get so carried away but I can't help feeling that there's something special between us. Maybe there was years ago as well, but we were both too young to recognise that we could be good together. I suggest we resume this, er... chat' – he smiled – 'in a more private place in the very near future. I'm going to be around for a while, until the sale of the manor house is underway.'

'OK,' said Clara, pulling down her T-shirt and swallowing hard. Now the kiss was over, excitement was giving way to awkwardness. 'Do you think your developer contact will want to buy the manor?'

Bartie brushed his fringe from his hot forehead. 'I expect so. It's an amazing opportunity for a top-class development in a beautiful, secluded location, and I know this developer will offer above the odds for it.'

'Will the developer just focus on the house? They won't build in the grounds, will they?'

'No, absolutely not. I've made it very clear to the developer that the grounds are out of bounds and need to be preserved. That's one of Geoffrey's sale stipulations.'

'I'm not surprised because he loves his gardens, and it would break his heart if they were destroyed.' A thought suddenly struck Clara. 'Once the development of the manor house is finished, I know the grounds will be private property but do you think the developer might give us permission to hold the charity fete in the grounds every year?'

'That is a definite possibility.' Bartie suddenly sat up straight. 'Actually, I've just had a brilliant idea. There's no reason why your cottage should have to be demolished if the grounds are being preserved, and it's far enough away from the manor that I can't see it would matter if you and your mum stayed there.'

'Really?' Clara felt her heart speeding up. 'That would be amazing. My mum would be so happy to stay in the house because it holds so many happy memories for her. And also, there's the whole being homeless and having to find somewhere else thing.'

'Of course.' Bartie gave her a bright, white smile. 'No promises, but I'll do what I can, for your mum but mostly for you.'

'Thank you. I'd be so grateful.'

'Yeah.' Bartie leaned forward again and kissed her briefly on the lips. 'And now I've got to go.'

'I thought we were going to discuss this year's fete.'

'I'd love to, but there's a lot to do before the developer arrives, especially if I need to twist their arm about your cottage. That's OK, isn't it?'

'Of course,' said Clara, feeling it would be ungrateful in the extreme to complain when he'd just promised to try and save her home.

When he reached across her, to grab a bottle of water, Clara spotted River at the far side of the green. He'd come after all.

She raised her hand, to beckon him over, but gasped when cold water sploshed over her legs.

'Sorry,' said Bartie, picking up the large bottle which had fallen onto its side. 'I hadn't put the top back on properly. Who are you waving at?'

Clara squinted into the distance but River was nowhere to be seen.

'No one. I thought I saw River but I must have been wrong.'

'Never mind. He probably got tied up on another call to his girlfriend. Will you be all right here on your own?' he asked, getting to his feet and brushing the creases out of his chinos.

'Of course.'

''Til the next time, babe, when I look forward to us being in a more private location.'

Bartie cupped her warm cheek in his hand before sauntering off across the grass.

Clara watched him go before lying back on the picnic rug and staring at the sky. Bartie had just kissed her and called her babe – twice. She laughed out loud, imagining her expression at fifteen if she'd known then what was going to happen in the future. She also pictured River's adolescent face and him miming sticking two fingers down his throat at what he would deem Bartie's cheesy chat-up lines.

There had been no chat at all before River had taken her by

surprise and kissed her as they'd sat by the stream in the darkness.

Clara huffed out loud, cross with herself for thinking of River when he hadn't even bothered to turn up for the picnic. She would think of Bartie instead, she decided, closing her eyes against the glare of the sun. Bartie, who had kissed her and who was doing his best to save the cottage that she and her mum called home.

18

RIVER

The irony was he'd been looking for Clara, tramping all over the manor house and grounds to find her after turning tail and running from her and Bartie on the picnic rug earlier that afternoon. But now that he had found her, he wasn't sure he wanted to speak to her after all.

She was sitting with her back to him, high on the moors, with her knees pulled up under her chin. The sun was still beating down but a straw hat was shielding her from the glare.

River ran a hand through his hair. He should have worn a hat too. *A gentleman never goes out in the afternoon sun without a Panama.* That's what his father had told him when he was growing up, along with *Boys don't cry.* He'd also promised: *One day this will all be yours*, which, as it turned out, was *really* ironic.

His childhood memories were coming back now he was at Brellasham Manor. He'd blocked them out in Australia – they were a painful reminder of a life that was no more, and of people who were gone for good.

But now memories, good and bad, were flooding back, triggered by a smell of damp in the drawing room, and the clatter of pans from the kitchen – or the sight of Clara sitting with her back to him on the wild moors they'd once roamed as children.

Taking a deep breath, he swallowed his misgivings and started walking towards her.

She glanced up when he reached her, squinting under the brim of her hat.

'Have you escaped?' she asked simply. Just as she used to almost twenty years ago, when he'd been running from his parents' constant bickering.

He nodded. 'Is it OK if I sit down?'

'Of course. It's a free country.' She glanced at him. 'How did you find me? That is, if you were looking for me in the first place. Or were you just out for a walk?'

'Both,' lied River. He looked out across the scrubby grass and huge slabs of granite that littered the countryside. They were high up here, and the sea was a glittering swathe of blue in the distance. Far below them, the roof of the manor house was just visible, and the whitewashed walls of Mrs N's cottage. 'I thought I might find you here. The moors and the castle ruins in the village were always your favourite places.'

'They still are,' said Clara. 'Look at that view. It's so vast, so wildly beautiful, it puts life into perspective somehow.' She wrinkled her nose. 'Does that sound pretentious?'

'No, I know what you mean and I can't imagine you ever being pretentious anyway.'

'I do hope you're not implying that I'm chippy.'

River grinned. 'As if I would.'

When they lapsed into silence, broken only by the chirping of birds and the rush of a warm wind, he stole a glance at her. She was wearing navy blue shorts and a strappy yellow T-shirt and sandals. Her skin was a light golden brown, apart from her cheeks, which were flushed from too much hatless sun at lunchtime. She looked amazing.

'How was the picnic?' River asked when the silence went on for too long.

Clara's cheeks flushed a brighter pink. 'Bartie and I had a good time. It's a shame you couldn't make it.'

River opened his mouth to say that, actually, he had gone along at one o'clock as arranged, only to see that Bartie and Clara were there already, enjoying a passionate kiss. Then he closed his mouth again. What Clara got up to was none of his business and she wouldn't thank him for meddling in her affairs.

But he couldn't help wondering what was going on. Were she and Bartie having a fling? Bartie was certainly angling for a short-term relationship, and maybe that was what Clara wanted too. She'd always had a bit of a thing for him. No wonder his own adolescent kiss had been poorly received.

'River?' Clara was staring at him. 'You're miles away.'

'Sorry. What did you say?'

'I said, did your phone call go well this morning?'

River frowned. 'Yeah, it was OK.' He'd rung his mother earlier, to tell her he was still alive, but that was all.

'Good,' said Clara, waving away a fly that was dive-bombing her. 'I expect you miss her, being so far away.'

'Um. I do, yes, and I know she misses me.'

'I bet she does.'

'But I'll see her again soon, so that's good.'

'Yeah, of course.' Clara picked a blade of grass and rolled it between her fingers. 'How do you feel about Brellasham Manor, then? Have you missed it?'

'I did, at first. Then it all kind of faded as I built a new life in a foreign country.'

'What did you and your mum do when you first arrived in Australia?'

'I think I mentioned that we lived in a couple of communes, which were, basically, people living off the land and sharing produce.'

'Your mum always was a bit of a hippy.'

'That's true. She still is, only now her cause is saving the planet. She's become something of an eco-warrior.'

Clara smiled. 'Yeah, I can see your mum doing that.' She paused. 'So, were the communes all right?'

River nodded. 'I guess so. Mostly I remember them as being unbearably hot.'

'I bet.'

'But then Mum got a job in Sydney after a couple of years so we moved to the city and we've been there ever since.'

'So were you too busy building your new life to give a monkey's about the people you'd left behind?'

River suppressed a smile. This was awkward but it reminded him so much of young Clara, who would say exactly what was on her mind. He'd presumed she would develop more of a filter as she got older, but apparently not – and, in spite of the awkwardness, he was glad of it.

'I did give a monkey's. I...' He swallowed, remembering how isolated and lonely he'd felt at first. 'I did miss Brellasham Manor.'

And you, he wanted to say, but an image of Bartie lying on top of Clara, his hand snaking beneath her T-shirt, sprang into his mind.

So he said instead, 'But I didn't realise just how much I'd missed the manor and my father until I came back.'

'How long do you think you'll stay?'

'I'm not sure,' he said, distracted by the flecks of amber in her eyes. Had they always been that beautiful colour? 'I was going to book a return flight but I haven't got round to it yet.'

'Right.' Clara nodded and stared to her right, at the moors stretching away into a smudgy purple haze. Then, she suddenly turned towards him. 'I forgot to say, Bartie has had a brilliant idea about Mum's cottage. He said the gardens and grounds will remain intact so he's going to do his best to get the developer to allow us to stay on.'

'Is he now? That's great.'

River raised an eyebrow because it had been his idea, actually, but saying so might make him sound petty. And the most important thing was that Clara and her mum could stay put once the manor was sold. That was all that mattered.

So, remembering why he'd been looking for Clara in the first place, he moved on.

'I wanted to ask if you're still trying to find out information about Audrey.'

'Why?' Clara's gaze turned on him. 'Do you want to tell me again not to bother? Only apparently Audrey was never seen around Heaven's Cove, even though her husband was out and about, lording it up, and Claude reckons a body would usually wash up after someone had drowned.'

'Claude?' River blinked. 'Scary Claude?'

'He's not so scary once you get to know him properly. He's just a one-off.'

'I'll take your word for it,' said River, remembering how he'd avoided the fisherman with wild hair who glared at teenagers and always had an air of melancholy about him. 'But I'm not here to tell you not to bother. I'm here to give you this.' He reached into his pocket and pulled out the folded marriage certificate and the photos he'd found on the drawing room floor. 'I thought they might be useful.'

Clara took them and studied them intently for a moment. 'Where did you get these?' she asked, lifting her face towards him.

'I found them in the house. I thought Audrey's maiden name might help if you're searching online for her. And the photos are interesting.'

Clara peered at the picture of Audrey in the library. 'What

book is she staring at so intently? It looks like the dictionary that's on her lap in her portrait. Don't you think?'

'I don't know. It's hard to tell. Possibly.'

Clara put the photo down. 'Thanks for these, but I thought you were against me delving more into Audrey's past.'

'Yeah, well, I changed my mind.'

'Why?'

Because if it's important to you, it's important to me.

'I just did,' he said.

Clara pushed her hand into the pocket of her shorts, bit her lip and narrowed her eyes. River remembered that expression, which usually preceded one of Clara's wilder ideas.

'What is it?' he asked.

She said nothing for a few moments and then pulled something from her pocket. 'Guess what I've got.'

'I have no idea.'

'Now don't freak out,' she said, which had always been one of her more disconcerting phrases, 'but I've got hold of this.' She unfurled her fingers to reveal a key with a long brass barrel and elaborate curlicued head.

'Is that...?'

'Yep. It was hanging in the store cupboard, behind a load of tins and boxes. I knew there must be a key to the third floor somewhere because Glenda, the cleaner, is allowed up there occasionally.'

'Can't Glenda tell you all about it?'

'Afraid not. She's totally tight-lipped, as if she's signed the Official Secrets Act or something.'

'Does your mum know you've got the key?'

'No, and I'd like it to stay that way, please.'

River sighed. 'I'm not going to tell on you, Clara, but is it a good idea to break into Audrey's suite of rooms?'

'Break in is rather a loaded phrase, don't you think? I'm not so much breaking in as having a quick look to try and solve a mystery and I thought, seeing as you're interested now, that you might like to come with me.' She got to her feet and brushed grass from her backside. 'No one will ever know, and you'll be back in Australia soon anyway.' She walked a few steps before looking back. 'Are you coming?'

River sat for a moment, deliberating what to do. On the one hand, his father would be furious if he ever found out, but on the other, it was just like the old days when he and Clara would go off in search of adventures.

And he really did want to know what was on the mysterious third floor.

19

CLARA

The key turned smoothly in the lock and the door swung open. Behind it lay a narrow wooden staircase leading up into darkness.

'These must have been the backstairs for the servants,' said Clara, her heart pounding.

'I guess so,' said River, peering over her shoulder, his breath hot on her neck. 'Are you quite sure about this, Clara?'

'Yes, absolutely,' she replied, though she wasn't sure at all. Who knew what lay above their heads? 'You don't have to come if you don't want to.'

She waited for his reply, praying that he wouldn't back out. Having him here made her feel braver but, whatever his decision, it was too late to turn back. She would go alone, if she had to.

River groaned quietly. 'I'm not going to let you go up there on your own, am I?' He glanced back at the grand staircase that led from the hall. Someone was walking upstairs, their feet a dull thud on the carpet. 'Just get a move on before someone sees us.'

Clara stepped through the door, waited for River to follow,

and closed it behind them. She couldn't see him in the darkness but she could hear him gently breathing and sense his body close to hers as the footsteps outside got closer.

The sound of River's breathing stopped, and Clara held her breath too. How could she explain the two of them being alone together in the dark? A secret rendezvous, perhaps, so they could kiss each other senseless in private? She swallowed, aware of the heat coming from River's body. This had been a terrible, *terrible* idea. Geoffrey would be furious and her mother would kill her.

She only started to relax when the footsteps receded, and she blinked when River turned on the torch on his mobile phone.

'That was close.' His face loomed ghost-like in the light. 'Come on, let's get this over with.'

He began to climb the stairs and Clara followed, her hand gripping the smooth bannister. Her grandmother, Violet, must have used these stairs when she was needed on the third floor – and when fleeing from Audrey's bedroom with her diary.

Clara stopped climbing as a wave of grief for the grand-mother she'd lost washed over her. If only Violet had talked to her about what had gone on that night. If only she'd felt able to share her secrets.

'Are you all right down there?' River asked over his shoulder.

'Yes, I'm fine. I'm right behind you.'

Clara sniffed back tears and kept on climbing until the gloom lessened and the stairs opened out onto a wide landing.

'Wow!' she murmured, overcome by the sight in front of her.

Daylight, filtering through half-open curtains, dappled on a thick, blue carpet that was covered in cream swirls. It looked retro, opulent and untrodden. Gilt-framed oil paintings of moorland hung on the walls and a large grandfather clock stood in a corner, its hands not moving. Time seemed to stand still up here, in this place which had been under lock and key for almost seventy years.

'Should we take off our shoes?' Clara whispered to River, who was gazing around him.

'Maybe we should,' he whispered back, 'seeing as we're not supposed to be up here. We don't want to leave dirty footprints for Glenda to find.'

Together, they slipped off their shoes and padded along the plush carpet.

'It's amazing, isn't it?' said Clara, her voice a little louder.

'It is, though I still can't believe you managed to get me up here.' River stopped to peep out of a window that overlooked the gardens and the sea.

'Think of it as revenge. It was you who encouraged me to climb the tallest tree in the garden when I was ten.'

'I didn't realise you'd get stuck and my father would have to call out the fire service to get you down.' River grinned. 'Do you remember how angry he was?'

'There was steam coming out of his ears. He thought I was a bad influence on you.'

River waved an arm at their surroundings. 'I think you still are, Clarissa.'

'Hey! Don't call me that.'

When Clara punched him on the arm, River laughed. 'You might have grown up but you still hit like a girl.'

'And you're still a sexist pain in the backside.'

'Nice. Always ready with an insult. That hasn't changed either.'

'You and Bartie always deserved it.'

Clara had said something wrong because the smile slipped from River's face.

'Anyway,' he muttered, moving away from the window, 'we

shouldn't be up here, so let's have a quick look and get the hell out.'

They walked on in silence, past closed doors, until their way was blocked by a floor-to-ceiling brick wall.

'I think the main staircase must be behind here,' said River, knocking on the bricks. 'My grandfather sealed them off completely after Audrey died.'

'Even if he was grief-stricken, you have to admit that's odd behaviour.'

'He can't have been grief-stricken for long because he married again very quickly afterwards. Though she died a few years later and he moved on to wife number four.' River groaned. 'Don't look at me like that, Clara. Just because three of his wives died, it doesn't mean he did away with them. Edwin, who, don't forget, was a close relative of mine, was not a serial killer.'

'Of course not,' said Clara, hoping she sounded convincing. It was time to change the subject. 'Let's see what's in here,' she said, opening the door nearest to the blank brick wall.

The door opened onto a large bedroom. Charcoal curtains were pulled almost fully across the window, allowing in a thin shaft of sunlight that fell across the floorboards.

There was no furniture apart from a double bed draped in a midnight-blue eiderdown, a bedside table, and a desk with a green leather inlay. No possessions. No hint of the person who'd once slept here.

'Do you think this was Edwin's bedroom?' whispered Clara. 'It's got a masculine feel to it.'

'Probably. The Brellashams tend to have separate bedrooms, including my mother and father when they were married. Personally, I prefer to sleep with my partner.'

Clara blinked as an image of River sleeping next to his girl-friend, his tanned arm draped across her bare shoulders, popped into her mind. Why was she thinking of River's love life? A door banging downstairs drove the image away.

'Come on,' said River. 'Let's make this quick before we're missed.'

The next door off the landing opened onto an opulent bathroom, the likes of which Clara had never seen. At the centre of the room stood an enormous claw-footed bath with gold taps. The walls were covered from floor to ceiling in white tiles edged in black and gold, and a double basin had been placed beneath the curtained window. The brass towel rails were gleaming but empty.

'I think you could fit my bedroom into this bath,' said Clara, stepping into the room and running her fingers along its rolled edge. She had an urge to clamber in and try it out for size, but River was tapping his watch, so she grudgingly left the amazing bathroom behind and walked to the only door left on the landing that was yet to be opened. This had to be Audrey's bedroom.

Taking a deep breath, she pushed down the handle and the door swung open to reveal a bedroom which was, presumably, still as Audrey had seen it, on the night that she disappeared.

'Woah!' said River beside her. 'Now, this really *is* amazing.'

Clara went inside, crossed to the window and, after peeping outside to make sure she wouldn't be seen, pulled back the cream curtains. When light flooded into the room, it was easy to imagine that Audrey had stepped away for a moment and would soon be back.

In stark contrast to the minimalism of Edwin's room, all surfaces here were covered with Audrey's personal possessions. Framed photos of her, Edwin, and Geoffrey as a boy were displayed on a tall wooden chest of drawers. A cerise silk scarf was draped over the back of a chair, and a silver-backed hairbrush, blonde hairs tangled in its bristles, sat on her dressing table, along with a gold necklace and a glass perfume bottle.

Glenda was doing a good job of cleaning up here because there was barely a speck of dust in sight.

Clara picked up the heavy bottle and sniffed in a rich, musky scent. She closed her eyes for a moment, picturing the woman who had stood in this spot and sprayed herself with this perfume.

'Come and look at this,' said River, who was standing next to a door, by a floor lamp with a green fabric shade. 'There's a whole dressing room in here.'

Clara followed him into the small room which was lined with wardrobes, all painted white. She opened one and gasped at the treasure trove of 1950s fashion that greeted her. The wardrobe was crammed with dresses: striking dresses in jewel colours, made from satin and silk, with nipped-in waists and full skirts.

She pulled one out – a blue short-sleeved dress with a white collar – and held it against her. Audrey must have been about the same height but, judging by this dress, her shoulders and waist were tiny. Clara was quite slim but she would never fit into Audrey's clothes.

She put the blue dress back and began to rifle through the other wardrobes – through skirt suits in pastel hues, Capri trousers, pedal pushers, and sleeveless cotton tops – until she reached a rack of long dresses and spied the dress she was looking for.

The lemon-yellow gown that Audrey was wearing in her portrait – the one she wore to the ball – felt soft when Clara ran her fingers across the satin and chiffon. It was a beautiful dress for a beautiful woman, whose ending still remained a mystery.

Clara carefully closed the wardrobes and went back into the bedroom. Then she sat on the four-poster bed before swinging her legs up onto the silk eiderdown and lying down.

'We don't have time for you to have a rest,' said River, a hint of anxiety in his voice. 'We really need to get out of here.'

'I'm just trying to get into Audrey's head, to understand what she might have been thinking before she left this house for good.'

River pulled the curtains back across the window, to erase any sign of their visit, before sitting down on the bed beside her. 'Do you think it's a good idea to try and get into the head of a woman who was so troubled, she walked into the sea?'

'Probably not,' Clara admitted. Who could ever know what Audrey, whose mental health could have been adversely affected by a whole range of issues, was thinking that night?

'I'm getting a bit worried about you, Clara,' said River gently. 'You do seem obsessed with a dead woman.'

Clara closed her eyes. It *was* beginning to feel as if her interest in Audrey was edging from curiosity towards unhealthy behaviour. But soon, any connection she felt to Audrey would be severed anyway, when the house was sold and she was no longer able to roam its rooms. Presumably, this forgotten ghost floor would be emptied and turned into a swish apartment for someone with far more money than she had.

She opened her eyes and swung her legs off the bed. 'You're right. We've had a look and there are no answers here.'

Her eyes fell on the book that was sitting on the bedside table. *Rebecca* by Daphne du Maurier, one of Clara's favourite novels and the book which was by Audrey's side in her portrait.

Clara picked it up and began to leaf through it. This was presumably the last book that Audrey had ever read: a story set in a grand country house, where a lonely young heroine lived in the shadow of a former wife whose death was cloaked in mystery.

Did it resonate with Audrey? This book that had sat for the last sixty-seven years next to her bed? Clara had to accept that she would never know.

Putting the book back in its place, she got to her feet and ran her hands across the eiderdown to smooth any creases. 'OK, it's time to go.'

She took a few steps before turning back and, on a whim, pulling open the drawer of the bedside table. Her grandmother had kept Audrey's diary, something that was important to her, hidden in the drawer of her bedside table. What did Audrey keep in hers?

Unlike her grandmother's drawer of tat, there was nothing in there except for another book – a large book bound in brown leather, which looked familiar. As she picked it up, Clara realised it was the ancient dictionary that Audrey was holding in her lap in her portrait.

Clara could understand why Audrey might want to re-read *Rebecca* at bedtime. But why take an old dictionary from the library and keep it close while she slept?

'Come on, Clara. We've pushed our luck already,' said River from the doorway. 'If my father finds us up here, he'll go absolutely bananas.'

'Why do you think Audrey kept this old dictionary next to her bed?' asked Clara, tracing the cracked binding with her fingers.

'I have no idea.'

'It's not exactly bedtime reading, is it?'

'It wouldn't be my choice before I settle down to sleep. I'd prefer the latest Harlan Coben.'

'So why keep it close, rather than in the library?' asked Clara, but River had already gone.

'Come on!' she heard him call.

'Right behind you,' she called back.

There had to be a reason why this book was important to Audrey and she really wanted to know what that reason was. Clara made a snap decision. Her grandmother had taken a diary from this bedroom and she was about to take a dictionary.

Tucking it under her arm, she pulled the bedroom door closed and hurried after River, down the narrow staircase.

After emerging onto the second floor, Clara closed and locked the door and dropped the key into her pocket.

'What are you two doing, huddled at the end of the landing?'

Bartie had just appeared at the top of the grand staircase. He walked towards them, a frown creasing the skin between his dark eyebrows.

'Nothing,' said Clara, taking several steps away from River.

'We were admiring the portrait of Audrey Brellasham,' said River smoothly. 'Have you seen it? She's Geoffrey's stepmother, who disappeared years ago.'

'Yeah. Great,' said Bartie on reaching them. He didn't even glance at the portrait. 'What are you carrying?' He was staring at the book under Clara's arm.

River glanced at Clara and rolled his eyes. 'Yeah, Clara, what have you got there?'

'Just an old book I found,' said Clara brightly. 'I'm going to return it to the library.'

Bartie stared at them both, suspicion etched across his face. But then his features relaxed and he smiled.

'I've been looking for you both to let you know that my developer contact is coming to view the manor later this week. She's very excited about this house and has lots of potential plans for it already. I think getting her to sign on the dotted line is going to be a slam dunk.'

'Really?' Clara felt flutters of panic in her stomach because the sale suddenly felt very real. 'Do you think she'll be amenable to leaving our cottage intact and letting Mum stay on there?'

'Clara told me about your great idea,' said River, an unfamiliar edge to his voice.

'Did she?' Bartie laughed and caught hold of Clara's hand. 'I said I'd try to save your home, Clo, and I'd never renege on a promise, especially to you.' He gave Clara a beaming, perfect-teeth smile. 'But there are no guarantees, of course. All I can do is my best.'

Clara was surprised that hearing her nickname from Bartie's mouth slightly put her teeth on edge. He'd never used it when they were teenagers together, though, thinking about it, he'd hardly ever spoken to her back then. He'd always made her feel like River's annoying little friend who insisted on tagging along. But people could change.

'Your best will be fantastic,' she told him. 'Thank you. I really appreciate it.'

'You're very welcome,' said Bartie, dropping her hand.

'What kind of development is your contact interested in pursuing with this house?' asked River, frowning.

'Nothing too radical. She's very into preserving the history and heritage of these magnificent buildings.'

'And the grounds around them?'

'Yeah, absolutely. There's nothing to fear. The house will be turned, tastefully and respectfully, into luxury apartments, and the grounds will be preserved as Geoffrey has stipulated.' He looked at Clara and winked. 'Maybe the Heaven's Cove charity fete can still be held here every year.'

'That would be amazing.'

Bartie hooked his arm through Clara's. 'Come on down with me and we can discuss this year's fete.'

They walked to the staircase and Clara looked back but River hadn't moved. He was still standing in front of the portrait, watching the two of them.

'Come on, slowcoach,' Bartie called, but River shook his head.

'I'll be down in a bit. You two go on without me.'

Once they reached the hall, Bartie unhooked his arm and,

leaning forward, kissed Clara on the cheek and let his skin rest against hers for a few seconds before straightening up.

'I hope my cousin hasn't been boring you to death up there with fun facts about tedious ancestors.'

'Not at all,' said Clara. 'He's been great, and I find some of his ancestors fascinating.'

Bartie's brows knitted together. 'Really? Well, each to their own.'

This was the moment to tell Bartie about how interested she was in Audrey's story and how much she wanted to solve the mystery of her disappearance, but something held Clara back. Probably anxiety that he wouldn't understand her interest or, worse, would think she was weird. River already knew she was weird so it didn't make much difference with him.

'So, how are the arrangements for the charity fete going?' asked Bartie, glancing at his phone that he'd just pulled from his pocket.

'Really well. I think most things are in hand. I need to contact stallholders and make sure they know the fete is still going ahead in spite of the manor being up for sale.'

'That's good,' said Bartie, swiping through emails on his phone screen.

'Then, it's just a case of erecting the stalls on the day before the fete.'

'Yeah, cool,' said Bartie, still swiping and not looking up from his phone. He didn't appear to be listening.

'Though I still need to book the talking llama, of course.'

'Excellent,' said Bartie, confirming Clara's suspicions. 'It sounds great. Hey. There's an urgent email here and I need to make a call. Can we catch up about the fete some other time?'

'Yeah, sure.'

Clara watched him walk away, disappointment blooming. Despite Bartie's pre-picnic claim that he wanted to help with the fete, that didn't appear to be the case. He wasn't interested in the event or, it seemed, in her, particularly. In fact, he'd just been dismissive and quite rude.

Her mum suddenly bustled into the hall, her arms filled with freshly washed linen. 'Don't just stand there, Clara. Do something useful. Put that book down and help me to put these sheets away, will you?'

Clara was so focused on Bartie, she'd almost forgotten the dictionary under her arm. The book she'd stolen from Audrey's bedroom. Not *stolen*, she told herself. She'd merely borrowed it and would soon return it to the library.

As her mother hurried upstairs, Clara shoved the dictionary into the coat cupboard, beneath a jumble of wellies. She would retrieve it later and try to work out why this unassuming, nothing-out-of-the-ordinary book had been so important to Audrey.

20

GEOFFREY

Geoffrey didn't often walk into Heaven's Cove. The place was heaving with tourists and, even worse, locals trying to elicit any gossip emanating from the manor. Not that there was any – not usually.

His marriage break-up had once been the talk of the village, of course. And his stepmother's disappearance in the 1950s must have set tongues wagging. But, since then, there had been very little to interest people. Just him and Julie and various other helpers and tradespeople rattling round the manor as it gradually fell into disrepair.

But now, his son had returned and the manor was going to be sold, which was rich fodder for locals like Belinda, who was bearing down on him fast.

Geoffrey cursed his decision to walk into the village before dinner. He was supposed to be sorting out paperwork to support a potential sale. But it had become too depressing after a while, and he'd suddenly craved fresh air and the familiarity of Heaven's Cove's jumble of ancient cottages and cobbled streets.

Perhaps what his father had once said to him was true: *You don't appreciate what you have until it's gone.*

Geoffrey had always taken Heaven's Cove for granted but he'd miss its picturesque beauty and air of permanence – though some of the villagers, maybe not so much.

'Good afternoon, Belinda,' he said as she bustled up to him. She was wearing sensible lace-up shoes and a brown corduroy jacket in spite of the heat.

'Good afternoon, Squire. We haven't seen you around in the village for a while. How are you?'

'I'm doing well, thank you. And you?'

'Can't complain.' She pushed grey hair from her eyes. 'My sister, Freya, and I are on the committee that's organising next week's charity fete which I hear is still going ahead in the manor grounds.'

'That's right. Let's hope the heatwave continues and we don't get any downpours on the day.'

Otherwise, everyone would want to escape the rain by coming into the manor and having a good look round. He knew the fete and open day raised lots of money for charity, but he still hated everyone gawping at his home. Not that it would be his home for much longer. Soon, a bunch of strangers would be living in the manor and he wouldn't even be able to visit.

'Are you sure you're doing well?' Belinda asked, her face collapsing into a sympathetic pout. 'You're facing so many changes – moving out of the manor that's been home to your family for generations, your estranged son returning but only for such a short while, leaving Heaven's Cove behind... I assume you will be leaving us behind?'

Geoffrey swallowed at Belinda's habit of putting people's problems into such distinct focus and nodded. 'Yes, I'll be moving on. It would be... difficult living so close to the manor but not in it.'

'I believe your young relative Bartie has some business

contacts, and the plan is to develop the manor into apartments while leaving the grounds and gardens intact.'

'That's right,' Geoffrey confirmed, marvelling at Belinda's ability to know *everything*. Her reputation as the biggest gossip in the village was well earned.

'Couldn't you buy one of the apartments and continue to live at Brellasham Manor?'

Geoffrey blinked. He hadn't even considered staying on, but he knew immediately that this wasn't the answer. It would be too painful to be faced every day with his failure to save his family's beautiful home from being lost and ripped apart.

'It's a thought,' said Geoffrey noncommittally.

Belinda waited for more information and, when that wasn't forthcoming, declared: 'It must be a great comfort to have your son back with you.'

'It's wonderful. Anyway, I must get on. Lots to do. It's good to see you, Belinda.'

'You too.' Belinda grasped hold of his hand. 'And, if I don't get the chance before you leave for good, I wish you all the best in your new life.'

Murmuring his thanks, Geoffrey pulled his hand away as gently as he could before walking away.

Belinda meant well, he supposed, but she was wrong about River because it wasn't a comfort having him back at Brellasham Manor. It was wonderful to see him, of course, but every time Geoffrey looked at his strapping adult son he knew there was something he should tell him that he never could.

The sun was low in the sky and the air was heavy with pollen and the rich perfume of stock, sweet rocket and honeysuckle.

The golden hour was what people called it, mused Geoffrey, shifting on the wooden bench that sat in the middle of his

garden. That time just before sunset when everything took on a
golden sheen, and anything seemed possible.

He liked to sit here, at this time of day, to appreciate the
beauty around him and enjoy the peace. And his daily sojourn
into the garden had taken on a new poignancy now that his time
here would soon come to an end. He would miss this place, with
its memories good and bad, just as he would miss Heaven's
Cove.

All of the villagers he'd met this afternoon had been warm
and seemingly genuinely sorry that he was leaving. He should
have made an effort to be more involved in the local community
while he could. Another opportunity missed.

Geoffrey closed his eyes and had begun to doze in the
warmth of early evening when he felt the air shift around him.
He opened one eye. Bartie had sat down next to him on the
bench.

'Are you OK, sir?' he asked.

'Of course,' Geoffrey replied, fighting the irritation he felt at
being interrupted. Bartie was here to help him and he must
remember that.

'It's a beautiful garden.' Geoffrey stayed silent as there was
no need to agree with such a patently true observation. 'I can
only imagine how sad you'll be to leave it.'

'It will be a dreadful wrench, but I'll take comfort in the fact
that this garden will survive and the new occupants of Brellasham Manor will enjoy it as I have.'

'Yes, of course.'

A rush of overwhelming anxiety suddenly whooshed
through Geoffrey, from his head to his toes. He couldn't
breathe. This was too much emotion for him to cope with. It
made him feel sick, as though he might be dying.

He turned on the bench to face Bartie and tried to keep any
panic from his voice as he sought reassurance.

'Selling this place is the right thing to do, isn't it? I keep thinking I'm making a dreadful mistake, that I'm missing an obvious way to maintain the status quo.'

Bartie put his head on one side, as though he was seeing Geoffrey in a whole new light, and sucked air between his teeth.

'I think we have to face hard facts here, Geoffrey. You've lost a lot of money on business deals that didn't pan out, and the costs associated with securing financial loans would be prohibitive. They also wouldn't solve the issue of how this house continues to thrive as you grow older and – forgive me for being blunt – become less able to cope, with no son around to provide support.'

He smiled. 'But, looking on the bright side, you'll have enough money from the sale to fund a very comfortable life for yourself elsewhere. Perhaps you could consider emigrating to Australia so you're closer to River.'

Geoffrey couldn't imagine moving to the other side of the world at his age, and River wouldn't want him closer anyway. But he nodded, even though he knew that he would end up living alone in a part of England he didn't know, surrounded by people who were strangers.

'Hannah, my developer contact, will be here the day after tomorrow,' Bartie continued, 'and I have high hopes that she'll see the potential in this place and will make us a great offer.' He patted the older man's hand. 'It really is for the best, Geoffrey. You're doing the right thing.'

'Yes, of course I am.'

Geoffrey breathed deeply in and out, relieved that the surge of anxiety was lessening. He only hoped that Bartie hadn't realised how panicky he'd felt, as if everything in his life had turned on its head and nothing made any sense. How his father would have berated him for displaying such weakness.

'That's all OK then.' Bartie got to his feet. 'I'd better go and check that everything's in order for Hannah's visit.'

'Thank you so much for all of your hard work on this,

Bartie. It's good of you to go to so much trouble. I won't forget it.'

Bartie smiled. 'You're welcome, Geoffrey. I have such fond memories of my time here and I love being a part of the Brel-lasham family. You've been so good to me. I've almost felt like a surrogate son since River disappeared from your life.'

Had he? Geoffrey tried to hide his surprise. He'd hardly seen Bartie over the last few years, but he felt warmed by his words. He'd got so much wrong with River, but perhaps he had done something right with Bartie.

21

CLARA

Clara sat in the middle of her bed with Audrey's diary on one side, the paper bearing numbers written by her grandmother on the other, and the ancient dictionary found in Audrey's room on her lap.

There had to be some link between all three – she could feel it in her bones – but she couldn't, for the life of her, work it out.

She leafed through the dictionary again, being careful not to damage its pages that had become fragile with age. She shouldn't have brought the book home with her, after rescuing it from the coat cupboard when her mother wasn't looking. But, then again, she should never have removed it from the drawer next to Audrey's bed in the first place.

As for breaking into the manor's 'ghost floor'... Did using a key constitute breaking in? she wondered. Especially if the son of the man who owned the house – for the time being, at least – was with her.

She smiled at the thought of River exploring the forbidden rooms too. For a while, it had been just like the old days, and she'd felt safer with him beside her.

In her mind's eye, she saw him turning towards her, his body silhouetted in the soft light falling through Audrey's bedroom window. In some ways he was so familiar and yet, after so many years away, he was a stranger too.

Their friendship was broken, so why had he bothered to look out Audrey and Edwin's marriage certificate for her? It was kind of him, which was why she hadn't revealed that she'd already found the certificate online, along with Audrey's birth certificate. They had revealed that Audrey's maiden name was Greene, but a search for that name had yielded few facts, and none of them useful. Audrey seemed to have had no close living family left by the time she walked into the sea so there were no descendants to track down. It was another potential avenue of information that could be crossed off.

But the old photographs that River had given her were perhaps a different matter. The stiff poses of husband and wife hinted at a marriage less than happy, but maybe Clara was reading too much into a formal photo taken so long ago.

Clara rubbed her eyes, yawned and focused again on the dictionary lying nearby. This might be her last chance to work out the truth about Audrey and she wasn't about to give up.

Twenty minutes later, Clara was ready to renege on her 'no giving up' resolution. She'd tried various ways to make sense of the numbers but they remained just that – numbers whose meanings were lost in time. Perhaps they didn't mean anything at all. Unless...

Clara looked at the first hyphenated figure written on the piece of paper by her grandmother: 49-6. She turned to page 49 in the dictionary and ran her finger down the first few words described. The sixth one was 'boat', which she jotted down.

That word seemed random but she did the same with the next figure, more in desperation than hope. It led to the word 'off', and the third was 'headland'.

Clara's heart began to hammer as she continued with the remaining figures, and then she sat back against the pillows and looked at the phrase she'd jotted down. It read: *Boat off headland point at seven on Tuesday.*

On what day of the week had Audrey disappeared? Clara reached for her laptop, googled the information and her jaw dropped. Audrey Brellasham walked into the sea on the seventeenth of September 1957, and that happened to be a Tuesday.

She'd cracked the code! Violet had written a note to Audrey, telling her there would be a boat waiting for her. Clara had an urge to rush up to the manor house and find River, but she didn't yet have enough to tell him. Because if Audrey did go into the sea in the hope of reaching a boat that stormy night – a boat Violet had helped her arrange – the most pressing question of all remained: why?

Clara began to decipher the numerals that littered Audrey's diary and soon she had her answer. Audrey was frightened of her husband's explosive temper and the physical abuse he had begun to mete out.

At first, references to his abusive behaviour were infrequent and brief: *More bruises to hide*, she wrote in March; *he hit me again*, in April. But she began to elaborate as the year went on and his behaviour seemingly escalated: In May, *Not allowed to leave manor on my own or speak alone with house staff*, and, three days later: *I feel like a prisoner. I am so unhappy.*

Poor Audrey. Clara continued deciphering the cries for help of a woman whose privileged, comfortable life had not been what it seemed. Even being openly honest in her own diary had felt impossible, and she'd been compelled to outline the truth about Edwin in code. No wonder she'd been overjoyed when he'd allowed a ball at the manor. The dance would have brought joy and company into her home. But what had happened to spark her flight so soon after the dance was over?

As Clara carried on deciphering the numbers with the help of the dictionary, Audrey's secrets continued to reveal themselves.

Two days after the fateful ball, the bottom of one diary page was covered in scrawled numerals: *Jealous. Held me around throat and promised to kill me. I believe him. No one will believe me. I am alone.*

Clara paused, feeling overwhelming sorrow for Audrey, who had suffered such abuse and fear. But fortunately she'd been wrong in thinking that she was alone. Violet, Clara's grandmother, had been on her side and had sent her the coded note which offered her a way out.

Turning the pages, Clara reached Tuesday, September the seventeenth, the fateful day that Audrey had disappeared. There was another line of numbers scrawled across the centre of the paper. But these, when decoded, made no sense at all: *Can a flower bloom in the snow? Only time will tell.*

Clara gave up trying to work out its meaning and closed the diary, her mind buzzing with what she'd just learned.

People assumed that Audrey had wanted to end her life that night she'd walked into the sea, and they were right. But it was only her life as Edwin's wife that she'd been so desperate to bring to a close. She planned to swim to the boat organised for her by Violet, but did she make it that night or did the sea claim her?

Clara slid off the bed and walked to her window. Tonight the sea was calm and lit by a full moon, but it still looked foreboding, with depths riven by currents and scattered with sharp rocks. And the headland, where a boat had been waiting, was a long way from the cove.

How good a swimmer was Audrey? Clara wondered. And how had she and Violet become so close that her grandmother had aided her escape?

Clara watched as moonlight cast a silvery sheen over the waves. She knew now why Audrey had chosen to walk into the sea at that time on that particular night. But, after finding out about Edwin's abuse and the planned escape, one huge question remained: did Audrey live or die?

22

RIVER

It was a long time since he'd been alone with his father. River tried to remember the last time the two of them had talked in private as he approached Geoffrey, who was sitting on a bench in his beloved garden.

It must be three years ago, when his father had made a brief stop in Sydney while chasing some business deal in New Zealand. They'd met in a hotel bar near the airport and had talked for a couple of awkward hours about nothing in particular – Geoffrey's flight, the weather, the increasing cost of maintaining Brellasham Manor.

River remembered asking after Clara and Mrs N and being told that they were keeping well. That was all, 'keeping well', and his father could elaborate no further. People's emotional lives were lost on Geoffrey, including his own.

Tonight, he was sitting still as a statue, staring at the beds of bright begonias and delicate campanula that were edged with ornamental trees which had been expertly pruned. Everything in this garden was ordered and symmetrical, which was completely unlike real life, thought River. The ensuing conversation would be proof enough of that.

He swallowed and sat down on the bench. Geoffrey, staring into the distance, glanced round and frowned at his unexpected visitor.

'Oh, it's you. I thought you were Bartie, coming back. Is something wrong? Has his developer contact got cold feet at the thought of taking on such a huge project?'

'Probably not, but I have no idea. I'm not here on Bartie's behalf. I just thought it would be nice to have a chat.'

Surprise – or was it panic? – flickered across his father's face. 'If you like.'

'So, how are you feeling?' River asked, before mentally kicking himself.

What sort of inane opening enquiry was that to a man who never discussed his emotions? Clara would have rolled her eyes. And he felt sure that Bartie had initiated a much more appropriate conversation when he'd been sitting here.

'I'm feeling the same as I was this morning,' said Geoffrey, patently not intending to make this conversation any easier.

'The garden's beautiful,' said River, trying a more neutral opening and already regretting giving his father another chance to be a halfway decent parent.

'It's always a riot of colour at this time of year, and very peaceful.'

'Is that why you like to sit here? Because of the peace?'

Geoffrey sniffed. 'Probably.'

He seemed irritated by his son, just as he had been when River was growing up. He hadn't made a great deal of effort to stay in touch over the years, but then neither had River, whose own lack of contact had played its part in their estrangement. It had been hard for both of them, being a world apart.

River took a deep breath. 'The house must get lonely sometimes.'

He was venturing into emotional territory again but he wanted to know more about his father. The two of them had almost nothing in common but, much to his surprise, he still cared about the old man. That was why he'd travelled across the globe after finding out that he was in trouble.

Geoffrey gave him a sideways glance. 'There are often people around – Mrs Netherway, Clara, various people working on the house and gardens – and I keep myself busy. One of the benefits of living in a falling-down house is that there's always a lot to keep one engaged. Though it appears that won't be the case for much longer.'

'Unless we can think of a way for you to keep the house, rather than sell it.'

'Even if we could, what's the use, really?' Geoffrey stared at River, his eyes pale in his lined face. 'You don't want this house. You don't care about it. So what would happen to it once I've died?'

River sat silently for a moment. Coming back here had shown him that he did care about this house, which was the biggest surprise of all. He'd thought the manor cold and forbidding as a child, with echoing spaces and rooms never entered. Yet now, seeing it through adult eyes, he could appreciate the grandeur of the place, and his family history that was imprinted on every brick.

It was far too large for one man, whether that be him or his father. But he would be sad to see it converted into flats and Geoffrey turned out.

'It's not that I don't want it,' he tried to explain. 'It's simply not been a part of my life for a long time.' River swallowed, feeling that he was floundering. 'But I know how important the house is to you. It must be full of memories.'

'I've lived in this house my whole life so, yes, it holds a plethora of memories. Some happy, some not so.' Geoffrey paused. 'I remember the day that you and your mother left.'

'Me too,' said River quietly, imagining the silence that must have descended as the sound of their car tyres on gravel had faded into the distance.

He had been heartbroken to drive away from this house back then. Scared to abandon his father, sad to leave behind Clara, who hadn't bothered to turn up and wish him well.

Then, a new life on the other side of the world had unfolded, one that was busy, chaotic, terrifying, exciting. And his life before that, his years in England, had, with encouragement from his mother, faded away until it all seemed like a dream.

'I haven't been the best of fathers,' said Geoffrey suddenly, staring straight ahead at the plants moving in the cool breeze coming off the sea.

River opened his mouth and closed it again, not sure what to say. He suddenly longed for Clara to be sitting here with him, saying the right things.

'I'm well aware of it,' Geoffrey continued, still not meeting River's eye.

River swallowed. 'I haven't always been the best son, and Mum can be a little...' He hesitated, searching for the right word. He felt great loyalty to his mother but recognised that she, too, had her faults. 'She can be a little unforgiving,' he said at last.

Geoffrey gave a snort of laughter. 'You're not wrong there. Your mother has many admirable qualities, as I remember, but forgiveness is not one of them.'

River felt his mouth twitch. 'That's fair enough,' he said, feeling his muscles relax. He hadn't realised how tightly he was holding himself. 'What were *your* parents like?' he asked tentatively. He was treading in uncharted waters here because his father rarely spoke about his past.

'My parents? I hardly remember my mother, who was dead before my fourth birthday. Then, my father married Audrey when I was seven and she was gone before I was ten.'

River felt his cheeks burn as he remembered snooping around Audrey's bedroom earlier that day.

'That must have been difficult for you and your father. What was *he* like?'

'He fed and clothed me and he sent me to the best schools. He did his best for me.'

'But what was he like as a man?'

'Why are you so interested in a man you never knew?' snapped Geoffrey, his brow creasing.

'I'm interested to know what kind of man my grandfather was.'

Geoffrey paused for so long, River began to think he wasn't going to continue the conversation. But then he said in a rush: 'Edwin Brellasham was an accomplished man. A scholar who excelled at business and had little time for those who didn't match his talents or intellect. I believe he cared about me, but he wasn't an easy man to live with.'

'Was he ever unkind to you or to his wives?'

Geoffrey swung around on the bench until he was facing his son. 'What exactly are you getting at?'

River almost ended the conversation right there. But he summoned up his courage and said: 'I suppose I'm wondering what prompted your stepmother to walk into the sea.'

Geoffrey narrowed his eyes. 'Have you been speaking to Clara about Audrey?'

'A little. We were looking at her portrait on the second floor.'

What would his father say if he knew that he and Clara had been exploring Audrey's bedroom that afternoon?

A shadow crossed the older man's face. 'Audrey suffered with her nerves and was troubled. My father did his best but he wasn't enough. *We* weren't enough.' When River put a comforting hand on his father's arm, Geoffrey pulled his arm away. 'Anyway, it was all a long time ago and best left in the past. Perhaps you could inform Clara of that if she raises the subject with you again. She has become rather obsessed with the whole thing. I've learned that it's far better to let sleeping dogs lie.'

The wind had changed direction and a sharp tang of the sea was swirling around them.

'It's getting late and the effects of jet lag can linger,' said Geoffrey. 'You really should have an early night.'

Feeling dismissed, River got to his feet. 'You're probably right. Well, I'll leave you in peace to enjoy your garden, shall I?' When his father said nothing, he added: 'Goodnight.'

River had walked only a few steps when he remembered another reason why he had wanted to speak to his father.

'I was wondering,' he said, turning back, 'if it might be possible for Mrs N and Clara to remain in their cottage after the manor is sold. Perhaps you could stipulate that their cottage remains as it is and that they can stay, paying rent to the new owner, of course. Bartie might have already mentioned it.'

'He hasn't,' said Geoffrey, 'but I don't see why that can't be arranged. It's a good idea that might stop Clara from chastising me in my own home.'

He turned back towards his beloved garden and River walked away, glancing back only once. His father was still as a statue, looking fragile and alone, his back slumped with age and his grey hair thinning.

He was a disappointed man, thought River. Disappointed that he was facing losing his family home. And disappointed that his only child was not the son he wanted.

23

CLARA

Clara rushed along the gravel drive towards the manor house, deep in thought. She'd cracked the code last night and knew what had driven Audrey to take such drastic action in 1957.

That should be enough – Audrey could now be consigned to history, as an abused wife who had taken desperate action in a bid to change her life. But had walking into the sea changed her life, or ended it?

Clara suddenly spotted River and Bartie, standing beneath the tallest oak tree in the garden, their heads bent together. Neither of them looked particularly happy but Bartie waved when he spotted her and his face lit up when she hurried over. He seemed really pleased to see her. Clara ran a hand self-consciously through her hair before she reached the two men.

'Clara, I was hoping I'd see you today,' said Bartie, his smile even wider.

'Why?' Clara asked, feeling herself growing hotter under his intense gaze.

'Just because.' He undid the top button on his blindingly white polo shirt. 'Seeing you cheers up my day. You bring a little sunshine into my life.'

Clara would have basked in the compliment if she hadn't noticed River glance up at the sun in a cloudless sky and roll his eyes.

'That's lovely of you to say,' she said, not giving River the satisfaction of knowing she'd seen his childish gesture.

'So why are you here today? Did you want me?' Bartie asked with a suggestive raise of an eyebrow.

'I'm heading for the house to help Mum. She's going through the books, trying to see where household savings can be made.'

'A waste of time, but admirable,' Bartie murmured.

'And I also needed a quick word with River.'

Bartie's smile became more fixed. 'Really? If it's something to do with the house, you'd be better off talking to both of us.'

'No, it's not about the house. It's a personal matter.'

Bartie stared at her, waiting for her to go on, while Clara panicked inside. She really hadn't thought this through.

'Um... it's about Michael, my brother. He's living in Canada now but he's planning a visit and is really keen to see River again. So I said I'd sort out a rendezvous. It's all boring, *boring* stuff, and I'm sure you've got meetings to arrange and... and other things.'

Bartie's smile was back. 'It doesn't sound riveting and I am a busy man, that's for sure. So I'll leave you and River to sort out the Michael rendezvous, and I hope to see you later, as planned.'

'Sure.'

What did he mean by 'as planned'? Did he mean somewhere more private to continue what they'd started on the picnic rug? Clara felt her cheeks begin to burn.

'Excellent,' he said, putting his hand briefly on her shoulder and giving it a squeeze. 'I'll catch up with you very soon.'

'Bartie,' she called after him, as he walked away. 'Have you managed to speak to Geoffrey about your idea?'

He looked at her blankly for a moment before understanding dawned in his grey eyes. 'Oh yes, we had a long chat about it yesterday evening and he's up for it. So, fingers crossed.'

'Absolutely,' said Clara, crossing her own fingers as Bartie wandered off.

'Do you mean his idea to save your mum's cottage?' asked River, leaning against the tree.

'That's the one.'

'Trust good ol' Bartie to come up with an idea like that and speak to my father about it.'

Was River being sarcastic? It was hard to tell because his face was giving nothing away.

'Don't you think it's a good idea?' she asked.

River hesitated and then smiled. 'Yes, of course it is. It'll be great if you and your mum can stay on in your home. Though the manor will be a building site for a while with lots of noise.'

He looked towards the manor house and sighed. There was an air of melancholy about him this morning.

'I hate to think of the house being knocked about and I'm sure you do too,' said Clara. 'But if there was a way of saving it, I doubt you'd want to take it on in the future, once your father's, you know... gone.' Clara kicked herself for being so blunt. 'You'll be heading back to Australia for ever as soon as the sale is sorted out, won't you?'

Clara waited for River's answer, realising that she cared what his answer would be more than she would ever admit. River was no longer a part of her life, and she still hadn't forgiven him for his heartless message from Australia. But, she had to admit to herself that there was something comforting about having him around.

'I wish my father could see out his days here,' he said after a while, not answering her question at all. 'That would mean a great deal to him. But once he's gone, as you so delicately put it,

I can't see myself rattling round in this place, raising money to keep it going. Can you?'

Clara shook her head. River had never been like his father, and his absence only seemed to have amplified their differences.

'Anyway.' River pushed himself away from the tree. 'What was that rubbish you told Bartie about setting up a meeting between me and Michael? I don't think we ever said more than a couple of words to each other when we were teenagers.'

'I'm sure he'd like to see you.'

'Really?'

Clara wrinkled her nose. 'Probably not. He's hopeless at keeping up with the local friends he's got.'

'Is he even coming over from Canada in the near future?'

'Nope. I have no idea when we'll next see him. He pops over occasionally but never stays for long.'

'So why the subterfuge with Bartie, who is so clearly dazzled by your sunshine vibe?'

Clara hit him playfully on the arm. 'I saw the eye roll.'

River grinned. 'Yeah, I thought you might.'

'The thing is, I wanted to tell you in private that I've worked out what the numbers in Audrey's diary mean.'

River's mouth fell open. 'That's amazing. How did you do it?'

'I finally realised that the numbers relate to pages and lines in that dictionary Audrey was so interested in and always kept close. Twelve dash five means page twelve, and whichever is the fifth word featured on that page.'

'That's clever! No one could crack the code unless they realised the significance of the dictionary and had a copy of it.'

'Which is probably why she removed it from the library and had it in her bedroom.'

River narrowed his eyes. 'You could have told Bartie about this.'

'And have him think that I'm a crazy woman who's obsessed with dead people?'

'There is that. Though I notice it's all right for me to think that about you.'

'It's fine because you know the real me already. You know what I'm truly like.'

Bartie's words at the picnic echoed in Clara's head: *I'm still looking for that one person who gets me for who I truly am.*

She and River had known each other inside out as teenagers – weirdness, neuroses, fears and all – and they'd still liked each other and found solace in one another's company. A wave of sadness for what the two of them had lost washed over Clara.

River leaned closer. 'Are you OK?'

'Mmm.' She nodded. 'Anyway, do you want to hear what I found out?'

'Of course I do. What secret was she hiding?'

'I'm afraid it's not very pleasant. The coded words reveal that Audrey was physically abused by Edwin and was incredibly lonely. He more or less imprisoned her in the house and it got to a point where she wasn't even allowed to talk to the staff.'

She paused with a lump in her throat as the injustice of Audrey's situation fully hit her. The poor woman had a husband who could treat her however he liked, at a time when domestic violence was a 'behind closed doors' secret that was rarely discussed, there were no women's refuges, and women who did speak out were often blamed or shamed.

River massaged his temples as if his head was aching. 'It's hard to believe that my grandfather was abusive.'

'I know, but why would Audrey lie about something like that?'

'My father spoke about Edwin last night and admitted he wasn't an easy man to live with, but he never said anything about him being abusive.'

'People don't always know, especially if they're not on the

receiving end of any violence. Your dad was only a child, and maybe Audrey was good at hiding what was happening.'

'Did Edwin hurt her?' asked River, sounding appalled.

'He hit her and she had bruises. That's all she says in the diary, except that he flew into a jealous rage after the ball and put his hands around her throat and promised to kill her.'

Clara blinked, feeling close to tears. She could imagine Audrey's terror and powerlessness in the face of such aggression.

'That's dreadful!' A deep crease appeared between River's eyebrows. 'Is that why she walked into the sea? Was she so frightened of my grandfather, so worn down by him, that she wanted to end it all?'

He sank down onto his haunches as if his legs no longer had the strength to carry him.

Clara stooped down beside him. 'She wanted to end her life here at Brellasham Manor, but not her life completely.'

'I don't know what you mean.'

'I also deciphered the note that's in my grandmother's hand-writing, that was in the back of Audrey's diary.'

'Please tell me it said that your grandmother was going to contact the police or get social services involved.'

'I don't think it worked like that in those days. I did a bit of research, and domestic abuse in the 1950s was swept under the carpet. There was a stigma attached to it. I know, I know.' Clara raised her hand as River opened his mouth to protest. 'It's awful and wrong, but that's the way it was back then. There weren't really laws to protect women or services to help those affected.'

'So Audrey was on her own.'

'She was until my gran stepped in. She wasn't allowed to speak to Audrey by that stage but she must have known about the code and used it to communicate with her. The note says: *boat off headland point at seven on Tuesday.*'

'So do you think—'

'She walked into the sea, planning to swim to the boat that was waiting for her. And she wrote something strange in her diary that day: *Can a flower bloom in the snow? Only time will tell.* Does that mean anything to you?'

River racked his brains but nothing came to mind. 'I'm afraid not, but the big question is, did Audrey make it to the boat?'

'I have no idea, but we need to find out if Audrey died that night or made good her escape.'

She frowned when River stood up and began pacing, his tall frame casting shadows across the lawn.

'I can do it myself if you haven't got the time, but you seem to want to be involved, and I thought you might be interested to find out what really happened.'

River stopped pacing. 'It's amazing that you've been able to decipher her code, but are you sure this is a good idea? What happened to Audrey is appalling but it was a long time ago and, even if she survived that night, she might still have died years ago.'

'I know that but I think Audrey's story deserves to be known, even if only by us. She had no one to tell when she lived here.'

'Except, it seems, for your grandmother.'

'Except for Gran,' said Clara. 'I only knew her in her later days but she was always a fierce advocate for women's rights, and she hated injustice. I can see why she would have wanted to help.'

'She did the right thing, whereas my grandfather...' River shook his head. 'It helps me to understand why my father is like he is.'

'He never hurt you or your mum, did he?'

'No, not physically, but it sounds as if he was brought up by a hypocrite who drummed into him the importance of repressing his emotions in public while, behind the scenes, he was abusing his wife. That must have damaged him.'

'Plus' – Clara cleared her throat – 'he saw his stepmother walking into the sea that night. He was in the library and he saw her from the window but couldn't do anything to stop her.'

River blinked. 'How do you know that?'

'He told me. I don't think he meant to but it slipped out while he was talking about her. He was meant to be having dinner with his father but he was excused to read a book because he wasn't feeling well and that's when he saw her. That's what he said, and I know he can be cold, River, but he looked haunted. Which is why I'm waiting for the right moment to give him Audrey's diary. I'm not sure he'll want to have it.'

River put his hands on his hips and gazed towards the sea, just visible through the trees.

'Maybe it's better to leave all of this, Clara. I've got involved but your search is uncovering too many secrets that are probably best left buried. My father wouldn't want it.'

Clara watched him for a moment, as he bent and brushed away grass that had stuck to the hem of his jeans. As a teenager, he'd have done the opposite of what his father wanted. But people changed. People grew up.

'What about Audrey?' she asked. 'I can see that our search might upset your dad but shouldn't the truth about what happened to her come out?'

'No.' River's tone was firm and uncompromising. 'This is my family you're talking about, and I'm saying definitely not. Sometimes, Clara, you can be a bit too—' He closed his mouth and started biting his lip.

'A bit too what?'

'A bit too stubborn and single-minded without taking into account other people's feelings.'

'And of course, you always take other people's feelings into account,' Clara shot back, remembering the postcard that had dropped onto her doormat from the other side of the world. The abrupt heartless words that had devastated her: *Probably best not to keep in touch now I've moved on. I really hope you have a good life. R.*

'I do my best,' said River, his tone frosty.

'I'm sure you do,' she replied, her tone matching River's. 'It's a shame that you don't always manage it.'

'You seem to be having an argument in your own head, Clara. I have no idea what you're going on about.'

He really didn't, and she wasn't about to remind him.

'Right, I'd better get on,' she said briskly. 'Mum will be expecting me and Bartie wanted to see me.'

'Yeah. OK. Um...'

'Was there something else?'

'Not really.' He ran a hand through his fringe. 'It's just, talking of Bartie, you have to be a bit... well, you know, with him.'

Clara stared at River. 'A bit, well, you know? No, I don't know.'

'What I'm trying to say is I know that Bartie is flirting with you and there's possibly more going on, and he's incredibly good looking and charismatic and you've always been a bit in awe of him, but you should be careful.'

'One, I've never been in awe of Bartie, and two, why do I need to be careful?'

'Well.' River shifted from foot to foot. 'Just in case he's—' He stopped mid-sentence. 'No, it doesn't matter.'

'Of course it matters. Just in case he's what?'

River breathed out slowly. 'Just in case he's trying it on with you but he doesn't really mean it.'

'He doesn't really mean it?' Clara blinked, annoyed with herself for suddenly wanting to cry. 'Why doesn't he really mean it? Because you can't believe that an extremely handsome and successful man like Bartie would be interested in boring little me?'

'No.' River frowned. 'That's not what I'm saying at all. I'm sure he would be interested in you. *Any* man would be interested in...' He trailed off and scuffed his feet in the grass. 'All I mean is, he can be disingenuous when it comes to women.'

'In what way?'

'He likes women, all women, and he likes them to like him.'

'So what you're saying is that he's not particularly fussy?'

'No, I'm not saying that, but it might be that you're around and available.'

'I'm around and available. Nice.' Clara puffed out her cheeks. 'Well, thank you so much for your advice on my love life and your ringing endorsement of my desirability to the opposite sex.'

'You know what I'm trying to say. That didn't come out right,' said River, but Clara was too angry to take any notice.

'You never liked Bartie much, even when we were kids. You were jealous of him then and you still sound jealous of him now.'

River looked up from his feet and caught Clara's eye. 'That's not true. I'm only trying to warn you that he doesn't always tell the whole truth.'

'Such as?'

'Well, I...' River looked as if he was floundering but then he pulled his shoulders back. 'He said it was his idea to try and save your mum's cottage, but actually it was mine.'

'So, you're saying he stole it.'

'Yes.' He wiped a hand across his face. 'That sounds petty and it's not a great example but it points to a... a... less than stellar moral compass.'

Clara held his gaze for a moment before looking away.

'Bye, River. I'm sure I'll see you around.'

Then she walked away without looking back, berating herself for mistakenly believing that she and River Brellasham could ever again be friends.

24

RIVER

A less than stellar moral compass. River winced, replaying his conversation with Clara in his head for what seemed like the hundredth time. How pretentious and prissy had that made him sound? He'd been trying to warn her about Bartie but had probably succeeded in pushing her even further into his arms.

'Nice one, mate,' he muttered to himself, dodging a family whose melting ice creams were dripping over the cobbled lane.

Heaven's Cove was busy at midday but he hadn't been able to settle to anything at the manor, and he didn't want to bump into Clara, so he'd come out for a walk instead.

It felt strange to be walking through the village because, although he was different after so many years away, this place seemed eerily the same. The whitewashed cottages, the ancient pub festooned with hanging baskets, the stone walls of the quay reaching out into the sea – nothing had changed.

Even lots of the people were the same, as he'd discovered on nipping into the mini-supermarket to buy himself a cold drink. Stan, the man who'd run the shop for decades, was still there, though now he had silver hair and was in a wheelchair. His son and young grandson were serving customers while he gave them advice and greeted customers from the sidelines.

To River's surprise, Stan had recognised him which made him feel warm inside. As if he belonged in this picturesque village that he'd rarely allowed himself to think about for years. Heaven's Cove still felt a little bit like home.

He walked on, past the quayside with its familiar smell of fish and sun cream, and along the lane that led towards the cove that gave the village its name. A steady stream of tourists accompanied him, past the old farmhouse whose fields almost reached the sand, and the high hedges that lined the road.

On arriving at the beach, he stopped and shielded his eyes against the glare of the sun. The cove was heaving with people on such a beautiful day, some of them locals, he supposed, but most of them sun-reddened visitors from out of the area.

They flocked to this village because it lived up to its name. River had thought it was heavenly, too, growing up in this picturesque part of Devon – until it wasn't. Until the fights between his parents had reached a crescendo and his mother had decided they should leave. Audrey had decided to leave Brellasham Manor as well, but her departure had been very different.

River sat down on a patch of empty beach and pushed his hands into the warm sand. Memories were coming at him thick and fast, tumbling through his brain and stirring up his emotions.

He remembered his mother leaving in a flurry of recrimination and driving too fast across the gravel while his father watched from the front steps. He would never forget the maelstrom of fear, excitement, sadness and longing that had hit him as Brellasham Manor disappeared from the back window.

Whereas, Audrey had left furtively while her violent husband was elsewhere. But her young stepson had witnessed her desperate break for freedom from behind a window and was unable to do anything to help her.

River felt a pang of sadness for his poor, repressed father, who had never dealt with the trauma. Maybe Clara was right to try to find out what had happened to Audrey, and the truth would set him free. Or maybe not.

River slipped off his trainers and socks and dug his toes into the sand. Did Audrey survive? he wondered, watching children running in and out of the gentle waves surging onto shore. Did she, like River and his mother, make a new life for herself far from Devon? Or did she perish in the sea, her body sinking unseen and for ever undiscovered into deep, dark water?

River ducked to avoid a stray frisbee thrown by a young boy who'd come to the beach with his family.

'Sorry about that,' said the boy's father, jumping to his feet and shaking sand from his shorts before wandering over to retrieve the frisbee.

'No worries. There's no harm done.'

River smiled as the man carried the frisbee back to his son and affectionately ruffled the lad's hair. Then, together, they walked to the sea and began to paddle, hand in hand.

It was such a tender scene, River's eyes began to prickle with tears, and he blinked hard. He had no memories of his father ever coming to this beach with him as a child, and if he had almost wounded a stranger with an errant frisbee, that would have elicited a furious lecture on being more aware of his surroundings.

But he'd been all right because he'd had his mother to cushion him with her love and affection. And he'd had Clara, who accepted him as he was and listened when life felt out of control.

They were firm friends from an early age: the housekeeper's daughter and the manor owner's son. Their friendship survived him being sent away to boarding school and, as they grew older, their friendship changed from climbing trees and swimming in the sea to talking about their feelings while swigging illicit cans of lager on the quayside.

They'd been sitting on the sea wall, at the age of fifteen, when he'd first realised that he really wanted to kiss her. But he hadn't summoned up the courage until weeks later, when they were sitting by the manor house stream under an inky sky. Then, the next morning his mother had told him they were leaving immediately and they'd driven away to a new life. A new life that didn't include Clara.

River closed his eyes and turned his face up to the sun, enjoying the warmth of its rays on his face. He should have kept in touch. He should have had the maturity to ignore that embarrassing kiss, that she'd obviously hated, and get their friendship back on an even keel. But she was more interested in Bartie, even back then, and he knew that she wouldn't miss him for long.

He opened his eyes, startled by the screeching of a seagull nearby. He'd upset Clara sixteen years ago, and he'd upset her this morning, too – by telling her to stop chasing Audrey, and by his clumsy attempt to warn her off Bartie.

Was he jealous of his cousin, as Clara had alleged? *Of course not*, was the answer that popped into his head. But he knew that he was lying to himself.

The truth was he'd been jealous of handsome Bartie for as long as he could remember. Not only because Clara had a teenage crush on him, but because he was the son that Geoffrey never had. With his suave good looks, charming manners and confidence, he was far more suited to life at Brellasham Manor than River ever was.

River couldn't dislike him for that. It was just the way that lucky, popular Bartie was. But he did dislike his cousin's attitude to women, and to Clara in particular. If Bartie broke her heart... He could never forgive him for hurting the woman he'd once thought of as his best friend in the world.

River rubbed a hand across his damp forehead and slowly got to his feet. The sun was hot and he was overdressed on the beach, in his jeans and T-shirt.

He would walk back to the house and see if he could help his father to decide where he might go after the manor was sold. He couldn't fully repair their relationship – that would involve him becoming a different type of person entirely in his father's eyes. Someone rather more like Bartie. But he could, perhaps, be the bigger person and mend a few bridges.

25

CLARA

Clara moved her head from side to side. She was sitting on the floor of the ballroom, staring at her laptop screen, and her neck was beginning to ache. She should move but she liked being tucked around a corner, where no one could see her if they came into the room.

She wasn't hiding. Not exactly. But she needed some time on her own after her run-in with River earlier. Their whole encounter had been upsetting – from his distress at his grandfather's actions to his assertion that Clara was hideously unfanciable.

Clara raised her eyebrows. OK, he hadn't exactly said that but he had implied, heavily, that Bartie was an amoral chancer who was only interested in her because she was available.

River was jealous, Clara decided anew. Jealous of Bartie's looks and charismatic personality that made him irresistible to women. *How many women?* asked the annoying little voice in her brain. *What if River is right?*

Determined not to dwell on what Bartie's motivations might or might not be, she went back to looking online for Audrey. She agreed with River that news of his stepmother might be too much for Geoffrey to handle, and she felt great sympathy for him. But it couldn't hurt him if he didn't know what Clara was doing. Chances were she'd never solve the mystery anyway. In fact, the more she searched for clues online, the more she realised what a herculean task it was.

It's hopeless, Clara thought, pushing the laptop away from her. Like searching for a needle in a haystack, when there might not be a needle at all. There was no proof that Audrey had survived that night and, even if she had, she could have taken on any name to avoid being discovered.

Can a flower bloom in the snow? Only time will tell. The last coded message in Audrey's diary – the one written on the day she made her escape – sounded in Clara's mind. But she still had no idea what it meant.

The ballroom door suddenly creaked open and Clara froze when footsteps sounded on the wooden floorboards.

'Oh, for goodness' sake!' It was a male voice. Bartie's, and he sounded annoyed. 'What's she playing at?' There were more footsteps and then she heard him bellow down the corridor. 'Clara! Where are you?'

She hesitated before calling out, 'I'm here.'

'Where?' He appeared around the corner and his face broke into a wide grin. 'Aha! There are you. Are you hiding from me, Miss Netherway?'

'No.' Clara's cheeks were turning pink. She could feel the burn which was both annoying and pathetic at her age. She'd had her share of boyfriends but there was something about Bartie, the memories of her crush on him as a teenager, that made the years fall away.

'Then why are you tucked away out of sight and sitting on the floor?'

Clara closed the laptop lid. 'I'm enjoying some peace while I get some work done.'

'Can't you work at home, in a chair?'

'I can, but my mum keeps popping in and out which wrecks my concentration.'

'Phew! You're avoiding your mother. I thought you were avoiding me for a minute.'

Bartie raised an eyebrow and grinned to make it clear that he hadn't thought that at all.

'What are you up to?' Clara asked, still feeling flustered.

'Apart from looking for you? I'm making sure I'm au fait with everything about the manor, ready for my contact's visit tomorrow morning.'

'Can't River help you with that?'

Bartie wrinkled his nose. 'Nah. Between you and me, I don't think River is one hundred per cent on board with this sale.'

'I don't think that's fair. I'm sure he wants whatever's best for his father.'

'Probably. Possibly. But he's changed a lot since we were last all here together, don't you think?'

'I guess so, but haven't we all?'

'True, but some of us have changed for the better.' Bartie leaned forward and gently brushed a strand of hair from Clara's burning cheek. 'You've *definitely* changed for the better, and yet I still feel that I know you so well. It's strange and rather lovely.'

He crouched down on his haunches and gazed into Clara's eyes. 'If you've got your work done, why don't you help bring me up to speed with everything I need to know before tomorrow? All the info I've got about Brellasham Manor is printed out and spread across my bedroom floor.'

Clara hesitated, her eyes still locked on Bartie's. It was both flattering and exciting to be sought out by Bartie and propositioned by him.

He *was* propositioning her, wasn't he? He'd mentioned his bedroom and his gaze was positively flirtatious but doubts had started creeping in, not helped by River's appraisal of her fanciability. Very annoyingly, his warning about Bartie was sounding at the back of her mind.

When Clara shook her head, to dislodge River's words, surprise registered on Bartie's handsome face.

'No?' He gave a disbelieving laugh. 'I can't believe you're giving me the elbow.'

'I'm not. I mean, I'm probably not. Sorry. The thing is... it's just River...'

'River? I really don't want to talk about River!' said Bartie, breaking eye contact and frowning. 'Perhaps you'd rather be reading your book.' He picked up the battered paperback lying near Clara. '*Rebecca* by Daphne du Maurier. Did you get it from the library here?'

'No, it's my own copy, from home.'

'Is it any good?'

'Yes, it's one of my favourite novels.'

Bartie turned the book over and peered at the back cover. 'Marries widower Maxim de Winter... moves into an isolated old house... haunted by a dead wife.' He dropped the book onto the floorboards. 'Yeah, sounds great but not as engrossing as spending the afternoon with me, surely?' He got to his feet. 'So what do you say, Clara?' He frowned. 'Clara?'

Clara blinked. 'Sorry.' She tried to focus on the man standing in front of her. 'I was distracted.'

'Distracted by my dazzling good looks, no doubt.' Bartie laughed and held out his hand. 'Come on, Clara. Let's have a lovely afternoon together.'

Clara looked at his hand and then at the battered paperback she'd read many times as a teenager. She'd loved it, just as Audrey had.

'Sorry, Bartie,' she said. 'I need to finish my work, so I'm afraid you'll have to mug up on Brellasham Manor on your own, or with River and Geoffrey's help.'

'Really?' Bartie's smile was fading. 'You know that I wasn't really talking about revising for tomorrow's visit, don't you?'

Clara nodded, her feelings horribly mixed – there was relief that she hadn't misread the situation, and disbelief that she was turning Bartie down. Her teenaged self would be horrified.

But something Bartie had said had sparked an idea that she couldn't wait to check out. If she was right, and Audrey hadn't perished that night, she might know exactly how to find her.

Can a flower bloom in the snow? Only time will tell. Audrey's final message was suddenly making far more sense.

26

GEOFFREY

Geoffrey trailed round after Bartie, feeling rather useless in his own home. Bartie had taken charge the moment his developer contact – a very attractive woman named Hannah – had arrived from London that morning.

He'd shown her the first and second floors, outlining the manor house's better points and skating over the patches of damp that were visible on some walls.

'We've experienced a lot of rain in the county recently,' he'd told her, even though Devon, like the rest of the country, was basking in a prolonged heatwave. Geoffrey wasn't sure if he was impressed by Bartie's chutzpah or disapproved of him lying. Hannah had simply nodded and moved on.

Now, they were scrutinising the ground floor and Geoffrey was looking forward to the whole visit being over.

'This is the drawing room which, as you can see, is a good size with high ceilings,' Bartie was saying. 'The old fireplace could be retained as a feature or I imagine it could be removed, and that wall could be knocked through into the small study next door, if you're looking for a more open-plan vibe.'

'Planning permission would be key, naturally,' said Hannah,

adjusting the jacket of her moss-green trouser suit. 'But I can see that this house has a great deal of potential.'

'My family used to congregate in this room after Christmas lunch and unwrap presents in front of the fire,' said Geoffrey, a sharp memory of young River ripping off paper and squealing with delight coming to mind.

'How sweet,' said Hannah, pushing her long ash-blonde hair over her shoulder. 'The Brellasham family stories attached to this building could add to its marketability as a luxury apartment development. People love to think they're buying a slice of history.'

Geoffrey harrumphed, not sure he wanted his family hawked around as a marketing tool. But Bartie and Hannah were too busy chatting to notice, and he really had little choice.

He needed to sell Brellasham Manor, and at least a sale organised by Bartie would preserve some of what he held dear – his beloved gardens, the unspoiled cove and, if possible, his housekeeper's cottage. It would give him some comfort to know that the Netherways were still close, keeping watch over what had once been his family home.

'Are you all right, Geoffrey?' Bartie popped his head back through the doorway. 'I'm showing Hannah the front hallway and then she's keen to have a look at the grounds.'

'She seems like a very switched-on young woman.'

'She is, and she's very good at her job. We're in safe hands with her, I promise.'

'Would she definitely preserve the look of the house, from the outside?'

'Of course.' Bartie laughed. 'Not that she'd have much choice. She'd never get planning permission to alter the external fascia of such an impressive-looking and historic building. Even with all my planning contacts, that would never be granted.'

Was that all that would stop her? Geoffrey wondered. 'And what about the gardens?' he added. He was asking questions he'd asked before but it seemed important to have them answered again.

Bartie's smile grew more fixed. 'As I reassured you earlier, Hannah has no plans or inclination to do anything with the grounds.'

'So you guarantee that there will be no more building or other development.'

'Absolutely.' Bartie walked into the room and patted Geoffrey on the shoulder. 'I know this is hard for you, sir, but Hannah is very clear that she's only interested in the house itself.'

'It's just that the grounds are large enough for more development, and business-wise—'

Bartie held up a hand. 'Let me stop you there, Geoffrey. Hannah sees the grounds and gardens as a marvellous enhancement to the new apartments, which will make them irresistible to city types looking to grab a slice of seaside life.'

'Only we hold the charity fete every year in the grounds, for the locals in Heaven's Cove. Can we make sure that can still go ahead?'

Bartie raised his eyebrows. 'I didn't think you were that bothered about the event. Is it important to you that it continues?'

Geoffrey had never thought so. In fact, he always dreaded the invasion and complained about it vociferously. But the tradition continuing seemed imperative all of a sudden. His family would be gone from Brellasham Manor but the fete they had accommodated for years would go on. It would be a lasting legacy of sorts.

'I think so, yes,' he said.

Bartie gave a reassuring smile. 'Then I'm sure it can be accommodated. I'll let Hannah know that hosting the annual fete is a deal-breaker as far as you're concerned.'

'Do you think she *will* put in an offer for the house?'

Bartie winked. 'I'm pretty sure she will, from the comments she's made so far. And I know she'll give us – give you – the best price.'

'Only River advised getting a few people in, so we can compare their offers.'

'We could do that, but some developers I've come across...' He paused. 'Let's just say that I would take what they say with a pinch of salt. They'll tell you one thing and do another. But I can vouch for Hannah and her trustworthiness and, being a member of the Brellasham family myself, you know I want only the best for this house and for you. I have so many happy memories here: me and River and Clara.'

Geoffrey nodded. He'd always felt secure in himself, even during the breakdown of his marriage. But right now he felt out of control and unsure of the best way forward. He felt old and, hard though it was to admit, horribly out of his depth. But Bartie's confidence was reassuring.

'Talking of River,' said Bartie, 'have you seen him this morning?'

'He came down for breakfast a little late and said he was going for a walk in the sunshine. He's been gone a while, so I expect he'll be back soon.'

Bartie started making for the door. 'In that case, I'd better go and catch Hannah before she comes across him. We all love River but he's not particularly business-minded, and we don't want him saying anything to scupper the deal, do we?'

Geoffrey followed Bartie into the hall where Hannah was staring at the Victorian stained-glass window.

'That was installed by my great-grandfather,' he told her. 'You wouldn't get rid of it, would you, if you end up buying Brellasham Manor?'

Hannah turned her bright white smile on him. 'Heavens, no. It's not double-glazed, so ripping it out and replacing it would make more practical sense. However, the planners might object' – she did a 'what are they like?' eye roll – 'and, anyway, an impressive window with history will add to the manor's—'

'Marketability?' interrupted Geoffrey.

'That's right.' Hannah smiled at him as if he was a schoolboy who'd just learned his times tables.

Geoffrey sighed and went to sit in his beloved library, while he could.

27

CLARA

Clara stepped into the doorway of a gift shop to avoid a throng of people – Heaven's Cove was heaving this afternoon – and licked the cone of salted caramel ice cream she'd just bought.

She urgently needed a sugar boost. Juggling freelance work with making sure that stallholders knew the charity fete was still on had kept her busy all morning. But that wasn't why her energy levels were low. It was everything else she was having to cope with at the moment – the manor sale, River being an arse, Bartie coming on strong, and now there was the added pressure of carrying a new secret about Audrey.

A *huge* secret that would blow people's minds, if it turned out to be true. A secret that had been revealed by unravelling the meaning behind Audrey's cryptic final message in her diary.

Clara swallowed a mouthful of caramel – which was hitting the spot, nicely – and, spying a gap in the steady stream of passers-by, darted across the cobbled street to sit on the sea wall.

What would people say if they knew what had really happened to Audrey since her break for freedom? she wondered, drumming her feet against the stone. What would Geoffrey and

River say, let alone her own mother? Everything had become so complicated. And now that an end to the mystery was in sight, she wasn't sure that she'd done the right thing in pursuing the truth.

She bit into the ice cream cone and tried to focus instead on people watching. A few locals who were out and about waved to her, but most of those passing by were tourists: many of them young couples wandering the narrow lanes hand in hand, and overheated children in sunhats being followed by frazzled parents.

Some villagers moaned about the annual 'invasion' which clogged local roads but Clara didn't mind it. An influx of visitors made Heaven's Cove hum with life from spring until autumn's end and it kept the local economy going.

But sometimes she longed for winter and crisp frosty days when she could walk through the village unhindered. When Brellasham Manor was decorated for Christmas and the gardens were covered in a blanket of snow.

Would she still be able to visit the manor this Christmas, Clara wondered, or would it be a building site with its innards torn apart and every reminder of Audrey on the third floor eradicated?

She suddenly noticed a familiar figure striding along the street that edged the sea wall. Bartie was walking with a young woman in a tailored trouser suit. The woman batted her blonde hair over her shoulder and laughed at something that Bartie was saying.

Clara blinked. This was potentially awkward, after not succumbing to Bartie's charms yesterday afternoon – another decision which Clara was not completely sure had been the right one, even though her hunch about Audrey's final message had paid off.

She stood up, ready to flee, but immediately sat back down again. She couldn't pretend she hadn't seen him. That would be childish in the extreme. So, taking the bull by the horns, she waved and called out, 'Hey, Bartie!'

His pace faltered and he waved back before wandering over.

'Fancy seeing you here, Clara.'

'In the middle of Heaven's Cove. Surprising, that.'

Clara smiled at Bartie, who gave a somewhat frosty smile back and then turned to his companion. 'Where are my manners? This is Hannah, from the development company that's interested in acquiring the manor. Hannah, this is Clara, a friend from years ago.'

Hannah put out her hand. 'I'm delighted to meet you, Clara.' Her voice was low and silky, her accent Home Counties.

'Likewise,' said Clara, shaking Hannah's outstretched hand while acutely aware that her skin was sticky with dripped ice cream.

Hannah's smile wavered slightly as she withdrew her hand.

'Clara's mother is currently the housekeeper at Brellasham Manor,' said Bartie.

'Oh dear.' Hannah's cherry-red lips formed into a pout. 'It's unfortunate that she'll lose her job when the sale goes through.'

'*If* the sale goes through,' said Bartie quickly. 'It's all very much up in the air at the moment.'

'Yes, of course,' said Hannah, staring at Clara's T-shirt which was spattered with salted caramel. 'It's entirely up to Geoffrey what he wants to do with the manor and I'm not counting any chickens before they hatch.'

'Hopefully, if your company does end up buying the manor, my mum won't lose her home as well as her job,' said Clara. 'Did Bartie mention her cottage to you? The whitewashed one in the grounds, near the gates?'

'Of course I did. That's all in hand,' said Bartie, but not before Clara had noticed the puzzled look that crossed Hannah's face. 'As I assured Geoffrey this morning, Hannah is very open to retaining the cottage and allowing your mother to stay there on a peppercorn rent. Isn't that right?'

He turned to Hannah, who nodded. 'Uh-huh. Absolutely. Peppercorn rent.'

'Did Bartie also mention the annual charity fete that takes place in the grounds, and how important it is to the local community?'

'I mentioned everything, just like I promised,' said Bartie, pointing out to sea. 'Wow! Look at that amazing boat over there.' A large yacht was a splash of white and blue in the distance. 'That must be worth a mint. I've always fancied owning a yacht.'

'Me too. A very large one in the Caribbean,' laughed Hannah.

Clara looked between the two of them as they began discussing the merits of sailing mega-expensive boats in exotic waters. Hannah seemed cool as a cucumber but there was something different, almost desperate, about Bartie as he kept the nautical conversation going.

'If Brellasham Manor is turned into apartments, what sort of price do you expect them to go for?' asked Clara, butting into their chat.

Hannah stopped conversing abruptly and turned towards her. 'Would you be interested in buying one?'

'I'd love to but I imagine they'll be very expensive.'

'They will be rather top-end, in such a marvellous location. I anticipate them being very popular with a prestigious international demographic, most of whom will likely be cash buyers. But if you can scrape the deposit together and secure a mortgage, absolutely anyone will be considered.' *Absolutely anyone.* Clara was beginning to feel patronised. 'Where do you live currently?'

'In the grounds of Brellasham Manor. With my mum, in the cottage that you're open to retaining.'

Hannah stared at Clara, as if she didn't know what to make of her, and then turned to Bartie. 'Did you say something about a Pimm's? I'm absolutely gasping for a drink.'

'Yes, of course.' He glanced at his watch. 'Time's ticking on and you're better off leaving Heaven's Cove before all the tourists head for home and the roads become a nightmare. So we'd better get moving and say goodbye, Clara.'

When he leaned forward and kissed her on the cheek, his musky aftershave tickled her nose.

'Don't worry about the cottage or the fete,' he whispered in her ear. 'I'm taking care of it and I'll see you later. I'm hoping you won't have so much work to do tonight.'

He winked before putting his hand beneath Hannah's elbow and leading her away, through the crowds.

Clara sat back down on the wall and folded her arms. The tide was coming in and waves were splashing against the wall. Fishing boats anchored offshore were bobbing on the swell and seagulls were wheeling overhead.

It was a perfect scene but Clara felt jangled. Something was very off and she needed to find out what, right now.

Hannah had mentioned having a Pimm's. Of course she had – Clara couldn't imagine her downing half a pint of lager. So Bartie would probably take her to The Smugglers Haunt.

Clara hurried through the lanes, not allowing herself to think too much or she'd turn around and go home. She had always been in awe of Bartie – River was right – and loath to challenge him on anything. But she couldn't shake the feeling that life was out of kilter.

The Smugglers Haunt, a low, whitewashed building festooned with bright hanging baskets, had tables set up outside. People were drinking and laughing in the sunshine but there was no sign of Bartie or Hannah.

Clara pushed her way into the busy pub and looked around. It was cooler in here and several people had chosen to drink out of the sun. When she went up to the bar, Fred, the landlord, glanced up from the pint he was pulling.

'A'right, Clara? You look like you could do with a drink.'

'Maybe in a minute,' she said distractedly, glancing around the bar. 'I'm looking for someone. Two people, actually. Bartie – do you remember Bartie, who used to visit Brellasham Manor when we were teenagers? – and a tall blonde woman in a green trouser suit.'

'They've gone out the back. There were a couple of tables left in the garden.'

'Thanks, Fred.'

Clara made her way through the throng to the back of the pub and out of the door into the Haunt's walled garden. It was baking hot out here, sheltered from the sea breeze, and people were sitting at tables beneath bright parasols.

All of the tables were taken but Clara couldn't see Bartie and Hannah. Perhaps they'd gone elsewhere for their drinks. She was about to head back inside when she remembered the table that had been shoved behind the trellis – there wasn't much space there but Fred tried to get as many customers into the garden as he could.

The trellis, dripping with a blooming purple clematis, provided cover which meant Clara could approach it unseen. And when she peeped around it, there were Bartie and Hannah at the hidden table, sitting with their heads bent close together. A glass of what Clara assumed was Pimm's stood in front of Hannah and Bartie had a pint, the outside of the glass dripping with beads of condensation.

Now she'd found them, Clara hesitated. They were deep in conversation and she wasn't sure what she wanted to say. She couldn't leap in and say she was feeling jangled. They'd both think she'd taken leave of her senses.

As Clara stood deliberating, Hannah sat back on her wooden bench and took a sip of her drink. Her voice was muffled by the trellis but her words could be made out clearly enough. 'So, are you sure that the old man will go for the plan?'

Bartie smiled. 'Absolutely, just so long as he doesn't *know* the plan, of course. He trusts my judgement and, at the end of the day, will do what I suggest.'

'What about his son? He seemed very interested in what I had in mind. Doesn't Geoffrey listen to him too?'

'I was hoping we'd manage to avoid River but I'm sure he was lying in wait for us in the garden. I wouldn't worry too much about him. He and his father have been estranged for years and River doesn't want to take on the house. I don't blame him, mind you. It's a financial millstone, and who'd want to live in this tiny place in the middle of nowhere? Except,' he laughed, 'people looking for luxury apartments who have more money than sense.'

Bartie suddenly glanced up, across the garden, and Clara stepped back, fully behind the trellis. People in other parts of the garden had noticed her and Florence, one of the village's oldest residents, waved from beneath her parasol. She looked confused by Clara's clandestine behaviour.

'Please don't tell my mother,' Clara murmured, giving Florence a wave and a weak smile. If Julie found out that she'd been spying, she'd never hear the end of it.

Maybe it was time to go and she could tackle Bartie later. But any plans to beat a hasty retreat were scuppered the moment Clara heard her own name being mentioned. She turned back to the trellis and peeped around it again.

'It was all very awkward when she asked about the cottage,' Hannah was saying. 'You should have warned me. River asked about the same cottage, too, but then that stupid dog came bounding up and almost knocked me over so I never actually answered him. I didn't know what he was going on about.'

'It's all fine,' said Bartie, his tone soothing and conciliatory.

'You don't have to worry about Clara either. I've got that covered.'

'Is she keen on you?' Hannah's tinkly laugh cut through Clara like a knife.

'She's completely nuts about me. I mean...' Bartie waved a hand over his body, 'who wouldn't be?' He grinned. 'But her feelings for me are useful because they mean she's very trusting.'

'She's also pretty, so you're quite happy to go along with it, I dare say.'

Hannah wasn't laughing any more. She pulled her mouth into a thin line and stared into her drink.

Bartie leaned forward and put his hand on top of hers. 'You worry too much, babe. You know I can be a bit of a jack-the-lad but it doesn't mean anything.'

Clara had heard enough and was finding it hard to breathe. River was right that Bartie wasn't to be trusted. She'd been dazzled by his faux charm, and flattered that, after all these years, he might be interested in her. But he was simply keeping her sweet, to ensure that the house sale went through, and that it was sold to this particular woman.

She suddenly went hot and cold at the thought of how close she'd come to spending yesterday afternoon with him. Thank goodness she'd chosen to focus on her search instead. It seemed that Audrey had saved her from making a massive mistake.

Clara was about to flee the pub garden when Bartie said: 'One thing I'm not sure about is how many homes you're planning on building in total. I know there are the ten luxury apartments in the house, but how many in the grounds?'

'As many as we can get away with, depending on planning regs. But I've had an off-the-record chat with a local planning official who seemed very keen on attracting more house buyers to the area. I think we can manage a small estate of executive four-bedroom houses, with half overlooking the sea and the rest looking towards the moors. It'll be catnip to the buyers we're planning to entice. The cottage will have to go, of course.'

'Obviously.' Bartie frowned. 'You didn't mention anything about housing estates to River, did you?'

'Of course not, Bartie. I'm not a novice at this. I'm very experienced.'

'Oh, I know that, sweetheart. That was evident from our first weekend together.'

When Bartie's hand snaked under the table and clamped Hannah's thigh, she giggled and took another sip of her drink.

Clara blinked back tears of sadness and rage. Not only were Bartie and Hannah in cahoots, trying to nab the manor and grounds under false pretences, he was also undeniably in some sort of relationship with her. Which made him kissing Clara even worse. He wasn't joking when he'd told Hannah 'it doesn't mean anything'. Clara was simply a means to an end.

She'd heard enough. Watched by a curious Florence, Clara rushed back into the pub and pushed her way through the throng at the bar.

'Did you find your friends?' called Fred. 'Were they in the garden?'

Clara nodded, not trusting herself to speak, and walked out into the street.

She turned her hot face towards the breeze coming off the sea and bit down hard on her bottom lip. She needed to let River know what was really going on, but she couldn't face the humiliation of admitting that he'd been right all along and she'd been a total fool.

28

CLARA

An orange sun was sinking into a silver sea, blazing a path across the swelling water. Puffs of cloud on the horizon were a vivid pink and purple.

'Completely beautiful,' whispered Clara, who was sitting on a ruined wall of the castle, swinging her legs. She loved this time of day, when shadows began to lengthen across the stones and the tourists had gone. It was easy to imagine the people who'd lived here long ago as the gap between then and now became wafer-thin.

But this evening, she felt too jittery to relax and enjoy the view. Too let down and deceived. She tapped her fingers urgently against the stone and berated herself for the hundredth time for being taken in by flattery and lies.

She'd been out for hours because she couldn't face going home. She'd texted her mum to say she'd be out for tea, and had eaten in a local café. But it was getting dark and she couldn't stay away from Brellasham Manor for much longer. She would have to face people soon and tell them the truth.

When two hands suddenly covered her eyes, Clara let out a scream and jumped to her feet.

'Steady on, Clara. It's only me,' said Bartie, who had sneaked up behind her.

'That was stupid,' spat Clara, her heart hammering in her chest. 'What are you doing creeping up on people like that?'

'It was only a joke! I didn't mean to make you jump. Would a hug with me help?' He opened his arms wide.

'No, I'm fine,' muttered Clara, taking a step back.

'Well, you don't look fine,' said Bartie, his arms dropping to his sides. 'Look, I admit that probably wasn't the best way to announce my arrival. I wasn't trying to scare you.'

'Well, you did.' Clara's heart rate was beginning to slow down. 'What are you doing here?'

'River and I took a walk into Heaven's Cove, seeing as there's not a lot to do at the manor, and I thought I'd see if you were here... the maiden in the castle. We saw your mum as we were leaving the estate and she said you were in the village.'

'But how did you know this was where I'd be?'

Bartie sniffed. 'I didn't, but River and I were discussing our teenage days and he mentioned that this was a favourite place for both of you. He said the two of you used to come up here and smoke illicit cigarettes. Not that you ever invited me.'

'You'd never have come with us anyway because we weren't cool enough for you.'

'That's not the case,' said Bartie, even though it was completely true. He gave Clara one of his megawatt smiles. 'I must say, you looked very peaceful sitting on the wall, like the queen of your domain.'

'Until you scared me half to death.'

'Which I've apologised for already.' He ran a hand through his hair. 'Come on, Clara. Don't be grumpy with me. I sneaked away from River so that you and I can, you know, enjoy a little time together as the sun sets.'

He gave Clara his sexiest wink which didn't have the effect

he desired. Once upon a time, Bartie winking at her would have made her knees wobble but now it just put her teeth on edge.

'Where is River?' she asked.

'He went into the pub to get us both a drink.'

'And you just walked off and left him?'

'He'll wait, like the good little boy he always was, and we can both go and join him. Not for a while though, hey?' He sat on the wall and gestured for her to sit next to him.

Clara stayed exactly where she was. 'Where's Hannah?'

'She left a couple of hours ago, before the mad tourist rush to vacate the village. She was very impressed with the manor and its potential for development. So much so, I'm pretty sure she'll soon be making Geoffrey an offer that he can't refuse.'

'Great.' Clara sounded flat and unimpressed but Bartie was too busy brushing dust from his suede loafers to notice. 'What did she have to say about the grounds and Geoffrey's beautiful gardens that he's poured his heart and soul into?'

Bartie looked up from his shoes. 'Oh, she loved them too. How could she not be impressed? Geoffrey has done such a fantastic job over the years. Well, his gardener has.'

'Exactly. So it would be a terrible shame if they were destroyed.'

'It would, but they won't be. Hannah only has plans for the manor itself, which is what Geoffrey wants.'

'So what about Mum's cottage?' Clara asked, fascinated by how easily lies were tripping from Bartie's tongue.

'Yeah, that's all sorted and fine,' said Bartie airily. He patted the wall beside him. 'Stop talking and get yourself over here.'

'Did Hannah enjoy her Pimm's?'

'I dunno. I think so.' Bartie laughed. 'Stop talking about Hannah, will you? You're killing the mood.'

'Did you enjoy your pint, tucked away in the corner of the pub garden?'

'Yeah, it was OK, though I prefer—' Bartie stopped talking

and began to blink very quickly. 'How do you know where we were in the garden? Have the Heaven's Cove spies been out in force?'

When Clara said nothing, Bartie hopped off the wall and walked over. 'I don't know what you're getting at, Clo.' He ran his hand down her arm. 'You seem very stern this evening.'

Clara watched his fingers sliding over her sun-warmed skin. 'I overheard you and Hannah at The Smugglers Haunt.'

He gave a short laugh and dropped his hand. 'What are you talking about?'

'I came into the garden to find you because I felt that something wasn't right and I heard what you and Hannah were saying.'

'Were *you* spying on us? That's not very nice.' Bartie's voice had taken on a harsher tone and Clara swallowed.

'It wasn't spying. Not exactly. I was looking for you and saw you behind the trellis but then I heard the two of you discussing the sale.'

'What exactly do you *think* you heard?' Bartie's voice was low and level.

'I heard you both talking about keeping Geoffrey in the dark about Hannah's real plans for the house and grounds. Yes, the manor will be turned into luxury apartments, but the grounds and gardens and my mum's cottage will be bulldozed to make way for an estate of... what was it? Executive-style homes.'

Bartie's smile had faded like the dying sun. He ran a hand through his fringe. 'You've misunderstood what we were saying.'

'I don't think so. I heard you both very clearly.'

'From behind the trellis?'

'That's right,' said Clara, pulling her shoulders back for courage. She was shivering, even though the evening was balmy.

'Honestly, you're over-reacting,' said Bartie, his tone an odd mixture of annoyed and conciliatory. He waved away a midge that was buzzing around his face. 'It's not that bad.'

'Yes, it is! You're lying to everyone, Bartie. OK, I can understand you lying to me about Mum's cottage and claiming we can still hold the charity fete in the grounds each year. You don't owe me or Mum anything. But Geoffrey and River are family. You often stayed with Geoffrey when you were a teenager and your parents were separating. And River tried to help you, even though you treated him with disdain half the time. So you do owe them.'

Bartie stared at Clara for a moment, his eyes cold. Then he said: 'Have you spoken about this to Geoffrey?'

'Not yet. I was getting my head around it, but I will tell him. I have to, even though it will upset him.' Clara rubbed at her eyes. 'Do you know, I've been sitting here, racking my brains about why you would deceive us and all I can think is that it's for money. You told Geoffrey you were facilitating the deal out of the goodness of your heart, because he's family. But I'm guessing your girlfriend is going to give you a hefty commission from the sale.'

'She's not my girlfriend,' said Bartie, stepping closer. 'You've got completely the wrong end of the stick, sweetheart. Hannah is simply a friend of a friend, an acquaintance I hardly know.'

'You know her well enough to put your hand on her thigh and talk about the first weekend you spent together.'

Bartie stood statue-still for a moment, his expression unreadable. Then his lips curled into a smile that left the chill in his eyes untouched.

'Oh, Clara. You've got this all wrong. That's what I'll tell Geoffrey, and who is he more likely to believe? Me, his blood relative, or you, the housekeeper's daughter who would say anything to save the manor that she likes to think of as her own? I mean, the Netherways don't have a great reputation. I heard on the village grapevine that one of your relatives was done for stealing jewellery from a member of the Brellasham family.'

'It was a false accusation. She was exonerated,' said Clara

defiantly, although she felt like crying. 'And River will believe me.'

Bartie tilted his head to one side. 'Will he, though? You were thick as thieves back when we were kids, but then he left and ghosted you, basically. And now he has another life in Australia while you've hardly moved on at all. Why would *he* believe *you*?'

'Because he doesn't trust you,' said Clara, trying to keep the wobble out of her voice.

'Of course he trusts me. He looks up to me as his older cousin who, let's face it, has always been way more savvy than him. Plus, I got in touch with him about his old man's financial worries because I care about Geoffrey.'

'But you care about your bank balance more. Am I right? Brellasham Manor is River's birthright and I don't suppose Geoffrey would agree to sell it without his son's blessing. That's why you had to get him involved.'

The sun was almost gone and Bartie's face was dark with shadow.

'Look, Clara,' he said, his voice now purely conciliatory. 'I should have told Geoffrey the truth about what Hannah's got in mind but, at the end of the day, he'll have the money to fund his old age and he'll soon forget the manor. To be honest, any developer willing to pay decent money is going to want to build in the grounds too. We're talking about prime land in a sought-after village with marketable charm.'

Clara ran a hand across her face. 'Maybe. But a different developer might want to build homes that local people can afford. Not executive homes beyond the reach of people like me.'

'Is that what this is all about? You haven't got any money and you'd like some? I'm sure we could come to some arrangement so you get a cut of my commission.'

Clara's mouth fell open. 'Do you really think that I'd sell out

River and Geoffrey for money? That I'd be fine with the manor being ripped apart and Geoffrey's gardens and my mum's home destroyed, as long as I benefited from the sale?' Clara began to walk away. 'You don't know me at all.'

'Clara!' Bartie called after her. 'Come back.' He grabbed hold of her arm and pulled her round.

'Let go of me,' said Clara, her breath catching in her throat. His fingers were tight on her bare skin.

'No, we need to discuss this and work out a way forward.'

'There is no way forward other than telling Geoffrey what you're up to.' She tried to pull her arm away but Bartie's grip was like a vice. 'Please let go of me.'

'You heard what Clara said,' said a voice from the shadows. 'Let go of her arm.'

When River stepped into view, Bartie laughed. 'Or what?'

'Or I'll make you.'

'You and whose army?' Bartie sneered, still holding on tightly to her arm.

'Just me,' said River, his voice low and controlled.

'Are you going to fight with me?'

Bartie sounded amused, and Clara noticed the muscles in River's jaw tighten.

'I'd rather not but I will if I have to.'

'You were always sweet on Clara but I'm afraid she was always far more interested in me – still is. Is that why you're coming to her rescue? So you can play the big saviour and hope she'll overlook what an idiot you are and swoon in your arms?'

Clara had heard enough. She aimed a kick at Bartie's shin and wrenched her arm free.

'Ow!' he complained, bending over to rub his leg. 'What did you do that for?'

'To shut you up, mainly, and I don't want any fighting.'

'There wouldn't have been any,' replied Bartie sulkily, sounding like a teenager again. 'Honestly, River, this is all

nothing but a misunderstanding. Clara's got the wrong end of
the stick and now she's trying to cause trouble. I've had enough
and I'm going back to the manor. Are you coming?'

'No,' said River.

Bartie hesitated. 'I think you should come back with me.'

'I'm not going anywhere with you.'

River sat down on the wall where Clara had been sitting
watching the sunset only ten minutes earlier. But a lot had
changed since then.

'Right. Suit yourself, then.' Bartie looked at Clara through
the deepening gloom and said quietly: 'Have a think about what
I suggested. You know it makes sense.'

'When did he become such an arse?' asked River as Bartie
vanished into the darkness.

Clara sat down beside River on the wall that was rapidly
cooling now the sun had dipped below the horizon. 'I'm beginning to think he always was.'

'But what's he so uptight about?'

'I overheard him and Hannah, his developer contact who's
actually a girlfriend, at the pub this afternoon.'

Clara outlined what she'd heard while River listened in
silence, his face in profile as he stared out to sea. The water, no
longer on fire from the sun's setting rays, was changing from
silver to blue-black.

'I was going to tell you and Geoffrey first thing tomorrow
morning,' she said, after relating the whole tale, 'but I was
ambushed by Bartie out here and then you came along.'

River squeezed his hands into fists. 'I knew I didn't much
like him but I kept telling myself that I was being unfair. He's
my cousin and we go back a long way. I know he can be arro-
gant and annoying at times, but I never thought he'd try to
screw over my father, who's always been good to him.' He
glanced at his watch. 'My father needs to know but I'll have to
tell him tomorrow. He's exhausted after Hannah's visit and told

me he was heading for bed early. Will you come with me first thing tomorrow morning to break the news?'

'Of course I will.'

'Thanks.' River glanced round at Clara. 'What did Bartie mean when he said "have a think about what I suggested" as he left?'

'He suggested that I keep quiet and go along with his and Hannah's plan and, in return, he'd cut me into his commission from the sale. But I could never deceive you or your father like that. You have to believe me.'

River caught her gaze and held it. 'Of course I believe you. I'd trust you with my life, Clara.'

'Yet you cut me out of your life as soon as you reached Australia.'

She wanted to add: *Even after you'd kissed me,* but the words remained unspoken. Today had already been enough of a blow to her self-confidence without factoring into the mix a kiss apparently so dreadful and regretted that the kisser had felt it best to erase the kissee from his life completely.

She probably shouldn't have said anything at all to River about their estrangement. Not when he was reeling from Bartie's deception. But it had been an upsetting day and she didn't feel particularly in control right now.

River shifted beside her. Then he said: 'I regret not keeping in touch. I was fifteen and an idiot. And I'm sorry if Bartie has broken your heart.'

'What makes you think he has?'

'I saw you kissing him the other day on the village green.'

'So you *were* there. I thought I caught sight of you.' A thought suddenly struck her. 'Did Bartie tell you that he'd changed the time of the picnic from one o'clock to twelve fifteen?'

'He did not,' said River drily. 'That detail must have slipped his mind.'

'What an absolute—'

Clara's shoulders slumped as it became even more clear that she'd been manipulated from the start. At best, she'd been a distraction for Bartie and, at worst, a potential obstacle to be managed.

'Also, have you got a girlfriend back in Australia?' she asked.

'No, why? Ah.' River breathed out slowly. 'Another of Bartie's lies, I suppose.'

Clara nodded miserably. 'Go on then. Aren't you going to say "I told you so" now it's turned out that Bartie is a nasty piece of work, just like you warned me?'

'Nope. You're not the first person he's taken in with his charm and hideously fabulous good looks.'

Clara could have kissed him then, for being kind. But instead she asked: 'How did you find us this evening?'

'When Bartie went AWOL, I waited at the pub for a while before realising he'd probably sneaked off to see you. I'm a total moron and had let slip where you might be. So I came to find you. Basically, I was worried about you and with good reason. He shouldn't have grabbed you like that.'

'Would you have fought him, if he hadn't let me go?'

River laughed ruefully. 'That was a bit gung-ho of me. Have you seen his muscles? He could probably floor me with one punch. But yes, in answer to your question, I would have fought for you, Clo. That's what friends do.'

Clara leaned against him in the darkness and he slipped his arm around her shoulder and pulled her close. They were friends again.

A bright moon was rising and they sat for a while, watching its light glint on the water.

'I have some news,' said Clara as one of the bats that roosted in the castle keep swooped above their heads. 'About Audrey. I know you said that I should let the whole thing drop but, well...'

'Let me guess, you didn't.' River let go of Clara and shifted round until they were face to face. 'That doesn't surprise me. You always were very—'

'Single-minded?'

'I was going to say bloody-minded but, yeah, single-minded will do.'

Clara grinned. 'It's just that I think I worked out what Audrey planned to call herself if she managed to reach the boat and start a new life somewhere else.'

Sitting there on the floor in the ballroom, it had all seemed hopeless until Bartie had barged in. He'd been offended that she'd apparently rather read her copy of *Rebecca* than spend the afternoon in his bedroom. But his flippant résumé of the story outlined on the novel's back cover had sparked an idea that Clara couldn't wait to explore.

River blinked in the fading light. 'How on earth did you work out Audrey's new name?'

'She told me, in the final entry in her diary: *Can a flower bloom in the snow? Only time will tell.* It didn't make any sense but then I wondered if she was referring to the new life she was hoping to build under a new identity and *only time will tell* if it would work.'

'OK, I get that, but what about *can a flower bloom in the snow*? How does that tell you what she planned to call herself?'

'"Flower" was easy – perhaps, as a reminder of my gran's help, she'd choose the name Violet. But I couldn't work out what her surname might be. I tried searching online for people with her maiden name but that came to nothing. Then I tried using the place where she was born as a surname but it turns out there aren't any Violet Dorkings online. Or, at least, I couldn't find any.'

'Dorking?'

'It's a town in Surrey. So then I searched online for her birth certificate and tried using her mum's maiden name instead, which still didn't work. But then I had a brainwave.'

'Don't keep me in the dark! What *was* the surname that she chose?'

Clara smiled. 'It was Winter, after Maxim de Winter, who's a main character in one of her favourite books, *Rebecca*. Bartie read out the blurb on the back of the book and, when he mentioned his name, it all fell into place. *Can a flower bloom in the snow?* Violet Winter.'

River sat in what Clara assumed to be stunned silence for a moment. Then he said slowly, 'O-K. Let's say Audrey did make it to the boat and she did choose Violet Winter as her new name. Where is she now?'

'Well.' Clara swallowed. 'That's the thing. I think I might have found her. At first, searching for Violet Winter took me to loads of horticultural websites, which was frustrating. Anyway, I drilled down a little deeper and I found a Violet Winter who's living in a care home for older people. She was mentioned in a local newspaper article about an event held at the home.'

Clara thought back to that moment of revelation. Her muscles were aching from sitting on the hard ballroom floor, but all pains were forgotten when she read the article and Violet's name leapt out.

'That's amazing, Clara, but there must be other Violet Winters of around the same age Audrey would be now if she'd survived. I expect some of them are living in care homes, too.'

'But probably not in a care home in Dorking.'

River's jaw dropped. 'Where she was born. Do you think she went back home?'

'Maybe not at first but perhaps she wants to end her days somewhere familiar, where her life began. What do you reckon? I'm sorry to land all of this on you but it was such a huge secret to keep and, to be honest, I don't know what to do next.'

Clara waited, hardly daring to breathe as River went quiet. If he told her to forget Audrey and move on, this time she would. For his and his father's sake, she would let the matter rest now she believed that Audrey had been found. The enigmatic woman in the portrait had survived that traumatic night and hopefully forged a happy new life for herself, far from Edwin's fists. That was enough.

River suddenly took hold of her hand as stars scattered across the inky sky twinkled high above. 'I think, Clara, that there's only one thing to do next, and that's to go to Dorking and see if Violet Winter is the woman you think she is.'

29

RIVER

River was pacing up and down the hallway, across the Victorian floor tiles that were gleaming after a Mrs N polish. He ran a hand through his hair, which was still damp from the shower, and pulled down his Sydney Opera House T-shirt.

He wasn't looking forward to the next five minutes, and only hoped that Clara would arrive in time to help take the heat.

Would she turn up at all? he fleetingly wondered. After all, she hadn't bothered on the day he left this house for Australia. Though perhaps that had been for the best. His father *and* Clara watching him and his mother disappear down the gravel drive would have been too much for his adolescent self to bear.

'She'll be here,' he murmured, keeping an eye on the stairs in case Bartie put in an appearance. He was probably still in bed, dreaming up another amoral get-rich-quick scheme.

River felt his whole body tense at the thought of Bartie's double dealings and his manhandling of Clara. He'd been prepared to hit him last night if he hadn't let her go and, though River wasn't a violent man, a part of him wished he had taken a swing.

'I'm not late, am I?' Clara hurried through the front door, which was flung open to let in a warm breeze. 'Mum's a bag of nerves about what's going to happen once her job and home are gone and she needed to let off steam. It was hard to get away.'

'No, you're fine,' River assured her. She was wearing a pink summer dress and white sandals which accentuated her tan. He smiled at her. 'Thanks for coming, especially if your mum needed you.'

'That's all right, though I can't say I'm looking forward to this.' Clara nervously fiddled with a shoulder strap on her dress. 'Your dad's going to be really upset.'

'I know, but it's better that he knows the truth. It would break his heart to find out about Bartie's deception once the grounds have been turned into a building site. So' – he felt his shoulders tense – 'shall we beard the lion in his den? What?' he asked when Clara grinned.

'Nothing. It's just that's what you used to say when we were teenagers and you had to speak to your dad about something difficult.'

'That was how it felt then, and how it feels now. Come on. Let's get it over with, shall we?'

He resisted the urge to grab Clara's hand before going to the door of his father's study and rapping on it sharply. There was a barked 'Come in,' and, with a final glance at Clara, he pushed it open.

His father was sitting at the walnut desk that had been placed near the window. A Tiffany-style lamp sat on the desk, along with a leather blotter, two fountain pens, and a small laptop with its lid closed.

'You both look very serious, and it's rather early.' Geoffrey swung from side to side in the leather chair behind his desk. 'Is this a delegation?'

'Not as such, but we need to talk to you about something

important,' said River, choosing not to faff about with small talk. The sooner this was done, the better.

Geoffrey raised an eyebrow. 'That *does* sound rather serious.'

'It is, and I don't think there's a way of broaching it without upsetting you.'

His father began rolling one of the fountain pens under his fingers, back and forth across the blotter. 'Is it do with Bartie, by any chance?'

'Yes, I'm afraid so.' He exchanged a look with Clara, who was biting her lip. 'Why do you think it's about him?'

Geoffrey stopped pen-rolling. 'He came to see me last night. Late. I was in my bedroom, asleep actually, when he knocked on my door and said he had to speak to me urgently.'

River groaned because Bartie had beaten them to it. But what story had he spun? 'What did he say that was so urgent it couldn't wait until morning?' he asked.

'He told me he'd just discovered that Hannah had plans to build houses in the grounds of the manor and—'

'*Just* discovered?' interrupted Clara.

Geoffrey gave her a cool stare. 'That's what he told me. He'd just discovered it and he had to tell me immediately so I'd be fully informed when making a decision on the house. He said his conscience wouldn't allow him to do otherwise.'

He ignored River's quiet snort of derision and continued. 'So I thanked him for letting me know and said I would think about how this information changed the situation. Anyway, that's what he told me and that's how things stand right now.'

River thought for a moment, feeling totally outflanked by his cousin.

'But that's not what happened,' declared Clara.

'I'm sure that it is,' Geoffrey replied in a low voice.

'No, it's not because Bartie already—'

She stopped speaking and frowned at River, who had just

nudged his foot hard against hers. She was about to tell his father everything, but River had changed his mind.

The two of them could insist that Bartie had known all along and Clara could repeat what she'd heard his cousin and Hannah discussing the day before. But his father suddenly looked so done in, it would almost feel like putting the boot in. Bartie was family and Geoffrey had trusted him. What good would be achieved by telling an old man, mourning the imminent loss of his home, that he had been deceived? What good would come from making him face that realisation when he clearly preferred to think otherwise?

River shook his head slightly and, when he caught Clara's eye, a look of understanding passed between them.

'OK,' he said. 'If that's how things currently stand, I expect that makes Hannah's potential offer on the manor a no-go as far as you're concerned.'

'Yes indeed. I won't be accepting any offers from that woman.' Geoffrey stood up, walked to the window and gazed out at the moors rising behind the house. 'But I woke early and have been considering my situation.'

He turned back from the window and pinched the bridge of his nose. 'There will be other offers from developers, but all of them will see the grounds of this house as prime building land. Of course they will. They'll want to make as big a return on their outlay as possible. My father would have understood that from the outset and he wouldn't be impressed that I've been deluding myself.'

He swallowed. 'You don't want this house, River, and I do understand why. It's not financially viable, and you have another life far away. But I am too old and worn out to keep the house on for much longer and I've come to terms with the fact that there's no way to save it or the grounds or, I'm afraid, your mother's cottage, Clara.

'Brellasham Manor will be turned into apartments and its

grounds and gardens will be bulldozed to make way for housing. I'm afraid that's practically inevitable. My father would say that's simply the way that business works, while also hating me for being so inept at business that I have lost the family home.'

He raised a hand when River went to speak. 'No, there's nothing more to be said. I know you must be keen to return to Australia but I'd be grateful if you could organise visits from a few speculative developers before you fly away. Developers who are trustworthy and truthful.'

River nodded. 'Of course, and I can stay to help with the visits.'

Geoffrey gave a weak smile before walking back to his desk and sinking into his chair. 'Thank you but that won't be necessary. And now I have a number of issues to deal with so I'd be grateful if you could leave me in peace to get on with them.'

When neither River nor Clara moved, he added briskly, 'I'm sure you both have other places to be and I certainly have a great deal to do. Good morning.' He picked up a letter lying on his desk and began to read it.

Without another word, Clara and River left the study and walked out of the house and into the gardens. The flowers seemed extra bright this morning, as though they knew what was coming and wanted to display their beauty while they could.

'That didn't go quite the way I'd imagined,' said Clara, whose face had paled beneath her tan.

'It's shown us that Bartie is even more of a snake than we thought he was,' said River, wiping a hand across his face. 'He knew we'd tell my father so he got in first and put all the blame on Hannah.'

'Or, as he put it, told the truth because his conscience wouldn't allow him to do otherwise' – Clara rolled her eyes – 'and your dad believed him.'

'He *wanted* to believe him. He's known Bartie since he was born and thinks of him as...' *As the son he never had* was on the tip of River's tongue but he couldn't say it. 'He thinks of Bartie as an upstanding Brellasham, successful and loyal. And I didn't have the heart to disabuse him of that. He looked done in already.'

'Yeah, he did and you were right to stop me from telling him. Unfortunately, Bartie is very good at pulling the wool over people's eyes and manipulating them.'

'He's an expert.' River gave a sardonic laugh. 'I'm really beginning to wish I *had* punched him last night.'

Clara nudged her arm against his. 'Talking of which, thank you again for sticking up for me.'

'Any time, Clo.'

He had a sudden urge to close the gap between them and kiss her on the cheek. No, not on the cheek. He stared at her mouth and then looked away. The last time they'd kissed it hadn't ended well.

Clara cleared her throat. 'So what happens now, with your dad and this house?'

'I guess he's right that, realistically, the manor needs to be sold and what happens to it after that is out of his hands.'

'So Bartie wins,' said Clara glumly.

'Not really. My father seems determined not to sell to Hannah, which means that Bartie will miss out on his commission. So all of his scheming and conniving will have been for nothing.'

'There is that. But it's cold comfort when your family will no longer live at Brellasham Manor, my mum will be out of a job and a home, and these beautiful grounds will become an overpriced housing estate.'

Cold comfort, indeed, but River tried to harden his heart. 'It's sad but that's life, I'm afraid. Things change but life goes on.'

'Yours in Australia and mine here in Heaven's Cove. Well, until Mum and I have to move somewhere else.'

River nodded, realising how much he would miss Clara after he left for Australia and she and her mother moved on to who knows where. He'd got used to being without her sixteen years ago and he'd have to get used to her absence all over again.

'I was thinking about the charity fete,' said Clara, pulling her shoulders back. 'Realistically, it's going to be the last one ever held here so we should make it a real celebration of all the money that's been raised over the years, and the link there's always been between Heaven's Cove and its inhabitants and the manor and the Brellasham family.'

'I'm up for that.'

'I'm not sure your dad will be.'

'I'm sure he can cope with an influx of local people one last time.'

Clara glanced up at River through her eyelashes. 'Will you still be around for the fete?'

That was a few days away and he really should get home to Australia after arranging for prospective buyers to visit. He was beginning to realise that the longer he delayed his departure, the harder it was going to be. But he smiled at the woman he'd known since she was a tomboy with scabbed knees, and made a decision.

'Yeah, I'll still be here. My dad needs me.'

Clara opened her mouth to speak but she was interrupted by the ringing of her phone in her dress pocket.

'Sorry,' she mouthed, glancing at her phone screen and frowning before answering the call. 'Yes?... Yes, that's me.' She listened for a moment, her brow creased. 'That's very helpful. Thank you very much for getting back to me. Goodbye.'

'Is everything all right? Who was that?'

'It was the residential home in Dorking,' said Clara quietly. 'I left a message asking if they still had a resident called Violet

Winter and if we could visit her. That was a care assistant returning my call who said that yes, Violet is still with them and visiting hours are between ten and six every day.'

'OK.' River brushed his fingers across the petals of a pink pelargonium. 'Then it looks as if we're going on a day trip to Surrey.'

'Are you sure?' Clara asked, her eyes opening wide.

'No, but I'm not sure about anything these days.'

Clara laughed as if he'd made a joke and River smiled even though he was being deadly serious. Everything had seemed fixed in Australia. Sorted. Settled. But his life had been in flux from the moment he'd first set foot back in Brellasham Manor.

There were ghosts from the past swirling around this place. The ghost of abusive Edwin, whose influence continued to stifle his repressed son; the ghost of the person River had once been – and now it seemed that he and Clara were going in search of another.

30

GEOFFREY

He wasn't born yesterday, despite what his son thought. Geoffrey padded along the landing and stood outside Bartie's bedroom door. He paused but only for a few moments before knocking loudly. When there was no reply, he knocked again – even more loudly this time – and pushed the door open. It swung widely, banging into the chest of drawers behind it.

Bartie, asleep on his back and spread across the bed like a starfish, grunted at the noise. Then he sat up, scrabbling at the duvet until it covered his bare chest.

'What?' he demanded, rubbing his eyes. 'What's going on?'

'You and I need to have a word,' said Geoffrey, walking to the window and wrenching back the curtains. Bright daylight flooded the room as he moved to the bed and sat down on it.

'Urgh.' Bartie, wincing in the light, smacked his lips together. 'I need a drink.'

Geoffrey passed him the glass of water on the nightstand without a word and waited while Bartie slurped it down.

'What's happened?' Bartie asked, passing the tumbler back and wiping the back of his hand across his mouth. 'And whatever it is, couldn't it wait until I'm up and dressed?'

'No.' Geoffrey ran his thumbs across the cool glass. 'I'm afraid not.' He took a deep breath, not relishing what was about to be said but resigned to the fact that it was necessary. 'The thing is, I know the truth about you and Hannah.'

Bartie sniffed and pulled the duvet higher. 'Yes, I told you all about it last night. I was terribly upset that she would deceive me like that – telling me one thing while planning another. It's shocking.'

'Yes.' Geoffrey nodded sadly. 'I'm very shocked by the duplicity. Both hers and yours.'

'Oh, I get what this is,' said Bartie, running his hands through his hair which was standing on end. 'I suppose you've been speaking to Clara, and probably River, too. I bet they came to see you first thing, looking all drawn and concerned, and they spun some tale about how I knew what Hannah was planning all along. Well, it's rubbish.'

When Geoffrey remained silent, Bartie blinked and continued. 'I don't like to speak badly of Clara but she's been all over me since I arrived, and she didn't take it too kindly when I gave her a firm no and told her I have a girlfriend in London. I think I've mentioned her before. She's called Mariella and she's very special to me. Possibly *the one*.'

When Geoffrey still said nothing, Bartie puffed air through his lips. 'Anyway, Clara got very upset and, frankly, a bit paranoid about my relationship with Hannah. She threatened to wreck any deal to buy the manor and said she would poison the relationship between you and me. And now she's spreading that poison to River. You really don't want to believe anything they told you about me this morning.'

'I did see them this morning.' Geoffrey carefully placed the empty glass on the nightstand. 'But they told me very little about you, Bartie.'

'Oh.' Bartie blinked rapidly. Geoffrey could almost see the cogs in his brain whirring ever faster. 'Well. That's OK, then.

Clara must have realised how ridiculous and unfair she was
being. She knows that you'd never believe such an outlandish
claim about a member of your own family. After all, we Brellashams stick together.'

Geoffrey sighed. This was proving to be more painful than
he had imagined. His instinct had been to avoid exacerbating
his emotional pain and to pretend, even to himself, that he
believed Bartie, who had been a dear member of his family for
years.

That was why he'd gone along with the boy's blurted-out
tale last night: Hannah was the one in the wrong who had
misled them about her plans for the grounds and gardens, and
Bartie was as much a victim of her lies as he was himself.

When River and Clara had come into his study that morning, Geoffrey was prepared to counter any information to the
contrary that they might present. Anything to preserve his
emotional equilibrium and to keep the Brellasham family, such
as it was, together.

But then his son had kept his counsel and said nothing
about Bartie's duplicity, even though he knew. Geoffrey could
see it in his eyes. In Clara's, too, and she'd attempted to be more
forthcoming before River had shut her down. They knew the
truth but were allowing him to continue seeing Bartie through
rose-tinted glasses because they didn't want to hurt him – and
he respected them for that.

'Say something, Geoffrey,' said Bartie, a hint of anxiety in
his voice. 'We can put Hannah behind us and I can bring in
another developer I know who I trust completely.'

'You told me you trusted Hannah completely.'

'I did trust her, which is why I'm so upset that she let me
down. But this new developer I'm thinking about is beyond
reproach. I've known him for years and I'd trust him with my
life.'

Geoffrey held up his hands, not wanting to hear any more.

'There's no need. From now on, River will be arranging all visits regarding potential buyers.'

'That's not a good idea, sir,' Bartie whined. 'River doesn't have a clue what he's doing. He knows nothing about this area of business whereas I'm very experienced.'

'That's probably the case, but the difference is that I can trust River but I'm sad to say that I can't trust you, Bartie.' Geoffrey suddenly felt close to tears and he swallowed hard, berating himself for being weak.

'That's not true.'

'I'm afraid it is and my mind is made up.'

'I'm completely trustworthy,' Bartie protested but he knew his time was up. That was evident by the scowl on his face.

'I assume there was money involved. Some promise of commission or similar?' When Bartie remained silent, Geoffrey had his answer. 'I think it's best if you pack up and leave before breakfast, don't you?'

'You're making a terrible mistake.'

Geoffrey got up from the bed and walked to the door which was still wide open. 'Sadly, I don't think so.'

'But I don't have a car here. I came with River.'

'Then I suggest that you call for a taxi.'

Geoffrey walked away, along the landing, down the stairs and out into what he liked to think of as his 'secret garden'. Tucked away around the corner of the house, it was a profusion of large, blowsy blooms at this time of year.

His father would have deemed the display vulgar but there was something about the unapologetic, in-your-face flowers that Geoffrey found comforting. Especially on days like this when his emotions threatened to overwhelm him.

The irony was that he'd intended to give Bartie some money from the sale anyway. More, he imagined, than Bartie's share in Hannah's commission would have been.

He leaned against the kitchen wall, closed his eyes and

breathed in the heady scent of peonies, hydrangea and rhodo-
dendron.

Several minutes later he heard a car approaching, its tyres
crunching on gravel. The slamming of a car door followed and
the crunching resumed, growing fainter as the vehicle moved
along the drive, until it disappeared completely.

31

CLARA

The dining room was noisy and smelled of overcooked vegetables. Around twenty people were sitting at circular tables, some eating or chatting and one or two seemingly asleep in their chairs.

Staff in blue tunics were moving amongst the diners, taking empty plates away and re-filling water glasses.

'Excuse me, is Violet Winter in here?' asked Clara, stepping aside to let a young man carrying two bowls go by. The residents of this care home on the outskirts of Dorking were about to enjoy treacle sponge and custard for pudding.

The man nodded distractedly towards double doors at the back of the dining hall.

'I think Violet has gone to the beach. She told us she wasn't very hungry today. Her appetite comes and goes.'

'The beach?' River frowned, as confused by this as Clara because the sea was miles away. 'We thought she'd be here.'

The young man smiled and pulled the wobbling bowls closer to his chest. 'It's our kind of beach. You can find Vi through those doors over there.' He glanced past Clara's shoulder and grimaced. 'Can't stop. Jim's about to kick off because he's waiting for his dessert.'

Still confused, Clara murmured her thanks and she and River wound their way past tables and diners to the doors that were painted navy blue. Someone had fixed a wooden sign above the lintel that read: I DO LIKE TO BE BESIDE THE SEASIDE.

Puzzled, she pushed the doors open and she and River stepped into a room that overlooked a garden filled with tidy flower beds.

'Ah, a beach!' whispered Clara, realising what the care assistant had been talking about.

One wall of this room was a bright azure blue, like the Mediterranean sky on a summer's day, and a blazing yellow sun had been painted at its centre. Sweeping green waves, topped by white horses, were depicted at the bottom of the wall, and the floor in front of this faux sea was covered with real yellow sand. A low wooden guardrail had been fixed to the floor – a three-sided rectangle to keep the grains in place, and faint squawks of seagulls were sounding from a speaker high up on the wall.

'It's an indoor beach,' said River beside her. 'For people who can't get out or who miss the sea. Absolute genius.'

A woman with a shock of white hair was the only person in the room. She was sitting with her back to them, staring out of the window at the garden's lone tree that was bending in the wind.

When Clara glanced at River, he gave her a small nod. This was her project, her passion. This was for her to do.

'Audrey?' she asked gently, her voice drifting across the room, along with the bird song. 'Audrey Brellasham?'

The woman's head lifted at that but she continued staring ahead for a few seconds before turning towards them.

Clara caught her breath. Any doubts she'd had, any worries that she'd misunderstood the diary's cryptic final message, were dispelled the moment she caught sight of the elderly woman's face.

The skin was lined and the pale blue eyes tired, but the tilt of her jaw, the shape of her mouth, and her direct gaze were the same as in the portrait of a much younger woman that was hanging at Brellasham Manor.

Almost seventy years after her tragic death, Audrey Brellasham had been found.

Neither Clara nor River moved. They stared at the woman, who gave her visitors the faintest hint of a smile before folding her hands into the lap of her pink dress.

'We're sorry to intrude but would it be all right if we had a quick word with you?' asked Clara, finding her voice.

Audrey gave a shrug and nodded at two chairs near her which were covered in blue and white striped fabric, to resemble deckchairs.

Taking that as a 'yes', Clara took a seat and River followed while she tried to gather her thoughts. She'd been working towards this for so long, suspecting that Audrey's drowning was not as it seemed. Yet now that this moment had arrived and a dead woman was sitting in front of her, she could hardly believe it.

Audrey was the first to break the silence.

'Nobody has called me that name in years. But I've been expecting you,' she said, her voice quiet but steady. 'I've been expecting you for a very long time.'

'We're not here to cause you any problems,' said River. 'We don't mean to disturb you or your life.'

'Then why are you here?' asked Audrey, raising a hand to her white bun and self-consciously checking that no hair had escaped the grips that secured it.

Why, indeed? The whole situation was so surreal, Clara was suddenly at a loss to know what to say. She'd been so focused on finding Audrey but not on what happened afterwards. She hadn't paid enough attention to how her need to know the truth might affect the woman in front of her.

'I'm sorry,' she murmured. 'We shouldn't have come.'

'But you have.' Audrey's pale eyes met Clara's. She seemed calm, resigned almost. 'So tell me why. You know my name so I presume you know some of my story.'

'The story everyone believes is that you drowned in 1957 in the sea off Heaven's Cove.'

'Not everyone believes it. You didn't or you wouldn't be here. How did you find me after all this time?' She leaned forward, staring into the faces of her visitors. 'You have an advantage over me. You know who I am but who are you? We've never met, yet you both seem oddly familiar. What are your names?'

When Clara placed a hand on her chest, she could feel her heart beating extra fast. 'I'm Clara, Clara Netherway.'

'Netherway, you say.' Audrey's gaze became unfocused, as if she was remembering something from another time. 'I knew a Netherway once. Are you any relation to Violet?'

'I'm her granddaughter.'

'Did she send you?'

'I'm afraid not. Gran died a while ago.'

Audrey leaned back in her chair, a frown creasing her fore-head. 'I'm sorry to hear that. Your grandmother was a good woman, one of the best. And I can see the resemblance between you now, with your freckles and pretty eyes.' She turned her gaze on River. 'And you? Why do I feel that we've already met?'

'I'm River Brellasham.' Audrey's breathing grew more shallow and her already pale face blanched. She looked like the ghost that everyone had assumed she was. River and Clara exchanged worried looks and he pushed his chair back, farther away from the elderly woman. 'I'm sorry. Do you want us to leave?'

'No.' Audrey began to fidget, her hands lacing and unlacing

in her lap. 'I'm afraid your surname took me by surprise. I haven't seen a member of that family for a very long time. But no, I don't want you to go. I always thought someone might come one day, and today is that day.' She peered at him more closely. 'Who exactly are you?'

'I'm Geoffrey's son.'

'Little Geoffrey?'

'Yes, that's right. Though he's not so little now.'

Audrey looked River up and down before declaring: 'You don't look much like your father.'

'I'm told I look more like my mother. I have her fair hair and brown eyes.'

'Her long hair too, I dare say, and you're very tanned for Devon.'

River stifled a grin. 'I've lived in Australia for almost twenty years.'

'With Geoffrey? He couldn't cope with the heat of an English summer as a child.'

'No, my mother and I left and he stayed on his own in Heaven's Cove, at Brellasham Manor.'

'Ah, I see.' Audrey paused. 'I dare say I could have found all of that out if I'd tried. They say you can find everything on the internet these days. There's a computer here in the home and the staff encourage us to use it but I don't often bother. Is the internet how you found me?'

'Eventually,' said Clara. 'Though it took us a while.'

'You haven't said yet why you've come looking for me.'

'I... I...' Clara blinked, unsure how to explain her motivation to the woman who had been in her thoughts for so long. 'I saw your portrait which is hanging in the manor. The one of you in a yellow dress, and I became interested in you and your story.'

'I never imagined that my portrait would still be on display.'

'I believe that was my father's doing,' said River. 'He insisted on it.'

Audrey's lower lip trembled and her next words were so indistinct, Clara barely caught them. 'So, he didn't forget me, then.'

Clara had an urge to put her hand on Audrey's, to comfort this elderly woman who had left behind a child she held dear. But she wasn't sure that any show of affection would be welcomed from her or River. They were strangers to Audrey, and the three of them were walking an emotional tightrope between the past and the present.

'How is Geoffrey doing?' Audrey asked River, her voice more steady now.

'He's healthy and still living in the manor house for the moment. But the costs involved in keeping the place repaired and running mean that it'll soon have to be sold.'

'Brellasham Manor no longer belonging to the Brellashams?' Audrey shook her head. 'Edwin wouldn't like that. He wouldn't like that at all.'

Hearing Audrey speak the name of her abusive husband gave Clara a jolt. Would she want to know what had happened to him after she'd left? Clara had just decided it was best not to mention him when Audrey said unprompted: 'I know that Edwin is dead. It said so the one time I looked up his name, a couple of years ago. I'd never tried before then to find out what had happened to my husband. I was frightened that if I asked any questions he would hear of it and find me.'

'And you didn't want to be found,' said Clara.

'It wasn't that I didn't want to be found. I *couldn't* be found. But I don't expect you to understand.'

'The thing is, Audrey, we do understand, more than you think... is it all right to call you Audrey? Perhaps I should be calling you Violet or Ms Winter? Whichever you prefer is—'

Clara stopped talking, realising that she was babbling because she was nervous. What she was about to explain would lead to her confessing that she'd read this woman's diary, and her mother's words were echoing in her mind: *It's a gross betrayal of trust.*

'I think at this point Audrey is fine.' The elderly woman folded her arms, curiosity written across her face. 'What exactly is it that you understand?'

Clara hesitated until a discreet nod from River gave her the courage to carry on. 'From the outside, your life at Brellasham Manor looked amazing – a beautiful house, a handsome husband, ballgowns and dances. But we know that things weren't what they seemed and Edwin wasn't the loving husband he appeared to be.'

'And how do you know all of that?' asked Audrey, shifting in her seat.

'We know because of your diary,' said Clara, pulling it from her bag that was looped across her body. 'I found it in my grandmother's belongings after she died. She must have taken it from your bedroom.'

Audrey took the book in shaking hands and began to leaf through it. And as she ran her fingers across the words she'd written so long ago, her eyes began to brim with tears. 'But how... how did this diary lead you to me?'

This was the part that Clara was dreading the most. How would Audrey react when she found out that the two strangers in front of her knew intimate details about her life and marriage? Details that she'd deliberately made unintelligible because they were a secret. Her secret. But Clara knew she'd come too far and this woman was owed both an explanation and an apology.

'I'm so sorry but I read your diary,' she blurted out. 'I know it's a terrible invasion of privacy, a gross betrayal of trust even, but I reckoned it was OK because you were dead, or so I thought. And then, when I saw the numbers you'd written and the coded message my gran sent you I was intrigued. I managed to decipher the numbers, using the dictionary we found in your bedside table and your final coded words, *Can a flower bloom in the snow? Only time will tell,* along with your love for the novel *Rebecca,* suggested to me that you might have chosen the new name Violet Winter, and I knew from your birth certificate that you had a link to Dorking.' Clara swallowed. 'I have a reputation for being stubborn and not letting things drop.'

Fake seagulls squawked from the speaker as Clara waited for Audrey's response. She was expecting anger, upset, outrage even, but all Audrey said was: 'So you know what Edwin was really like.' Clara nodded, angered afresh by the lifelong effect that Edwin's abuse had wreaked on this softly spoken woman. 'And you too?' Audrey asked River.

'Yes, and I'm so sorry for what my grandfather did to you.'

Audrey regarded him for a moment, her eyes unbearably sad. Then she reached over and patted his knee. 'It's not for you to apologise for the actions of a man who's long gone. His flaws aren't your responsibility.'

'I guess so.' River's voice was husky with emotion. 'But I'm sorry all the same.'

'Everybody's sorry. You on behalf of a man you probably hardly knew, and you,' said Audrey, turning her attention to Clara, 'for reading a diary that I meant to destroy. But I suppose that reading the diary of a dead woman is allowed, and I'm impressed that you worked out my code. You're a clever girl. Just like your grandmother.'

Clara felt her shoulders relax. She'd been holding herself tight, waiting for condemnation from Audrey that wasn't coming.

'I forgot to destroy my diary before I left and I was so worried it would get Violet into trouble. If Edwin had realised the message was in her handwriting...' Audrey grasped hold of Clara's hand. Her skin was cool and ridged with blue veins. 'He never did find out, did he? She didn't lose her job?'

'No, he never found out and Gran didn't lose her job. But

she was spotted in your bedroom and was under suspicion for a while of stealing the diamond necklace that went missing when you did.'

Audrey pulled back her hand. 'Of course Violet didn't steal the diamonds. That must have been dreadful for her. I'm terribly sorry, after she'd helped me so much.'

'Do you mind me asking how exactly my grandmother helped you?'

'Violet knew about Edwin's temper and, when she noticed that I sometimes had bruises, I began to confide in her. But as Edwin's paranoia increased, he forbade me from talking to the staff and began to limit who I could see and when. I could only see people if he was present too. He was morbidly jealous for no good reason and, after a while, I wasn't even allowed to go out of the manor grounds on my own.' She paused. 'It was a difficult time, to say the least. But your grandmother was kind. She risked dismissal by speaking to me when she could and, when that became ever more challenging, we began to communicate using coded notes.'

'I'm glad you had Violet,' said Clara, feeling an overwhelming rush of love for her brave, big-hearted grandmother. 'But everything seemed to come to a head after the ball.'

'Ah, the ball.' Audrey closed her eyes and her body began to sway, as if she could hear music from long ago, from another life.

'I was so excited when Edwin agreed to having a grand ball at the manor,' she said, opening her eyes. 'The house was so lonely, I craved company. I was only twenty-four years old and full of life.'

'Why did he agree to the ball at all?' River asked.

Audrey blinked at him as if she'd forgotten he was there. 'It suited him to invite people with whom he was hoping to do business, and maybe he realised that he couldn't keep me cooped up for ever? I don't know. I didn't ask any questions in case he changed his mind. I simply threw myself into the preparations.'

'The ball sounded wonderful from your description,' said Clara, fascinated by Audrey's memories.

'It was the most magnificent evening,' she declared, her eyes shining. 'The ballroom was lit by hundreds of candles and a string orchestra played for hours. Our guests were resplendent in long gowns and black tie and tails, and I wore my beautiful yellow dress and was so happy.' She smiled, lost in her memories. 'But afterwards...'

Audrey's hands had begun to shake and Clara put hers on top of them. She and Audrey no longer felt like strangers, not when so much was being shared in this room that pretended to be the seaside.

'You don't have to tell us anything more. We've found you, and that's all that matters.'

Audrey turned her pale blue eyes on Clara. 'But don't you understand that I want to tell you? That's why I've been so open since you arrived. I've carried this with me for the last sixty-seven years. I've been living a lie and the truth needs to come into the light before I die. Will you please both listen to my story?'

When Clara and River glanced at each other and nodded, Audrey continued.

'I was getting ready for bed, after the ball. I'd finished writing my diary and was in the bathroom when Edwin appeared in a rage. He'd drunk too much and was slurring his words. He accused me of flirting with William Jenkinson, an older man who had actually been kind to me.

'Edwin was busy all night talking to business associates and William took pity on me. We danced a few times and he fetched me some food. We talked about his children and his wife, who was unwell so hadn't accompanied him. We discussed the challenges of being a parent and I confided in him that I sometimes felt awkward around Geoffrey. I cared about him but wasn't sure how he felt about me. That was all that happened.'

'Did Edwin believe you when you told him that?' asked River.

'No. He became more angry than I'd ever seen him before and, when I tried to get past him, he pinned me to the wall by my neck.'

She cleared her throat as if Edwin's hands were still around it, chasing the breath from her.

'He finally released me when I began to cry but he promised to kill me if I so much as looked at another man ever again, and I believed him.'

'That's appalling,' said River. 'Was there someone you could tell about his threats?'

'Who would I tell? Domestic abuse was rarely talked about and certainly not amongst well-off families. Everyone thought I lived a charmed life with nothing to complain about, and plenty of people thought I was a money-grabber who'd married a much older man for his house when, in fact, I'd married him for love. So who would have believed that I was terrified of my husband?'

'My grandmother,' said Clara.

Audrey smiled. 'That's right. Wonderful Violet, who noticed the marks around my neck and knew I had to get away. She knew I was desperate to escape, one way or another.'

'One way or another?' Clara probed gently.

'I just wanted my life in that house to end because I couldn't go on like that. Looking back, I can see how depressed and frightened I was.'

'So my grandmother helped you.'

'And your grandfather did, too.'

Clara blinked at this bombshell but bit back questions about her grandfather's involvement because words were still spilling from Audrey's mouth.

'I was trapped at Brellasham Manor. Edwin had even hired security staff – thugs really – to patrol the border of his land. He said it was to keep burglars out, but I knew it was to keep me in. Then Violet offered me a lifeline. She sent the message you found in my diary because she'd found a way out for me.

'Edwin could stop me leaving by land but he couldn't stop me leaving by sea. A boat pulling into the cove would have been noticed, but not a lone figure walking into the waves. But someone must have seen me. I saw newspaper articles soon afterwards that said I'd drowned.'

'Yes,' said River quietly. He'd taken a back seat, letting Clara take the lead, but now he leaned forward. 'My father saw you walking into the water.'

'*Geoffrey* saw me?' gasped Audrey. 'That can't be right.'

'He was in the library, looking out of the window.'

'No, no, no.' Audrey was shaking her head. 'That definitely couldn't have happened. I timed my escape so that Geoffrey was in the dining room, having his evening meal with his father. Edwin insisted on it every night.'

'That night my father wasn't feeling well so he was excused to sit quietly and read a book. That's when he saw you wading into the sea.'

'I'm sorry. That was never the plan.' Audrey's face crumpled. 'Poor Geoffrey.'

'He's all right,' River assured her, but Clara knew that wasn't really the truth. His father was an unemotional, lonely and unhappy man – but how much of that was due to seeing the stepmother he loved apparently drown herself would never be known.

Audrey sat quietly for a moment, composing herself. Then she said: 'The sea was so cold that night, I thought I might drown. But I managed to swim to the headland, to where your grandfather was waiting for me in his boat, Clara. My rescue was a Netherway family affair and I will always be grateful to your family for saving my life.'

'Where did you go?' Clara asked, curious about what the last almost seven decades had been like for a woman with a new life and no past.

'Here and there. I spent much of my life in rural parts of Ireland. I had no close family, so I was able to disappear.'

'Did you marry again or have children?'

Pain flickered across Audrey's face. 'No. I was still married to Edwin, even if he didn't know it.'

'You survived,' River interrupted, 'but you left my father alone with an abusive man.'

There was no accusation in his voice but Clara had once known him so well she recognised anger in the tightening of his jaw.

Audrey turned to face him. 'Edwin was abusive to me but I knew he'd never lay a finger on his son. He was proud of his boy and he loved him. If I'd taken Geoffrey with me, Edwin would never have stopped looking for us. And I couldn't expect a young boy to walk into the sea with me that night when I didn't know if I would live or die. I was right to leave him behind.' She glanced up at River, fear in her eyes. 'Wasn't I? Edwin never harmed Geoffrey, did he?'

River shook his head. 'As far as I'm aware, he never hurt Geoffrey physically.'

Emotionally, it was probably a different matter. But Clara was grateful that River didn't elaborate because Audrey sighed with relief. 'Does Geoffrey know that I've been found?'

'No. We thought it best not to say anything, until we'd spoken to you.'

'Then, I'd ask that you don't tell him. It was all a long time ago and he has moved on. He doesn't need me back in his life, stirring up the past.'

'He might *want* to know,' said River, but Audrey waved away his words.

'I doubt it. You must care a great deal about your father because you've come to find me. But sometimes the best thing we can do for the ones we love is to protect them from the truth. Please promise me that you won't say a word,' she pleaded. 'My life hasn't been easy but I think I can finally put Audrey Brellasham to rest now I've told you what happened. I'm Violet Winter, who wants to live out her final days in peace.'

River looked at Clara, who nodded because they owed Audrey that at least. 'Of course,' he said. 'We won't tell my father. You might be right that he's better off not knowing.'

Audrey's shoulders slumped and she folded her fingers around the diary in her lap. 'Thank you.'

Her eyelids were fluttering as if she could hardly keep them open. The poor woman was exhausted after reliving so many painful memories, and Clara's heart ached for her.

'We'll let you get some rest,' she said, getting to her feet. Lunch was done in the next room and a couple of diners had just pushed open the door. 'Thank you so much for seeing us and for sharing with us what happened. That can't have been easy.'

'Not easy, but necessary.' Audrey gave a small smile. 'Now you know that I didn't perish in September 1957. I survived then and I'm surviving still, if that's what sitting in front of a painted beach amounts to.'

'Will you be all right? Would you like me to send someone in to be with you?'

'No, thank you. I'll just sit here quietly for a while.'

River and Clara had started walking away when Clara had a sudden thought and looked back. 'Audrey... I'm so sorry. I have one more question. What happened to the diamond necklace that my grandmother was accused of stealing?'

Audrey didn't look round. 'I was wearing the necklace

when I left but it was dragged from my neck by the current and the diamonds are now at the bottom of the ocean. Just as well, really.'

≈

'Wow, that was intense,' said Clara as she and River walked away from the care home. She felt punch-drunk from the intensity of the last twenty minutes and she could sense that River felt the same way. He was breathing heavily beside her, as if he'd just been for a run. 'I can't believe that we found Audrey. I only hope we did the right thing in coming to see her.'

Clara knew she was seeking reassurance but she was still worried that her need to know the truth about Audrey had trumped her concern for the elderly woman's well-being.

'I think it was the right thing,' said River, his footsteps falling into synch with hers. 'It was emotional but Audrey said herself that she wanted to share the truth before it was too late. She wanted to tell us what had happened, and she seemed more at peace, somehow, once she'd got it off her chest. She's been waiting for the truth to catch up with her for almost seventy years and hopefully she'll feel better now that her secret's been shared.'

'It's been a big secret to keep,' Clara agreed, thinking of her grandmother who had guarded it 'til her dying day. 'One that's shaped her whole life.' She glanced across at River, whose breathing had slowed. 'A part of me wishes we could tell your dad, though.'

'Me too.' He shrugged. '*We've* got a big secret to keep now. The baton has been passed to us. But we promised Audrey and she's probably right when she says it's better that he doesn't know. He's got enough to cope with at the moment and, as far as he's concerned, the trauma surrounding Audrey's apparent death was dealt with ages ago.'

'I guess so,' said Clara, although she wasn't sure anyone could ever deal fully with such a traumatic event. But River was right; they'd promised Audrey so there was nothing to be done.

'Did you leave the diary with her?' asked River.

'Yeah, it's hers and she can do what she likes with it – keep it or destroy it,' Clara answered, remembering how her mum had dumped the book into the bin with the vegetable peelings. Audrey would never have been found had it stayed there. But perhaps the diary had now done its job and it was time for it to disappear for ever, along with Audrey Brellasham.

They walked a little further along the busy street before Clara asked: 'Do you believe her about the diamonds?'

'I don't know,' said River, side-stepping a woman with a buggy. 'Maybe she sold them to fund her new life. I wouldn't blame her.'

'Or they're resting on the seabed somewhere off Heaven's Cove.'

Clara could picture them glinting in shafts of sunlight that filtered through the depths.

River suddenly stopped in the middle of the pavement. 'It was hard to hear how badly my grandfather treated Audrey.' He turned to face Clara, ignoring tutting passers-by who had to walk around them. 'Do you think I'm like him? I lose my temper sometimes and I can be stubborn and single-minded and—'

Clara grabbed hold of his arms. 'River, listen to me. You're nothing like Edwin. You're kind and sensitive and caring. You hardly ever lose your temper, you put up with me for years, and you didn't even thump Bartie when he was being horrible. There's no resemblance, honestly. You're two very different men.'

River breathed out slowly and nodded. 'OK. Thanks,' he said gruffly.

They walked on towards the car park and neither of them made any comment when Clara slipped her hand into his.

32

RIVER

'How many stalls are there in all?' River asked, wiping sweat from his forehead. 'One thousand? Two?'

He and Clara had been busy all morning, helping a team of volunteers to build the market stands that local traders would use at the fete tomorrow – and the task seemed never-ending.

'Thirty-three,' said Clara, her eyes shining when she laughed. 'We usually only have twenty-five, tops, but people in Heaven's Cove are pulling out all the stops because they know this year's Brellasham Manor Charity Fete and Open Day will be the last.'

Her smile faded. 'Talking of which, what's happening with prospective buyers for this place?'

'It's all in hand. I've been in touch with a couple of specialist estate agencies who know how best to handle this kind of sale. They're visiting next week to take down all the particulars and get photos, and then it's just a case of finding the right buyer.'

'What did they say about the grounds?'

River frowned. 'I'm afraid they say the grounds are a prime

spot for development and that's what buyers will be interested in, as well as the manor house itself.'

It was inevitable, thought River, but depressing, especially on a day like today when the land surrounding the manor house looked so magnificent. The breeze was rustling through the branches of the tall trees that edged the cove and his father's beloved gardens were a blaze of colour, with the moors rising up beyond them.

Clara folded her arms, looking thoroughly fed up. 'Yeah, I thought they'd say that. How long is a sale likely to take?'

'It depends who's interested in the deal but, when the right person or company comes forward, I'm told it can all be dealt with pretty quickly. I'm sorry I can't be more specific than that.'

'It's not your fault. We're dealing with a lot of unknowns, which is what Mum is finding so hard. She could be out of a job and a home in two months' time, or six months, or perhaps not for a year. It's all making her very anxious.'

'She won't have to worry about money, not initially anyway, because I'm sure my father will arrange a good redundancy package.'

'I know and that's great, but it's the upheaval and uncertainty about everything that's stressing her out. That, and having to leave the home she shared with my dad for decades. I've been trying to get her to meditate.'

'Your mum?' River couldn't help smiling at the thought of pragmatic Mrs N sitting on a bean bag, chanting.

'Yeah, it's not all sitting on bean bags, saying "om", you know. It would do her good to give her mind, and me, a rest.'

Once again, River was struck by how much in synch he and Clara were. As teenagers, it had seemed at times that they could almost read each other's minds. He'd thought they'd lost that connection but, over the last few days, since meeting Audrey, they'd felt closer again. Perhaps the two of them keeping such a huge secret meant they would be for ever linked.

Thinking about Audrey made him jittery. 'I still feel conflicted about not—' He looked around to make sure they couldn't be overheard. Keeping secrets made people paranoid. 'About not saying anything to my father about... you know.'

Clara, unfazed by his abrupt change of subject, nodded. 'I know what you mean. I keep going back and forth in my mind, wondering whether it would be better for him to know or not. But I guess we don't have a choice. Audrey's been through a lot already and we made her a promise. Though keeping it won't be easy.'

She paused and winced. 'Sometimes I wish we'd never found her at all. I should have done what you and my mum told me and left the whole thing well alone.' She frowned when River laughed. 'What?'

'It's just the thought of you doing what you're told and backing off. That's not the Clara I know of old.'

'Maybe I've changed,' she said, clearly trying to look terribly affronted but failing miserably.

River tilted his head to one side and smiled at the woman in front of him. Her ponytail was falling down and her denim dungarees were coated in dust. A large streak of oil marked the side of her face and her white T-shirt had a rip at the shoulder.

Clara was the same tomboy he'd always known, and yet she was subtly different. Still stubborn and chippy, of course. He doubted that would ever change. But her sharper edges had been smoothed over the years by what life had thrown at her. All of the joys and sorrows she'd experienced had turned her from a great teenager into this amazing woman whom he desperately wanted to kiss.

River closed his eyes. He was turning into a hopeless romantic idiot, and his Aussie mates would take the mick mercilessly if they knew. When he opened his eyes again, Clara was staring at him.

'Are you all right? Have you had too much sun?'

'You think this is sun?' he retorted, keen to ease his vulnerability with humour. 'You've obviously never spent twenty-four
hours lost in an Australian desert with a duff phone and a water
bottle that's sprung a leak.'

'This is true, and it sounds like a terrifying experience. Did
that really happen?'

'It did and it was a bit hairy at the time.'

'Talking of terrifying experiences, I heard that you fight
blazes in the Australian bush.'

'That's right. I'm a volunteer firefighter,' said River,
surprised that Clara knew. 'Who told you that?'

'Belinda in the village saw an online photo of you being
heroic and told my mum.' She wrinkled her nose. 'You know
what small villages are like for gossip.'

'We tackled a huge blaze last summer that got—'

They both swung around – his story for ever untold – as a
metal pole clanged to the ground. The man who'd dropped it
raised his hand in apology.

'I think we'd better stop chatting and go and help Corey,'
said Clara. 'We could do with more manpower to put all of
these stands up and I never thought I'd say this, but I wish
Bartie was here to pitch in.'

'He'd be far too busy wheeling and dealing to get his hands
dirty.'

'You're probably right. Has your dad said anything about
him upping and leaving like that, without a word?'

'Nothing except that Bartie left a note saying he had to get
back to London because of an urgent work problem.'

'An urgent work problem?' Clara guffawed loudly. 'He
probably thought we'd tell Geoffrey the truth about Hannah's
plans. Though I like to think that he felt too guilty to face us
after the showdown at the castle. At least that would prove
there is some decency in him.'

'That's probably it,' said River, although he had his doubts.

His cousin had never seemed the type of person overly bothered by a conscience. But he hoped that his father was still none the wiser about Bartie's deception.

They'd almost reached Corey when Clara stopped and turned to River.

'Thanks for your help with all of this. I really want tomorrow's fete and open day to be the best one ever which raises loads of money for local charities. I want everyone in Heaven's Cove to remember this amazing place as it is now, before everything changes. I want my mum and your dad to make happy memories. And I want to make sure that you don't forget us all when you go back to Australia.'

As if he could. River smiled. 'It's going to be amazing, Clo. Just you wait and see.'

33

GEOFFREY

Geoffrey had been dreading the fete and open day, even though he knew it raised much-needed money for charities in and around Heaven's Cove.

It was good, of course, to see so many locals enjoying themselves in the sunshine. It would be curmudgeonly in the extreme to think otherwise. But he disliked them wandering around his home, pointing at things with their mouths open. And he lived in fear of youngsters trampling all over his flower beds – which was ironic when the majority of those beds would be flattened soon enough by a bulldozer.

He threw another dart, which didn't even reach the dartboard at the back of the stall, and gave a tight smile when the stallholder, pub landlord Fred, declared loudly: 'Ooh, that's a shame. No prize for the Squire, I'm afraid.'

'I can live with that,' Geoffrey murmured, heading for the refreshments tent. There was only so much taking part in proceedings that he could stomach, although people were being extremely nice to him. Were some of them sad to see him go? he wondered.

He looked around him, at children laughing and eating

candy floss and smiling villagers he'd known for decades, and his bad mood suddenly lifted.

Clara had done a grand job, with River's help, and the fete was proving a great success. The least he could do was to make an effort, especially as it was for the very last time. The Brellashams would leave Heaven's Cove with their heads held high.

He decided to go back to the manor, to help show people round, and he'd almost reached the door when local eccentric Claude stepped in front of him, blocking his way.

'Claude, I'm surprised to see you here,' said Geoffrey, taking a step back from Claude's dog which was shedding hairs everywhere.

'I got invited by Clara, if that's a'right with you, when she was asking me about dead bodies,' said Claude, his words softened by a strong Devon accent.

Geoffrey blinked in the bright sunlight. 'Dead bodies?'

'That's right. Not much idea what she was going on about but she told me to get myself along here, so I have.'

Claude hadn't spoken to him in years, Geoffrey realised, as the old fisherman stroked a hand down his wild grey beard. Not as far as he could remember. Or perhaps it was more a case of Geoffrey not having spoken to him.

A shudder of shame went down his spine. His family had been a part of this village for generations and yet there were long-term residents of Heaven's Cove that he didn't converse with from one year to the next.

'You're very welcome here,' he told his grizzled visitor. Too little, too late.

'I heard you're leaving.' Claude gave his shedding dog a pat on the head.

'Yes, sadly that's the case.'

'Staying in Heaven's Cove, are you?'

'No, I'll be moving away.'

Claude sniffed. 'That's a mistake.'

'Possibly, but I've decided to move on.'

When Claude stared at him for a moment, Geoffrey had the uncomfortable feeling that the old eccentric could see into his soul. He curled his fingers into his palms, rather disgusted with himself for being so... new age. He'd be joining the wokerati next. He wasn't quite sure who or what the wokerati was but he knew that he wouldn't want to be a part of it.

'It'd be hard to see everything your family's built up being changed,' said Claude. 'It'll be strange, the Brellashams not being a part of Heaven's Cove after so long.' He sniffed again, more loudly. 'Well, I wish you well though you'll hardly be on the breadline after selling this place.'

Claude was obviously not a man to mince his words.

'Thank you,' said Geoffrey briskly, now wanting this conversation to end. 'I'd better get on. I'm helping with tours of the manor. Um... would you like to have a look around?'

Claude sniffed. 'Nope. What's the point?' And with that enigmatic farewell he sloped off with the dog at his heels.

Geoffrey watched him go, the flash of shame he'd felt morphing into something new. It was regret, he realised, that he hadn't been a bigger and better part of the local community. That he hadn't got to know its characters, like Claude, or spent time drinking in The Smugglers Haunt. He might even have made a few friends.

But he'd had his chance and he'd blown it. He'd virtually locked himself away at Brellasham Manor following the departure of his wife and son and it was too late now to make up for lost time. Claude's parting words *What's the point?* rang in Geoffrey's ears.

With a heavy heart, he walked into the grand hallway of his home and nodded at the woman from the bakery who was gawping at his great-grandfather's stained-glass window. He would find River and Clara, who were shepherding people around his home, and offer to help. That would show willing on his part.

Geoffrey walked through the manor, searching for his son amongst all the people who were wandering from room to room. Several locals stopped him to wish him well and the regret in his heart grew heavier with every encounter.

On reaching the ballroom, he spotted River pointing out the intricately plastered ceiling to a group of visitors. Clara was standing nearby with another small group, gesturing at something out of the window.

The room was filled with a hubbub of conversation and Geoffrey had the strange feeling that the manor had come alive. This house had been dozing for decades but now it had woken from its slumbers and was happy.

Geoffrey looked around the busy ballroom and rolled his eyes at his own stupidity. Fancy ascribing feelings to a pile of bricks and mortar! He wasn't sure what was happening to him these days.

He felt sad to be leaving the manor. Of course he did. Anyone would. But, he realised, he also felt upset on the house's behalf, as if he were abandoning it and Brellasham Manor did not approve.

Geoffrey couldn't quite understand it. He'd long prided himself on being an unsentimental man, yet all kinds of emotions were now bubbling to the surface of his mind, like bleached bones rising from the depths of the ocean.

Most distressingly, he couldn't stop thinking about Audrey. He'd pushed down his memories of that tragic night and had fought his sorrow by focusing on the family talent for maintaining a stiff upper lip. *It's the Brellasham Way*, his father had told him in the days following Audrey's disappearance, ignoring Geoffrey's need for reassurance that he hadn't been to blame. That it wasn't his fault for not rushing to the cove to save his stepmother.

Then, a couple of weeks later, he'd packed his son back off to boarding school with a handshake and an instruction: *Best not to dwell on the past.* And they hadn't. His stepmother was rarely mentioned again.

At first, Geoffrey had blamed Clara's questions about Audrey for dredging up memories. But the truth was he'd never really stopped thinking about his stepmother, the woman he'd lost whom he should have saved, and the prospect of leaving the manor appeared to have opened the floodgates.

What he couldn't get out of his mind, in particular, was that when developers moved in, the third floor he'd long avoided would be opened up. And the thought of that was so unsettling, he'd been having nightmares about hordes of ghosts being unleashed. It was all very distressing and not the Brellasham Way at all.

Geoffrey tried to focus on the people in front of him to clear his mind of these thoughts that served no purpose. But his mind flew back to the night of the ball in 1957, when he'd been a child peeping through the door before bedtime.

The memory was so vivid, he could picture the ball as though it were happening right now: dozens of candles were casting flickering light into the corners of the room and reflecting off the glass chandeliers that hung from the ceiling. A small orchestra was playing on a raised dais at the end of the room, next to a table groaning with food, and people were whirling around the dance floor.

Audrey was dancing with a man he didn't recognise, her pretty yellow ballgown swirling around her ankles. While his father was in a corner, a cigar between his fingers, talking animatedly to some of the businessmen he'd invited. There was an atmosphere of anticipation and excitement; both Audrey and his father were alive, and his life was still full of possibilities.

Sadly, present-day reality was that his years were now far more limited and he would for ever be known as the Brellasham who sold this magnificent manor house and ended his days alone. If only River weren't going back to Australia.

Geoffrey felt a sudden visceral longing for the years that were behind him and the people long gone. If only he could rewind time and avoid the mistakes that had derailed him.

He would swallow his pride and run after the car taking his wife and son away and beg them to stay. Lucia might still have chosen to go, but at least River would have known how much he was wanted and loved.

Geoffrey sniffed and tightened his shoulders. Now wasn't the time to go harking back to the past, not when he was on show to so many people. Now was the time to smile and be grateful that the charity fete and open day was providing the house with a good send-off.

He glanced across the once-busy dance floor at his son, who looked handsome in his jeans and sweatshirt. And Clara, not far away, looked stunning today. She was wearing emerald green which shone iridescent in the light streaming through the window, and she'd swept her hair up into a bun which revealed her long neck.

As Geoffrey watched, River caught Clara's eye and, when he smiled at her, she gave him a sunny smile back. They were still close, even after all these years and thousands of miles of separation. He wished he could say the same about himself and River, but he'd blown that too.

Geoffrey glanced at his watch, feeling tired. He was of no use whatsoever and surely no one would notice if he took himself off to his bedroom – a room that was out of bounds to the people exploring the house. The youngsters were in charge now, and this house had stood before his birth and would stand long after he had left it behind. Geoffrey Brellasham was now redundant.

Disappointed with himself for being so self-pitying, he was

about to slip away when his attention was caught by a door opening at the far side of the ballroom.

A new guest had come in and Geoffrey's eyes narrowed as he looked her up and down.

The woman, far shorter than him, was using a walking stick, and there was a young man beside her. She was simply attired in a knee-length dress made of navy fabric, and she was old. Older than Geoffrey, with white hair piled into a bun and a silver necklace at her throat. A navy bag, that matched her dress, was hanging from her shoulder.

Geoffrey had no idea who the woman was and yet there was something familiar in the way she held herself. Perhaps she was someone he'd seen around Heaven's Cove. Another villager he hadn't bothered to speak to.

The woman caught his eye and began to walk slowly towards him, and suddenly, he was finding it hard to breathe.

It couldn't be. The person walking towards him was a ghost unleashed from the third floor, the woman he had watched walk into the sea almost seventy years ago.

Her face was lined and her steps hesitant, but there was no mistaking the shape of her mouth or the pale blue of her eyes.

'Hello, Geoffrey,' she said, on reaching him. 'Now that I'm here, I don't quite know what to say.'

'Is it you?' he croaked, his breath coming in short gasps. Out of the corner of his eye, he spotted River and Clara hurrying towards him.

'Yes, it's me.' When the woman took hold of his hand, her skin was warm. He couldn't understand what was happening but he knew that this was no ghost risen from a watery grave. 'I'm so sorry, my dear boy,' she said, tears in her eyes. 'I'm so sorry that I had to leave you.'

'Audrey,' he managed. Then his arms were around the woman he had mourned in silence for so long and he was pulling her towards him. Her head went onto his shoulder and he felt her body shake as she cried.

People were watching, curious about what was going on. But he didn't care. It was a miracle. Audrey, his stepmother, was alive and the guilt he had carried for decades was sliding away.

'Come with me.'

River's hand was on his arm, and Clara's on Audrey's, and they were being led downstairs into the library.

'We need this room,' River said to Lettie, the red-haired woman who ran the village's cultural centre. She'd volunteered to keep an eye on the ground-floor visitors. 'Can you make sure that everyone stays out?'

Lettie cast a curious eye over Audrey before nodding. 'Of course. That's no problem.'

Still led by his son, Geoffrey walked into the centre of the library and Audrey, led by Clara, did the same.

When Clara went and closed the door, the hubbub of people outside faded away as Geoffrey and Audrey stood looking at each other. Reunited after almost a lifetime apart.

34

GEOFFREY

'You'd better sit down here,' River urged, grabbing Geoffrey and pushing him into his favourite seat by the window.

'I'll get you a drink,' said Clara, taking the stopper out of the whisky decanter. 'You've had a shock.'

That was putting it mildly, thought Geoffrey, watching his long-lost stepmother walk around the library, leaning heavily on her stick, as if reacquainting herself with the room.

She stopped in front of the photograph of herself and stared at it. An old face gazing at the young. A ghost studying an imprint of the past.

Geoffrey tried to catch his breath as past and present smashed into each other. His brain couldn't take in that Audrey was here. He'd watched her walk into the sea. He'd banged on the window and screamed at her to stop. He'd seen his father and locals from the village search the cove in fishing boats and come back empty-handed.

'Why don't you sit here, Audrey?' said River, dragging a chair closer to Geoffrey's. 'Then the two of you can talk.'

'How do you know who she is? Did you know that Audrey was still alive?' asked Geoffrey, taking the large glass of whisky that Clara was proffering. He noticed her exchange a glance with his son before River knelt down beside him.

'Clara and I found out that Audrey had survived, but only a few days ago. Clara tracked her down and we went to see her.'

Geoffrey could hardly believe what he was hearing. First, Bartie had deceived him and now his own son was sneaking around behind his back. 'You should have told me,' he said gruffly.

'I'm sorry but—'

'It's my fault,' Audrey interrupted, waving away the glass of whisky Clara was offering. 'I made them promise not to tell you but now I can see that was wrong.'

'Yes, it was.' Geoffrey took a large swig of his whisky, its warmth offering some comfort as it slid past his throat. 'But I still don't understand.'

'I came across Audrey's diary from 1957,' Clara blurted out. 'It was in my grandmother's belongings. That's what she took from Audrey's bedroom on the night she disappeared, not the diamond necklace.'

'Why would she take a diary?'

'The diary contained a coded message, sent to Audrey by my grandmother, which told her where my grandfather would be waiting offshore for her in his rowing boat.'

'A boat, you say?'

Geoffrey took another large gulp of his drink as the pieces of the puzzle began to fall into place. So it had all been worked out between them. Audrey had planned to go and leave him behind.

He bit down hard on his lower lip, almost overwhelmed by the emotions boiling inside him. *You're not nine years old any more,* he told himself. *You mustn't cry. Stiff upper lip. It's the Brellasham Way.*

But he felt like a child again, here in the library, watching the stepmother he loved walking away from him, into the cold sea.

'Please don't be cross with River and Clara,' said Audrey, the soft lilt of her voice familiar even after all these years. 'I'm sure they didn't want to upset you by telling you the truth. And I made them promise not to tell.'

'Yet you're here now.'

Geoffrey knew his tone was harsh but he couldn't help it. Everything he thought was true had been turned on its head. It felt as if black was white and up was down. Nothing made sense any more.

A long-forgotten memory suddenly began spooling through his mind: Violet putting her arm around his nine-year-old self and telling him, 'Please don't be too sad about your stepmother. I'm sure she's in a better place.' And though he'd longed for comfort, he'd felt embarrassed to be embraced by the house-keeper. He'd thought her words were a platitude – the sort of thing the village vicar kept spouting. But it turned out she'd been trying to comfort him with the truth.

'Yes, Geoffrey, I'm here,' said Audrey, snapping his mind back to the present. Her hands were clasped in her lap and he noticed that they were shaking. 'I'm afraid my resolve not to interfere in your life has been stretched to breaking point over the years. And meeting Clara and your son was the final straw that made me want to see you above anything else. So that I can explain and apologise.'

'Who's the young man you arrived with?' asked Geoffrey, trying to deflect the conversation that he knew was coming.

Part of him wanted to know what had happened in 1957, but he felt scared. Something bad must have caused Audrey to risk her life by swimming to a boat that evening. Something bad that was pricking at the edges of his brain, like a memory that he'd locked away.

'That's Charlie, who works at the residential home in

Surrey where I'm seeing out my days. He's a very caring young man and he offered to bring me here when I told him my story... well, a version of my story.'

'And you decided to arrive during an open day when half the village are present.'

Geoffrey racked his brains. Had he seen Belinda this afternoon? If she was here, rumours about his mysterious visitor would be all round Heaven's Cove by the day's end.

'I know that arriving when we did wasn't ideal and I apologise for that too.' Audrey started fiddling with the buttons on the cuff of her sleeve. 'Charlie and I arrived in Heaven's Cove at lunchtime and are staying overnight at Driftwood House, up on the cliff. Rosie, the owner – you probably know her: a lovely woman, heavily pregnant – mentioned that she was coming here to the fete, not knowing my link to you and the manor.

'I didn't tell her anything about us, of course, but after she left, I couldn't wait any longer, knowing that you were so near. I was planning to try to see you this evening or tomorrow morning, but I persuaded Charlie to bring me here this afternoon instead.'

She raised her head and looked him directly in the eye. 'I'm so sorry, Geoffrey. This must all be very hard for you to take in.'

Do you think? Geoffrey drained his whisky and motioned for Clara to get him another.

He rarely drank before his evening meal and certainly never had two whiskies in the afternoon, but normal rules didn't apply today. That was obvious by the fact that his dead stepmother was sitting in front of him, telling him she was sorry.

After Clara had thrust another drink into his hands, River got to his feet. 'Would you like us to leave you both alone?'

Whisky slopped from Geoffrey's glass when he shook his head. He was devastated that River and Clara had kept such a huge secret from him, but the two of them provided a familiarity that was anchoring amidst the upset of the afternoon.

Audrey leaned forward. 'Please may I tell you what happened that September night?' When Geoffrey nodded, she continued. 'I didn't want to leave you behind, Geoffrey. You were so dear to me. But I needed to get away from your father and I knew that he would never let me go.

'Did you realise that he was having me watched and he forbade me from leaving the estate on my own? He even stopped me talking to the staff in the house, people like Violet, Clara's grandmother.'

Geoffrey swallowed. 'My father was a possessive man but no, I didn't realise that he was doing that.'

'Why did *you* think I'd left?'

'I wasn't sure.' He paused, unsure if he should say out loud what he'd always believed. But he was beyond keeping secrets. 'I thought we weren't enough for you. That *I* wasn't enough for you.'

'Oh, Geoffrey.' Audrey reached out and took hold of his hands. 'You were the reason I stayed for as long as I did. But everything came to a head after the ball. Your father became irrationally jealous about another man I'd danced with and he became—' She stopped speaking.

'He became what?'

He didn't want to know. Not for sure. But he had to hear it from her lips.

Audrey sat up straighter. 'He became seriously violent and threatening towards me and that was when I knew that I had to leave.'

'He wasn't a violent man,' said Geoffrey, feeling that he, as Edwin's son, should protect his father's reputation.

Audrey's smile was sad and sympathetic. 'Not towards you, and I was always grateful for that. But he was abusive towards me many times. And I know he was your father but that's the truth of why I left. You don't have to believe it.'

Geoffrey thought of his father and realised that he could

believe it. Edwin had never laid a hand on his son, but there was a simmering fury beneath the surface that had seen off many of his business rivals and silenced him as a child.

It was a source of great disappointment to Edwin that his son did not have the same talent for business dealings as him. But at least, thought Geoffrey, he had a more equitable temper and didn't have Edwin's repressed rage. He had made sure of that by smothering all of his emotions.

'You could have taken me with you,' he told Audrey quietly.

His stepmother's eyes glistened with tears. 'I thought about it. I truly did. But your father had parental rights to you which I didn't. And anyway, how could I take you away from everything you had here? My escape was dangerous and I wasn't sure where I was going. I planned to wait until I was settled somewhere and then write to you, to let you know that I was all right. But then...'

She looked out of the window, across the gardens and the trees to the sea which sparkled under a blue sky.

'But then people thought you were dead and it was easier to keep it that way,' said Geoffrey dully.

Audrey nodded. 'I realised that Edwin would never come looking for me if he thought I'd drowned that night.'

'But I saw you,' said Geoffrey plaintively, now more nine years old than seventy-six. 'Did you know that I saw you walking into the water?'

'No, not at the time. I wasn't sure if Edwin assumed I'd walked into the sea or if someone had seen me doing so. But I never thought for one minute that it would be you. I timed my escape so that you and your father would be eating in the dining room, on the other side of the house.'

'I wasn't well and wasn't hungry.'

'I know that now. Your son and Clara told me. I'm so sorry, Geoffrey. I've thought of you constantly over the years and have often longed to be in touch.'

'You could have contacted me after my father died.'

Geoffrey's voice still sounded plaintive, pleading even, but he didn't care.

'Perhaps I should have, but you were an adult by then and I thought you were better off without me. I was afraid that you wouldn't want to know me. And I was afraid because...' – she stopped and swallowed – 'I was afraid because I'm a thief.'

Geoffrey stared at her. 'What do you mean?'

'When I left, I took something with me, to fund my new life. I figured I was owed it because I would never have a proper divorce settlement. But then I realised that what I'd done could be viewed as theft.'

'What did you take?' Geoffrey asked, although he knew.

Audrey pushed her hand into the navy handbag still slung over her shoulder.

'This,' she said, thrusting out her hand. A muddle of gold and glinting diamonds nestled in the palm of her hand.

There was an audible gasp from the corner of the room and Clara stepped forward, out of the shadows.

'Is that the necklace that you told me fell off into the sea?'

'Yes. I'm sorry that I lied to you, Clara. But it was just one of many lies I've told over the decades as I became a different person to escape my past. At first I was frightened to sell the diamonds, in case they led Edwin to me, and then I felt too guilty to let them go because they weren't truly mine to part with.'

She turned back to Geoffrey, whose eyes hadn't left the sparkling jewels. 'Here,' she said, thrusting them into his hand. 'They're yours. They've always been yours.'

Geoffrey brushed his fingers across the diamonds that glinted like ice. The necklace was heavy in his palm.

'I've said what I came here to say and have done what I needed to do,' said Audrey, slowly pushing herself to her feet.

'But I have one final thing to ask. Have you had a good life, Geoffrey?'

The question took him by surprise and he paused. How could he sum up his whole life? Audrey waited, her eyes pleading with him to say yes.

Geoffrey nodded. 'I have. My father was distant but he provided well for me. I married late and had River but my wife and I divorced. She was much younger than me.'

He could see it clearly now: he'd been following in his father's footsteps. Young woman, older man. And although he'd never laid a finger on his wife in anger or prevented her from living her own life, he'd been cold, just as his father had been.

If only he could step through time and change the kind of man he was back then. Perhaps he wouldn't be the kind of man he was now.

'Anyway.' He cleared his throat. 'Since then, I've lived a comfortable life here at Brellasham Manor. Though I'll soon be leaving.'

'So I heard,' said Audrey, leaning on her walking stick. 'Which was another reason for seeing you and returning the necklace. I gave you nothing useful as a child, Geoffrey, but perhaps the diamonds will be useful now. Goodbye, my boy. Please take care of yourself.'

She turned and began walking slowly towards the door.

'Will I see you again?' Geoffrey asked.

She turned back and smiled. 'I do hope so, but that's entirely your decision to make.'

River and Clara went out into the hall with Audrey and the door banged shut behind them. Geoffrey was alone. He stared out of the window, hardly registering the children running towards the cove who were trampling over his prized petunias.

There was so much for him to process. So many assumptions to rewrite in his head. But all he could think about was Audrey being wrong when she'd said that she'd given him nothing as a child. In fact she'd given him so much that was precious: comfort, support and love. Which was why her disappearance had hurt so much. But he could understand why she'd had to flee.

Geoffrey looked down at the diamonds nestling in his palm. Today had focused on the past. But tomorrow, knowing what he knew now, perhaps he could focus on the future.

35

RIVER

The sun had only recently peeped above the horizon and the pearly sky was a vibrant palette of pinks, yellow and gold.

River had seen many wonderful sunrises in Australia but this one, over the Devon coast, seemed more beautiful, and more fragile. As if it might shatter into a million shards of light.

He walked quietly through the trees that lay between the manor house and the sea, until he reached the cove. But he came to an abrupt halt when he realised that he wasn't the only one up early after yesterday's fete and unexpected visitor.

His father was sitting on a jacket that he'd spread across the sand. Staring out to sea, he cut a lonely figure lit by the rays of the rising sun.

River's immediate reaction was to turn tail and creep away. Geoffrey might not want company, particularly the company of his son. He hadn't wanted to talk to him after Audrey's departure and had spent the rest of the day shut away in his bedroom.

But there was something about him there on the cool sand that drew River towards him. Perhaps it was the slump of his shoulders and the tilt of his head. Or perhaps it was the fact that their time together was coming to an end that propelled River across the cove.

Geoffrey glanced up when his son reached him. 'You're out and about early, River.'

'I could say the same of you.' River hesitated for a second and then sat down beside him. 'Couldn't sleep either, huh?'

Geoffrey gave a half-smile. 'My mind was busy with the goings-on of yesterday. A ghost rising from the grave does interfere somewhat with one's sleep pattern.'

'Tell me about it,' said River, although his sleep had been interrupted more by thoughts of Clara than Audrey. The warmth of her hand in his as they walked through Dorking. The way she wrinkled her nose when she laughed.

He turned his face to the sun, a blazing ball of energy in the dawn sky. 'I'm sorry that you found out about Audrey that way. Clara and I didn't like keeping it from you but we weren't sure what to do for the best, and Audrey was adamant that it should stay a secret. I think she was trying to protect you, in her own way.'

Geoffrey breathed out slowly. 'It was a huge shock, of course. But the more I think about it, the more I can understand her reasoning. I can understand a lot, actually.' His snort of laughter took River by surprise. 'Do you know what the funny thing is in all of this? It struck me in the middle of the night that my father went on to marry again, twice – which means he was a bigamist.'

River blinked. 'Is that funny?'

'Oh yes. If you knew how proper he was. How much of a stickler for keeping up appearances. He would have been horrified at the thought that he, Edwin Brellasham, was a bigamist.'

'A double bigamist, actually.'

The corner of Geoffrey's mouth turned upwards. 'Quite.'

The two men sat for a while in what felt like companionable silence until River asked: 'Would you like to see Audrey again?'

Geoffrey continued gazing out to sea as he replied: 'Yes, I would. I'd like to know more about her life after leaving this place. Where did she live? Does she have children?'

'She told us that she'd lived in Ireland for a long time and has no family, but that's all I know.' River hesitated before asking: 'Did what she told you about her life at the manor with your father come as a complete surprise?'

His father was likely to snap and tell him to mind his own business. But Geoffrey answered calmly, as seagulls screeched and wheeled in the pale morning light.

'I knew nothing about the physical abuse. At least I don't think I did. So many memories from that time are incomplete or indistinct. But I do remember hearing him shouting at her over nothing and hearing her sob. He was a possessive, probably quite insecure, man who demanded absolute loyalty on his own terms. It must have been difficult for Audrey, who was such a vibrant young woman and so full of life. She must have felt like a bird in a gilded cage.'

'So she left and took the diamonds with her.'

Geoffrey nodded. 'Ah, yes, the diamonds. Quite apart from their financial value, they meant a great deal to my father because they linked his family with the monarchy and he always was quite the snob. I rather think he missed the diamonds as much as he did Audrey.'

'And now they're back, too.'

'Yes, but not for long. I've decided to sell them. They should fetch a tidy sum.'

'Really? I didn't think you'd want to sell them,' said River, before realising that his father was not the kind of man to hold a sentimental attachment to a piece of jewellery.

'I think it's for the best though, of course, they belong to you too, in a way. I suppose they're a family heirloom.' Geoffrey shifted on the sand until he was facing his son. 'Would you *mind* if I sold them?'

'Not at all. We didn't know they still existed until yesterday and, with their links to royalty, those diamonds must be worth a small fortune. Selling them will provide enough capital to keep the manor going for some time, I imagine.'

'Not for long enough, I dare say, once repairs have been made and bills paid. But I'm hoping they'll buy me another couple of years or so in my home.' He glanced over his shoulder at the manor that was just visible through the trees. 'And after that, I'll sell Brellasham Manor to Hannah, or whoever wants it, to do with as they wish, and you'll receive a nest egg from the sale.'

'I don't want your money. That's not important to me.'

Geoffrey caught his eye and smiled. 'No, I thought as much. You and your cousin have a very different attitude to financial gain.'

Did he know the truth now about Bartie's deception? Geoffrey didn't elaborate. He grabbed a handful of sand and let the grains trickle slowly through his fingers.

Then he said: 'I do understand, you know, why you don't want to take on the manor after I get too old to run it. I've rather messed up the income stream that was keeping it afloat, with my poor business decisions recently. My father must be turning in his grave.'

River swallowed, aware that now was the time to say what he'd wanted to say since he was a child. He clenched his hands into fists on the sand and blurted it out.

'I'm sorry I haven't been the son that *you* wanted. I know I've always been a great disappointment to you and you'd rather that Bartie was your son and heir.'

Geoffrey's jaw dropped at this sudden onslaught. 'Bartie?' he said with a frown. 'Bartie, who lies to my face and was pushing me to sell to Hannah so that he could clean up with the commission?'

'So you *do* know about that. Clara and I thought you believed him when he told you he'd only just found out about Hannah's plans for the grounds.'

Geoffrey gave a snort of derision. 'I'm not completely gaga, River. Yes, I was taken in by him at first, with his offers of help. I got rather swept off my feet and surrendered control of the situation to him. But his crisis of conscience after discovering Hannah's dastardly scheme? Please give me some credit! He'd presumably been found out – by you and Clara. I'm only sorry I didn't listen when you tried to tell me.'

'It was Clara who found him out.'

Geoffrey smiled. 'That doesn't surprise me. That girl has always been a force of nature.' His smile faded. 'I'm fond of Bartie. He's family and I've known him since he was born. I've watched him grow up and I saw him occasionally when you were far away. But no, I've never wished that Bartie was my son and heir, not even before I realised how amoral and disloyal he could be. In fact, I...' He faltered and tried again. 'I...'

He gave up and stared out to sea for a moment. Then, he turned again. 'I have something I have to tell you, River, and it won't be easy for me to say it.'

'You don't have to tell me anything you don't want to,' River assured him, alarmed by the pain on his father's face.

'I do want to tell you because you'll soon go back to Australia and that will be it.' He swallowed. 'The truth is that I'm not disappointed in you, dear boy. I'm disappointed in me. As a father.'

He wiped a hand across his eyes. 'Rather disgracefully, I've turned out to be the same kind of parent to you as my father was to me.'

When River went to speak, he held up his hand. 'Let me get this out because I'm not sure I'll be able to say it again.'

He pulled in a lungful of sea air and continued. 'The truth is I missed you when you left for Australia all those years ago, but I was glad you'd gone. Not because I don't care about you, but because I do.

'The reason I kept in touch and saw you only very occasionally was because I told myself you'd fare better away from me – you were better off starting a new life with your mother, who knew how to love you. I hoped that it would break the cycle and, one day, you could become the father that I had never been to you.'

He cleared his throat. 'That's all true, that I wanted the best for you. But what's also true is that another reason why I didn't fight for you when your mother took you away was because I couldn't bear washing our dirty laundry in public, via courts and lawyers. It pains me to admit it but I thought more about the Brellasham family's reputation than about how you would feel when I just let you go like that.

'I know you think I'm a cold, unemotional man, River, and there are echoes of my father in me that are hard to ignore. But I very much regret the lack of closeness between us and not seeing more of you since you went away. I stepped back from your life and let your mother take you to the other side of the world. I can only hope that you've been happy there.'

'I have been. Mostly,' said River, stunned by the words streaming from his father's mouth. 'But I missed you.'

'Did you?' Geoffrey sounded genuinely surprised. 'I assumed you were pleased to be shot of me. You hardly ever wrote or rang.'

'I thought you'd more or less abandoned me and didn't care if I got in touch or not.'

'Oh, I cared,' said Geoffrey softly, a wistfulness in his voice that broke River's heart. 'But when we did meet up in Australia, I didn't know what to say to you.'

'Me neither. I reckoned you were fine without me, and I

knew that Bartie was still around to be the son I thought you wanted.'

Geoffrey raised an eyebrow. 'Bartie virtually disappeared after you took off. I've hardly seen him from year to year, until he heard that I was thinking of selling this place.'

'So, not a brilliant son substitute then?'

'A very poor one, I'd say.'

The two men smiled at each other as the rising sun turned the sea to shimmering gold. Then, they sat in silence while the sun climbed higher and the pink sky at the horizon faded into the palest of blues.

'When will you return to Australia?' asked Geoffrey after a while.

'Soon, I suppose, especially now you're going to sell the diamonds and you don't need to sell this place, not for a while anyway. I'll get a flight booked.'

'Right.' Geoffrey folded his hands in his lap. 'I hope you'll come to see me again before too long. Or maybe, if you don't mind, I could make more regular visits to see you in Australia? Make up for lost time. That kind of thing.'

River grinned, as the rising sun's rays warmed his skin. 'Yeah. I'd like that. I'd like that a lot, Dad.'

There was no outward sign that Geoffrey had noticed that River had called him 'Dad', except for the tear that trickled down his cheek.

36

CLARA

Her mother was not happy. In fact, Clara would go so far as to say that Julie Netherway was furious.

'You did what?' she demanded, even though Clara had explained it all very carefully.

Clara placed the tulips she was carrying on the ground, next to her grandmother's gravestone, and straightened up. Talking to her mother in public and in broad daylight so she wouldn't freak out didn't appear to be working.

'I told you, Mum. I fished Audrey Brellasham's diary out of the bin while you were in bed, which I know I shouldn't have done. Some of the things she'd written were in code but I managed to crack it and work out what she'd said.'

Julie stooped down and began to clear Violet Netherway's grave in what could only be described as an aggressive manner. Weeds that had dared to encroach on the area were yanked from the earth with force and thrown to one side.

'Why would you do that?' she asked, tearing out a dandelion. 'No, don't tell me. I suppose Audrey was speaking to you from some other dimension and saying her voice had to be heard? You losing your mind is the only possible explanation as to why you would go against my explicit instructions and do something that would horrify tragically bereaved Mr Brellasham while also dragging your hideously maligned grandmother back into the spotlight. Poor Audrey Brellasham is dead, Clara. Can't you let her rest in peace?'

'The thing is, Mum' – Clara swallowed – 'it turns out that Audrey Brellasham isn't dead after all.'

Julie stopped, her fingers wrapped around another unsuspecting weed, and looked up.

'What are you gabbling on about? Of course she's dead.' She released the weed and got to her feet, her face suddenly creased with concern. 'I understand that life's very stressful for you at the moment, what with the manor being sold and River heading back to Australia soon. It's a tough time. But I'm getting worried about you, Clara.' She put an earthy hand on her daughter's shoulder. 'Do you think talking to Dr Kellaway might help?'

'I don't need to see a doctor, Mum. I'm fine, and what I told you about Audrey is true. She needed to escape from the manor because her husband was abusing her, so she waded into the sea and swam to a boat that was waiting for her. She's been living in Ireland, mostly, but now she's back in England and settled in a care home in Surrey.'

Julie huffed, scepticism written across her face, but then her eyes narrowed and she moved her hand from Clara's shoulder.

'I hardly knew Edwin. He was unwell and bedbound for many years and I had little to do with him. But actually, I did hear things about him from my mother. Not much. Just a criticism here and a hint there but, you know your gran, she never usually had a bad word to say about anyone.'

'Gran knew all about Edwin's abuse, and she was one of the people who helped Audrey to escape. Grandad was the person rowing the boat that carried her to her new life.'

'Your grandad?' squeaked Julie.

Her mouth had fallen open but no sound was coming out so

Clara carried on while she could. 'Gran sent Audrey a coded message to tell her where the boat would be and that message was in the back of the diary. That's why Gran stole it from Audrey's bedroom.'

'Your grandmother wasn't a thief!'

'OK,' said Clara gently. 'Let's say that she liberated the diary before Edwin or the police got to it.'

'So that she could retrieve this message that you claim she sent.'

'Exactly, and maybe she also didn't want Edwin reading Audrey's innermost thoughts.'

'Then why didn't she burn the diary?' asked Julie. 'Why did she keep it for decades?'

'She must have been very fond of Audrey to help her escape. Perhaps the diary was a keepsake or maybe it was insurance, in case Edwin realised that his wife wasn't dead and made a fuss about her taking the diamond necklace with her. The diary notes some of the occasions when Edwin hurt her. It might have been useful to Audrey if Edwin ever found her and got legally nasty.'

Julie walked to the wooden bench that was pushed up against the churchyard wall and sat down heavily. 'Well, I never. Mum didn't tell me any of this. Dad, neither, though he died when I was quite young.'

Clara joined her on the bench. 'They didn't tell the police either, not even when Gran was accused of theft. They were determined to keep Audrey's secret from everyone and, as the years went by, Gran must have put the whole thing behind her.'

Julie sat up straight. 'Does Geoffrey know?'

'He does now because Audrey came to see him on Saturday afternoon, during the fete.'

'I *knew* there was something funny going on! Belinda nabbed me this morning in the village and was babbling on about some mystery woman who'd turned up and was acting peculiarly. I'd seen nothing out of the ordinary, having spent most of the fete in the kitchen, making teas. So I thought Belinda was inventing gossip, as usual, but she was insistent.'

'She was right.'

'Poor Geoffrey. He must have been overwhelmed.'

'He was, but I think...' Clara crossed her fingers behind her back. 'I really *hope* that finding out the truth will be the best for him, in the long run.'

'Audrey Brellasham, alive and well.' Julie whistled through her teeth. 'I can't believe it.'

'It's hard to take in, isn't it? River and I found it hard to get our heads around it too.'

'Have you been working with River on all of this?'

'Most of it, yes. We've done quite a lot together.'

Including going up to the locked third floor and exploring the ghost rooms. Clara decided that was information her mother really didn't need to know.

Instead, she said: 'The good thing is, Mum, that Audrey has returned the diamond necklace that she took with her.'

'I can't believe she still has it.'

'I think she was scared that selling such a distinctive necklace would alert Edwin that she was still alive, and she didn't feel that it belonged to her anyway.'

'It didn't,' said Julie fiercely. 'It belongs to the Brellasham family.' Her voice softened. 'Though I can understand why she took it after being abused by her husband. He doesn't sound like the sort of man who would have agreed to a divorce settlement.'

'Definitely not.'

'So the necklace is back where it belongs.' Julie stood up and, after walking to Violet's grave, laid her hand gently on the headstone. 'You're completely exonerated, Mum. You never stole those diamonds and now there's proof of it. You helped Audrey to escape and kept her secret until the day you died,

even after Dad had passed away. You were an amazing woman
and I miss you so much.'

Tears sprang into Clara's eyes as she remembered her lovely
grandmother who would do anything for anybody who needed
help. Her kind heart had been larger than any of them had ever
realised.

'Don't upset yourself, Clara.' Julie sat down next to her and
patted her knee. 'What's to become of us, I wonder? Jobless and
homeless. It won't be easy getting another job at my age and
there's not much call for housekeepers.'

'It'll be OK. I'll find us a new place to live and, if I can't get
enough freelance work, I can get a permanent job somewhere.
Whatever happens, you won't have to go through this on your
own, Mum.'

Julie looked into her daughter's eyes and smiled. 'No, I don't
suppose I will. I'm glad you're here and I know you probably
don't believe it but I do appreciate the sacrifice you made in
coming back home to look after your dad, and me. It can't have
been easy.'

Clara blinked at her mother's unexpected words, waiting
for the 'but'. When it didn't come, she patted her mum's arm. It
hadn't been easy giving up her whole life, yet all she said was,
'I'm glad I'm here too.'

Her mother sniffed before saying briskly, 'But Michael
would never have been so nosy, reading that old diary and stirring all of this up.'

And normal service was resumed. Clara allowed herself a
discreet eye roll.

'We'd better get back to the manor.' Julie stood up and
brushed her hands together to dislodge the soil still on her skin.
'Geoffrey needs tea and cake at four on the dot or his blood
sugar levels dip and he gets grumpy. I shall miss Geoffrey and
his curmudgeonly ways.'

'Curmudgeonly? You won't normally hear a word against perfect Geoffrey.'

'Actually, he can be a total pain but he's been my total pain for a long time, and I will definitely miss him.'

'Me too,' Clara admitted with a smile, bending down to pick up the carrier bag that held the trowel her mother had ignored in favour of her hands. 'I've grown quite fond of him recently.'

'I expect you'll miss River too.'

Clara shrugged, even though the prospect of River leaving was occupying her thoughts more and more.

'I suppose I will, a bit. But he'll be off soon without giving me a backward glance. He won't miss me. I'm just someone he used to know.'

'Are you sure about that?' asked Julie, nodding towards the churchyard gate.

Clara followed her mother's gaze and caught her breath when she saw River standing there.

'He's waiting for you,' said Julie.

'I'm not sure—'

'He's here for you, Clara,' her mother insisted, taking the carrier bag from her. 'Now don't keep him waiting.'

37

CLARA

Geoffrey was going to sell the fabulous lost diamonds that Audrey had dropped into his palm yesterday afternoon. Clara could hardly believe her ears. She'd assumed that the necklace would go into a safe somewhere and never be seen again. But she hadn't banked on Geoffrey's practicality and lack of sentimentality.

'How much do you think they're worth?' she asked, dipping her toes into the stream that cut through the manor grounds.

River had suggested they come here, and now the two of them were sitting on its banks, hidden from the manor by willow trees whose branches trailed in the fast-flowing water.

'We're not sure yet. I'm arranging to have them properly valued.'

'The necklace is stunning and if the story of Queen Victoria giving it as a gift to the Brellashams is true, it could be worth a small fortune.'

'I suspect the necklace will fetch a fair bit – enough for my father to get repairs done and live on at the manor for another couple of years or so. Sadly, it's not a long-term answer to his dilemma.'

'Maybe not, but your dad will love having more time here, and we'll have more time to come up with a better option than selling this place.'

'If there is one.'

'Yeah, if there is one,' Clara agreed, picturing the joy on her mother's face when she was told that her home and job were safe for a while longer, thanks to the diamonds.

River swished his feet in the cool, clear stream and winced when water splashed up Clara's leg. 'Sorry.'

Clara laughed. 'You're forgiven. What did your dad say about Audrey? I felt so sorry for him, being taken by surprise like that. He must have felt as if he'd stepped into some alternate universe.'

'I was worried he was about to keel over when she walked towards him across the ballroom, like a ghost.'

'Me too. I thought he took it remarkably well, considering. Has he forgiven us for keeping Audrey's miraculous resurrection a secret?'

'I think so. Maybe we should have told him about her from the start, but we'd promised Audrey.'

'We were in a very difficult position,' Clara agreed, 'and we weren't to know that she'd turn up out of the blue like that.' She batted away a fly that was buzzing round her face. Clouds had covered the sun and the weather had turned hot and muggy. 'Do you think your dad will see her again?'

'I don't know. Maybe, once he's got over the shock of it.'

Clara turned her face to River. 'I hope he will. It must have taken a lot of courage for Audrey to step inside the manor again, after all that went on in the house and the memories it must hold for her.'

'Mmm,' said River, sounding distracted. He swished his feet back and forth in the stream.

'What is it?' Clara asked. 'It sounds as though things are going pretty well, in the circumstances.'

Once, she would have nudged her arm against his, in a show of friendly solidarity, but today she kept her distance.

Years ago, they'd shared their first and only kiss in this very place. That had been quite a moment. The kiss was fumbling and awkward and lovely – and Clara had wondered at the time if she might actually be in proper love with him. However, she'd decided that she was mistaken and, actually, she hated him after he'd left Heaven's Cove and cut off all contact – adolescent feelings being so black and white.

Time plus maturity meant that hatred had faded to indifference by the time River returned but now... The closer River got to going back to Australia, the more she wanted him to stay.

But soon he would be gone again and she had to protect her heart – especially in this special place that held so much meaning for her. River had obviously forgotten the kiss completely or he'd never have brought her back here.

River cleared his throat. 'My father told me this morning that he loved me. Well, not exactly,' he added, seeing Clara's jaw drop. 'I've always thought he was disappointed in me, but he said that wasn't true and he was only disappointed in himself for not being a good parent.'

'Wow.' Clara sat quietly for a moment, letting the enormity of Geoffrey's words sink in. 'It sounds like your dad is finally getting in touch with his feelings.'

'Maybe.' River gave a wry grin. 'Better late than never, I suppose.'

'Definitely.'

It was sad that it was so late. Clara knew how much it would have boosted River's confidence as a teenager to hear those words from his father. But at least what he needed to hear had finally been said.

'He also said that he wouldn't rather have Bartie as his son and heir than me.'

'Of course he wouldn't.' Clara looked into River's eyes. 'Is that what you think? That your dad prefers Bartie to you?'

'It's what I've always thought.'

'Yet you never told me. I thought you told me everything, but you never told me that.'

River held her gaze. 'I knew how much you liked Bartie, even back when we were kids. He was bold and brash and exciting, and I suppose I was afraid that if I said he'd make a better son and heir than me, you'd agree.'

'I would never have agreed with that.'

'I should have trusted you and confided how I was feeling.' He thought for a moment and then, staring at the water tumbling past, asked: 'Are you terribly upset about Bartie?'

'What, that bold, brash, exciting Bartie turned out to be a bit of a rat? I'm glad that I know the truth about him.'

'I am sorry he upset you, though.'

Clara felt a rush of warmth towards the kind, gentle man sitting beside her. 'You are, aren't you? Even though I completely ignored your warning about him and let myself be taken in.'

'My father was taken in too, for a while.'

'But you never were. Not really.'

'Only because I was screamingly jealous of him when we were kids and it rather coloured my view of him.' River wrinkled his nose.

'You really didn't need to be jealous.' This time, Clara allowed her arm to nudge against his.

'Of course I did,' snorted River. 'I was a geek at fifteen, with spots and an inferiority complex, and he was this eighteen-year-old Greek god.'

'Granted, you were a bit geeky at fifteen. But I wasn't exactly a stunning extrovert. Do you remember my terrible plaits and how I used to blush all the time? But we've both grown up and improved. Well, I *hope* I've improved, apart from the blushing, that is. You've turned into this bronzed Australian Adonis who threatens to fight dragons to protect damsels in distress.'

She grinned, but this time River didn't smile back. He swallowed, his breathing ragged.

'You've grown into a beautiful, brilliant, feisty woman. But I always thought you were perfect, Clo.'

As he leaned towards her, Clara's eyes opened wide. Was he going to kiss her? She realised that she really hoped so. She wanted nothing more than to feel his arms around her, and yet...

When she moved her head away, River immediately drew back.

'Sorry,' he said. 'I thought...' He rubbed a hand across his face.

'You thought what? That we'd have a kiss and then you'd fly off to Australia and I'd never hear from you again?'

Clara pushed herself to her feet, slipped her wet feet into her sandals and wiped grass from the backs of her thighs. Her heart was hammering as she started walking away. How had she let this happen again?

'Hey, Clara!' River moved past and stood in front of her. 'Stop.'

'No.'

Clara went around him but he walked past her and blocked the path again.

'Please stop and talk to me. This isn't about what happened here sixteen years ago. We can both move on from that.'

So he did remember their first kiss. Clara took a shuddering breath. 'Can we move on? You kissed me and left for Australia the next day, and that was that. All I got was a postcard that said: *Probably best not to keep in touch now I've moved on. I really hope you have a good life. R.*'

'Oh God.' River closed his eyes briefly. 'Did I really send you such an idiotic, thoughtless goodbye?'

'Yes, you did.'

'It was so bad, you memorised it.'

'It's not the kind of message you're likely to forget,' said Clara, wanting to cry.

She still remembered her excitement when the Sydney postcard plopped onto the doormat of their cottage. He'd written, at last! Followed by a searing sense of loss, disappointment and grief as she'd read his words.

River ran a hand across his jaw. 'I really was an arse back then, wasn't I?'

Clara nodded, staring at her feet rather than look him in the eye.

'You kissed me and then left for the other side of the world, and you cut off all contact. How do you think that made me feel?'

'Horrible?'

'Yes, really horrible.' She lifted her head and glared at him. 'For ages I thought the kiss was *so bad*, *so wrong*, you didn't want anything more to do with me. I didn't kiss anyone else for ages. I had a total complex about it.'

River ran a hand through his hair in exasperation. 'But you didn't come to say goodbye the next morning when Mum was dragging me off to Australia. I thought you were furious with me for kissing you.'

'I didn't know you were leaving.'

'I sent you a text when my mum told me what she'd planned and said we'd be going at eight o'clock, but you weren't there.'

'I didn't receive any text. This place was like a black hole back then for a phone signal. The first I knew about you leaving was when my mum told me that you and your mum had gone for good.'

River's shoulders slumped. 'The truth is, our first kiss was amazing, Clo. It was everything I'd dreamed of. But when you didn't bother coming to say goodbye, I thought you didn't really want me. You'd never really wanted me because it was Bartie you were keen on.'

'I thought Bartie was cool but I wouldn't have kissed you if it was him I *really* wanted,' said Clara crossly, although she wasn't cross with River.

She was cross with stupid patchy phone signals and hasty assumptions that had pushed the two of them apart. She was filled with sadness about the time they'd lost.

River shook his head. 'I assumed you only went along with the kiss because you felt sorry for me, because you knew what life was like for me at home. The parental arguments. My dad being distant. I told you almost everything, except how I really felt about you.'

'You assumed a lot,' said Clara as River's final words hit home: *how I really felt about you.*

'I was so far away,' River continued, 'and I wanted you to be happy, so I was clearing a path for you to be with Bartie, as I saw it.' He shrugged. 'Though it wasn't all about me being self-sacrificing. The truth was I was heartbroken to be thousands of miles from you and I thought a clean break was the only way to stay sane. Why torture myself by staying in contact and hearing all about your boyfriends, when I felt I was never going to see you again?'

'Boyfriends, now, is it? Not just Bartie?'

'Of course, boyfriends plural. You were amazing, Clo. You *are* amazing, and I knew that any man would be honoured to be your boyfriend.'

'You'd be surprised,' murmured Clara, still trying to take in what River was saying as he stood, barefoot, his hair lit by sunlight dappling through the trees. He was still the boy she'd loved, and now he was the man who made her heart beat faster whenever she saw him.

'Anyway, that postcard I sent was completely out of order and I totally understand why me trying to kiss you just now freaked you out. I mean, in many ways we're strangers, and I live a long way away and—'

'Oh, for goodness' sake, shut up!' said Clara, flinging her arms around his neck. 'If you're not going to be an arse about it this time, just kiss me, will you?'

River looked down at her, the surprise on his face quickly replaced with amusement.

'Well, seeing as you asked me so nicely.'

His arms snaked around her waist and pulled her closer to him. And then he bent his head and kissed her, and this time it wasn't tentative or awkward. It was passionate and practised and loving. This kiss was just right.

EPILOGUE
AUDREY, SIX MONTHS LATER

Audrey sat at the library window with a cosy throw across her legs and smiled at the efforts going on in the garden.

Geoffrey had insisted that an extra fir was needed, although the manor already had a huge Christmas tree in the hallway. Julie had spent ages decorating it and it twinkled a welcome whenever anyone came into the house.

Yet Geoffrey was adamant that the drawing room needed additional festive pizzazz, hence the humongous tree that was currently being dragged through the snow towards the kitchen door.

'Pivot!' he yelled as they negotiated the gap in the wall that enclosed the herb garden. 'Now!'

Sadly, pivoting proved useless because the tree clipped the wall, River dropped the thick trunk he was holding and fell backwards into a snowdrift.

When Clara immediately doubled up with the giggles, Audrey couldn't help chuckling too. There was so much laughter at Brellasham Manor these days, and the sound of it had chased away any ghosts that remained of the past.

River pulled a screaming Clara into the snowdrift and they embraced, their breath frosty in the cold air.

'Come on. No slacking on the job!' called Geoffrey. He clapped his gloved hands together, startling a robin which had flown down to perch on the fallen tree. 'You'll be glad when the drawing room is looking marvellous.'

Audrey could still glimpse the serious little boy in Geoffrey, and he bore traces of Edwin that sometimes took her by surprise: a judging glance here, a barked order there.

But, overall, Geoffrey was far less like his father than he imagined himself to be. He was more open about his feelings – although that was a work in progress, according to those who knew him well. He was more gentle, and he was also more openly affectionate with his son. In fact, the more time father and son spent together, the better they seemed to get on.

Audrey watched as Geoffrey reached out his hand to pull River from the snowdrift. She had seen a change in her former stepson over the last few months, during her visits to this house. He seemed less rigid and brittle than the man she had first got to know.

As for River, his talk of returning to Australia had all but dried up and, seeing the way he looked at Clara, Audrey doubted that he would ever go back. Not for good, anyway.

Geoffrey had confided in her that he hoped his son might stay and take on the house when his time here was done, especially now it was in a much better state of repair thanks to the sale of the diamond necklace. And Audrey thought that he very well might.

Like her, River had fled Brellasham Manor, sure that he would never return. But here they both were, about to enjoy a family Christmas within its walls. It was strange how life turned out, thought Audrey, wrapping the throw more tightly around her legs.

What would Edwin think of it all? she wondered. Then, she

shivered and turned her attention back to the garden. It didn't matter what Edwin would think because he was no longer here to give his opinion. He was gone and the fear that he'd stoked in her had disappeared.

'Hey, Audrey!' Clara shouted, waving at her through the window. 'Did you see River take a tumble?'

Audrey nodded and waved back at the wonderful young woman whose drive and enthusiasm were behind the manor's new lease of life.

It had been her suggestion to build a children's play area in the grounds for the youngsters of Heaven's Cove, and also to provide new meeting facilities for organisations in and around the village. Hosting local weddings was another of her brainwaves that she was currently pursuing.

Geoffrey had been reluctant at first but he'd gradually come around to Clara's assertion that the manor should play a bigger role in the future of Heaven's Cove.

'You should pass on your privilege,' she'd told him, shutting down his protest that trying to stop a massive, grand old house from falling down was actually quite a hardship. 'Tell that to Claude, who lives in a two-up, two-down with dodgy electrics,' had done the trick.

So, from next month, local groups could book the manor's old boot room, apple store and scullery which had been converted into meeting rooms, and the play area would open in the spring. Audrey often saw children with their faces pressed to the manor gates, watching excitedly as their new swings, slides and climbing frames were erected.

Tourist visits to the manor were also climbing after she and River had persuaded Geoffrey to let people enjoy the house that he and his family had kept to themselves for generations.

Poor Geoffrey. Audrey chuckled. The 'squire' was being dragged into the twenty-first century whether he liked it or not. Though on balance, she thought that he rather approved.

Audrey got slowly to her feet, folded the throw across the back of the chair and tucked her book under her arm. She was re-reading *Rebecca* and would take it up to her bedroom so she could continue with it when she woke tomorrow with the dawn.

It was funny. She hadn't read the book for decades, not since she'd fled this house in 1957. But Clara had given her back her old copy and she was remembering why she'd once loved the book so much.

'Are you all right, Audrey?' asked Julie as the old woman walked slowly through the hallway.

'I'm very well, thank you,' Audrey replied, alarmed to see that Julie was adding yet more ornaments to the Christmas tree which was already festooned.

'Will you be going to the Christmas fair on the village green?' Julie enquired, concentrating on fixing a glass snowflake to an inch of bare branch. 'Everyone will be very pleased to see you.'

'Possibly,' said Audrey, gripping the bannister and beginning to climb the stairs. She'd become very popular in Heaven's Cove once the locals had realised who she was. Word had spread, and her story was proving quite a draw. She'd even been featured in a national publication, in an article that signposted various support groups and helpful information now available to people experiencing domestic abuse. That had pleased her.

She'd thought that Geoffrey would baulk at Edwin being shown in such a critical light. But after thinking about it and speaking to River, he'd simply told her: 'It's your story to tell and, anyway, if my father had behaved better there would be no criticism to level.'

That was when Audrey had known for sure that Geoffrey was far more like his mother than his father.

On reaching the top of the stairs, she stopped for a moment to catch her breath. She would have to take up Geoffrey's offer to set up a bedroom for her on the ground floor before too long, but for now she would push herself.

She was about to go to her bedroom when she had second thoughts and, leaving her book behind, she climbed even more slowly to the next floor. She rarely came up here, but there was something she wanted to see.

Audrey walked along the landing and reached the door to the third floor. The door was no longer locked but she felt no need to go up there.

Clara and River planned on opening up the time-slip rooms to tourists, with her beautiful 1950s clothes as the star attraction, and she was fine with that. It would bring in regular income that would keep the manor going once the money from the diamonds ran out.

Maybe one day she would climb the stairs and walk the rooms that she'd inhabited long ago. But for now she was happier to stay away. Perhaps a few lingering ghosts remained that it was best not to rouse. She smiled at her overactive imagination but passed the door as quickly as she could and walked on to the gilt-framed portrait.

'Hello,' she said before glancing around her.

People would be concerned if they heard her talking to a painting of herself. But Geoffrey, River and Clara were still in the garden, and Julie was weighing down the tree in the hall.

'Look what's become of us,' she said to the woman in the portrait. 'You were so scared and unhappy when you sat for the artist in your fine clothes. You couldn't see a way out. But I'm here to tell you that Violet and her husband will come up trumps and you will see Geoffrey again. I'm here to tell you that everything will be all right.'

With tears in her eyes, Audrey turned and made her way along the landing, towards the people waiting for her downstairs.

A LETTER FROM LIZ

Hello,

Thank you for reading *The Diary at the Last House Before the Sea*. Whether you've read all of the Heaven's Cove series or this is your first visit to the village, I really hope you enjoyed your stay.

I love writing about the goings-on in and around Heaven's Cove, and I'm drafting the next book in the series at the moment. If you'd like to keep up to date with that book and all my latest releases, just sign up at the following link. Your email address will never be shared and you can unsubscribe at any time:

www.bookouture.com/liz-eeles

Writing *The Diary at the Last House Before the Sea* was great fun, especially when it came to imagining Brellasham Manor. I can picture the grand house in my mind's eye, with its sweeping stone steps and elegant rooms, and the moors rising up behind it – I'd move in like a shot, if Geoffrey didn't mind. I also relished giving the inhabitants of Heaven's Cove a shimmering heatwave to enjoy, as I sat shivering at my desk in the depths of a cold, wet British winter.

If you did enjoy Clara's quest to discover the truth about Audrey, I'd be grateful if you could spare a few minutes to write a review. I'd love to hear your thoughts on the book, and your review might encourage other readers to visit Heaven's Cove themselves. Thank you so much.

Please do stop by and say hello on social media, if you get the chance. You can find me on the links below and I look forward to hearing from you.

Take care, and happy reading!

Liz x

www.lizeeles.com

 facebook.com/lizeelesauthor

x.com/lizeelesauthor

 instagram.com/lizeelesauthor

ACKNOWLEDGEMENTS

Thank you, Ellen Gleeson, for being the perfect editor for me: talented, collaborative, funny and unflappable. Your calming confidence is particularly appreciated when my nerves kick in shortly before publication.

Thank you, Bookouture, for taking a chance on me thirteen books ago. Thirteen! I can't believe you've published so many of my novels – or that I've written so many, to be honest.

Thank you to my friends and family, for always being interested in what I'm writing. And a special thank you to my husband, Tim, who read an earlier draft of this book and made supportive and helpful suggestions, even though women's fiction is not his genre of choice.

Thank you to my lovely readers all over the world, many of whom feel like friends now we've got to know each other on Facebook and Instagram. Your enthusiasm for my books is such a boost when I'm partway through writing a novel and not sure I'll ever reach THE END.

And finally, thank you to Eileen Carey for designing the beautiful cover of this book and all the books in my Heaven's Cove series. I love every one of them.

PUBLISHING TEAM

Turning a manuscript into a book requires the efforts of many people. The publishing team at Bookouture would like to acknowledge everyone who contributed to this publication.

Commercial
Lauren Morrissette
Hannah Richmond
Imogen Allport

Data and analysis
Mark Alder
Mohamed Bussuri

Cover design
Eileen Carey

Editorial
Ellen Gleeson
Nadia Michael

Copyeditor
Jenny Page

Proofreader
Becca Allen

Printed in Great Britain
by Amazon

48746501R00173